PROTECTORS

UNBOUNDED SIDE STORIES

AVA'S REVENGE
MORTAL BROTHER
SET ABLAZE

BOOKS BY TEYLA BRANTON

Unbounded Series
The Change
The Cure
Protectors
  Ava's Revenge
  Mortal Brother
  Set Ablaze
The Escape
The Reckoning
Lethal Engagement
The Takeover

Colony Six Series
Insight (prequel)
Sketches
Visions
Travels

Imprints Series
First Touch (prequel)
Touch of Rain
On The Hunt
Upstaged
Under Fire
Blinded
Street Smart
Hidden Intent
Checked In

Other
Times Nine

UNDER THE NAME RACHEL BRANTON

Lily's House Series
House Without Lies
Tell Me No Lies
Hearts Never Lie
Your Eyes Don't Lie
Broken Lies
No Secrets or Lies
Cowboys Can't Lie

A Town Called Forgotten
Kiss at Midnight

Noble Hearts
Royal Quest
Royal Dance

Finding Home Series
Take Me Home
All That I Love
Then I Found You

Other
How Far
I Don't Want To Eat
  Bugs

PROTECTORS

UNBOUNDED SIDE STORIES

AVA'S REVENGE
MORTAL BROTHER
SET ABLAZE

TEYLA
BRANTON

WHITE
STAR
PRESS

This is a work of fiction, and the views expressed herein are the sole responsibility of the author. Likewise, certain characters, places, and incidents are the product of the author's imagination, and any resemblance to actual persons, living or dead, or actual events or locales, is entirely coincidental.

Protectors (Unbounded Series #3)
Includes the Unbounded novellas Ava's Revenge, Mortal Brother, and Set Ablaze)

Published by White Star Press
P.O. Box 353
American Fork, Utah 84003

Printed in the United States of America
ISBN: 978-1-948982-19-1
Year of first printing: 2020

AVA'S REVENGE

AN UNBOUNDED NOVELLA

To my readers who have enjoyed the Unbounded series
and wanted to know more about the characters.

PART ONE

June 1745 - Near Williamsburg, Virginia

Ava's Change

CHAPTER 1

SIMON WAS IN A BLACK MOOD, THE KIND THAT EVEN AFTER thirteen years of marriage brought terror to my heart and made me want to flee. I had almost run away a year ago, but I couldn't do that now because of Hannah. I couldn't risk her.

I could feel him coming, imagined slights and impotent frustration clinging to him like sticky gray cobwebs. I felt the darkness as if I could see into his mind, as if I were a part of him.

He was late and dinner had long since cooled, despite my moving it on and off the heat for the past two hours. I hurried to stoke the dying fire, swinging the kettle back over the flames, praying it would reheat quickly. Simon had never been content with the customary cold leftovers from the larger afternoon meal but required all his food served hot. Though I'd originally made the roast in the oven built inside the fireplace, today I had reheated the meat in the kettle, nearly burning it when he didn't appear on time.

Stepping to the other side of the hearth, I peered out the window of our three-bedroom house—a house larger than those of our neighbors. Solid on the outside but reeking putrefaction on the inside. Sure enough, Simon was coming up the dirt road that led to our main fields, riding Old Bob. Simon's face was his normal red, and his thick, aging, slouch-shouldered body didn't appear any more tense than usual, yet the dark emotion remained lodged in my heart. Clearly, his planned discussion with our neighbor about our troublesome cow hadn't gone well.

Around his body was a glow I had been seeing around everyone since before Hannah's birth. Always the same white color—like twenty candles framing the body. I didn't know what it was, but every living thing had it, even animals and insects, except these were muted compared with the brighter human auras. It could be quite distracting at town council or in a church meeting, but for the most part I found it comforting, especially with Hannah. There was no glow around the deceased.

A sound stilled my heart. "Oh, no," I whispered. "Let me get him taken care of first." Because three-month-old Hannah knew nothing about our world and how it worked. Nothing about her father.

"Shush, my sweet." I scooped up the baby, thinking hard. I could take her to the woodshed, where her cries wouldn't be heard. I'd done it before, rescuing her as soon as possible, her face red and her fists clenched in indignation at being ignored. I would pay the price for not being in the house when he came home, but that would be preferable to his noticing Hannah.

Desperation clogged my throat. I'd lost too many babies. The first had been a boy, in my womb less than five months. Simon had cried real tears that day, his worn face sorrowful. I'd been eighteen and I'd believed the tears. Almost, I'd forgiven him.

The second baby I miscarried six months into the pregnancy, a little girl. Simon hadn't wept over her small corpse or apologized for hitting me, and that was when I began to suspect the depths of his depravation. The third baby I lost at two months after Simon kicked me in the stomach, and the fourth at five after he slammed me into the wall and locked me up for three days without food. Afterwards, Simon had been angry because I had lost another boy. He'd raped me that very evening in the effort to start another.

But that was it. No more babies. Not for me. No more victims for Simon. As the years went on, I was just Ava O'Hare Brumbaugh, the barren woman with the poor, hard-working husband, who really couldn't be blamed for stepping out at the brothel given his hardships.

Not that his attempt at showing his manhood protected me from his advances. Because he still wanted a son. I was just as determined not to give him one, so I took the herbs that women only talked about behind closed doors when their husbands and children couldn't hear. Just in case my body decided to heal.

Last year, at thirty, I discovered I was expecting again despite the prevention. Given the low life expectancy in Virginia and my volatile relationship with Simon, I was surprised I'd lived that long.

Hannah had fallen back to sleep, turning her lips toward my breast and making sucking motions, her bottom lip disappearing inside her mouth as she nursed in her dream. "Good girl," I murmured. "Please stay asleep." I stroked her soft cheek. Just once and only briefly. She was due for a feeding soon, but I couldn't have her awaken now, not with Simon in that foul mood. Unfortunately, Hannah was a fussy baby, and though I had ample milk, every day it was an increasing effort to keep her quiet.

To deepen her slumber, I held her as long as I dared. As Simon's boots sounded against the steps, I slipped her into the little cradle that lay inside the large corner cupboard where I had once kept cooking supplies.

Untucking my skirt from my underclothes where I'd put it to prevent it from catching fire, I hurried back to the fireplace.

I wasn't fast enough.

Simon's eyes pinned me as I bent to check the food, then strayed toward the cupboard, his eyes narrowing with the jealousy he showed toward anything that took my attention from him. Fury emanated from his body as prominently as the stench of his sweat.

I forced my jaw to unclench. "Good evening, Simon. How was your day? Dinner's hot and ready." This last was a lie, or maybe a desperate hope.

His eyes left the cupboard, and I nearly gave a sigh of relief, the knot in my stomach lessening slightly. "Rotten," he muttered. "Imbeciles. Barker and the rest. He had three of the others there to witness his demands for payment. It ain't my fault his old fences can't keep out my livestock. He even had the gall to ask me to fix his fence."

He looked at me expectantly, so I shook my head in commiseration. "What did you tell him?"

The potatoes and carrots were ready, and the new butter and the freshly baked bread I had struggled over all day would please him, but the meat wouldn't be as hot as he liked. I should have kept it warm, no matter his complaints about the wasted fuel. He could afford it, despite the setbacks he'd experienced lately with the crops.

Simon pulled out a chair and sat at the table, cursing under his breath as he removed his boots and tossed them by the door where I'd have to remove the caked mud later. "I told him he owes *me* for treating the cow for bloating."

I suspected that Simon had let our cow into Barker's field, or at least starved her into desperation so she would break through the fence. She was older and after the summer would become our meat for the winter. Fattening her up on Barker's grain would mean better eating for us.

Or for Simon. These days I had no appetite—a good thing because Simon seemed to begrudge anything that went into my mouth. That I hadn't lost weight or felt weak, I chalked up to a miracle.

Maybe I can find a way to leave with Hannah. He might not find us. I'd been saving every bit of money I could, but it wasn't enough to get us very far. Not yet. Simon was careful with what he gave me, and the only money I had was what I earned from my needlework for Mrs. Adamson. That tiny nest egg and the hope it represented—and sweet Hannah, of course—were the only things keeping me alive.

Because if we didn't go far enough, I knew he would find me. And he'd have help. Simon was a contributing member of our society, if not a friendly one, and most of our neighbors and acquaintances would work together to return a runaway wife. I belonged to him like the chickens or the cows.

He was proud of me in his own way. My face maintained much of my youthful beauty, my blond hair was long and lustrous, and I didn't carry extra pounds. The scars he'd given me over the years had disappeared, and even the deep bruises he now gave me faded overnight. I worked hard and needed little sleep. As long as I didn't linger too long with any of the local farmers or their sons, he was willing to take me out to church or other town functions and show me off. He even endured Hannah's presence during the outings because she represented his prowess of fathering a child.

No, the only way Simon would let me leave was in a pine box.

Like his first wife.

Until Hannah arrived, I had begun to think of the first Mistress Brumbaugh as the lucky one.

"Well?" Simon looked at me expectantly.

I swept up a plate, but instead of going to the stove, I approached him, my mind scrabbling to find a delay so the meat could heat thoroughly. "Maybe we can go for a walk this evening. Would you like that?"

He studied me, his face turning a deeper shade of red. Simon wasn't an ugly man, but there was nothing remarkable about him. His height was average, or perhaps slightly less so. He was wide and his arms thick, but his strength was also average by comparison. He looked no more or less worn than any of the other wrinkled, leather-faced men who spent their entire lives toiling under the sun.

Simon's very averageness might have fueled his ever-present anger. Maybe if he'd been taller, he would have been more confident and not so quick to take offense. If he'd been stronger, he might not have needed to prove his domination over me. If his eyes had been more compelling or his face less red, perhaps he wouldn't regard my every interaction with other men as flirting. If he'd been wealthy, instead of just slightly better off than the rest of our neighbors, or if we lived in one of the big, fancy houses in town and he was a doctor or politician instead of a farmer, maybe everything would have been different.

I didn't really believe that.

His hands fisted on the table. "Someone you want to see?" His muddy eyes felt like the cigars he'd once burned into my skin. Scars that had also disappeared—at least on the outside.

"No. You had a hard day. A stroll might help you relax, that's all."

"I'm tired. I just want my dinner. Bring it."

No more delay. Praying the flames had done their job, I glided to the fireplace, my movements seemingly unreal, a dream. I cut the bread on the hearth first, as slowly as I dared, and then filled his plate.

As I set it down on the table in front of him, his hand whipped out and gripped my breast. The knot in my stomach quadrupled in that instant. "I know what you can do to relax me," he said, squeezing tighter.

I wanted to vomit. I wanted to jerk away or tell him he was hurting me, but I knew from experience that would only make it worse.

His hand moved down to my stomach and back up again, rubbing and squeezing. "You like that, don't ya? Yeah, you live for it. I know you do." He chuckled and released me, his hand going for the knife. He sliced off a chunk of meat. "I got a few new things in mind tonight. To relax me, as you say." He chuckled as if we shared some kind of special joke. "I got more of that tranquility potion. Remember the one from a couple years back? You'll take it after you clean up dinner."

For a man who had never shown an ounce of creativity

in other areas, he knew all sorts of depravity in the bedroom—or living room, or kitchen, or barn—things that I had never dreamed existed in my girlish fantasies of married life. The idea of taking his potion, bought from some traveling snake oil salesman, frightened me beyond belief. It brought complete immobility, made me an observer to whatever indignities he would subject me to. And it would last for hours. What if Hannah needed me?

Simon had been forty when we married, just weeks short of my eighteenth birthday. At the time, I was nearly a spinster in the eyes of my parents, who had given me away like a foal to a new master. After the first year of being sadistically raped by Simon, I'd stopped talking to my parents. They should have been able to see behind the face he showed the world, the life he kept just for me in the privacy of our home. I knew it was a man's right to keep his woman in place, but that wasn't the relationship I'd dreamed about. Or planned with my first and only love, Gabriel, who at sixteen had been too young and penniless to prevent my fate as Mrs. Brumbaugh.

Maybe it was my double black eyes or the choke marks around my throat, but after losing baby number four, my widowed father had finally taken my side, realizing far too late what he had condemned me to. For my father, it was no longer the broken arm, the black eyes, or the bruises that could be explained as a man keeping his spirited young wife under control, but the slaughter of his posterity—the future.

I didn't let myself believe it stemmed from love. That was too dangerous.

He'd confronted Simon, and they'd fought. A year later my father was dead, still suffering from the leg injury he'd earned that day. His farm passed to Simon. I didn't mourn my father. I was nothing more than a corpse myself, unable to feel anything but fear. Until Hannah.

Simon took a bite of food and grunted with enjoyment. I moved to get myself a plate with a thin slice of meat and only two small pieces of potatoes. He liked my company so he could brag about the day, and he would be angry if I didn't eat or if I ate too much.

"I'm planting the south field next week," he said. "You'll bring out our food. I'm hiring Wilson's boys to help."

A rustling from the cupboard clogged my response in my throat, but there was no cry, so Hannah was probably just moving in her sleep.

I still didn't know how she'd happened, but the moment I'd realized I was expecting, I'd talked nonstop about the son Simon would have and what people would say. How he'd have someone to bestow his legacy upon. I'd made sure plenty of witnesses were at the birth, and when it was a daughter—after the fear subsided—I was fiercely glad. A daughter I might be able to protect from his anger. A daughter wouldn't follow in her father's footsteps.

But whenever he had to hire other men's sons, he remembered that Hannah wasn't the heir I'd promised.

He'd never forgiven me for what he thought of as my betrayal.

"I'll do that," I said. It'd actually be nice to cook for someone who might appreciate the effort.

Simon took a second bite of meat, and this time his face furrowed. He swallowed and took another mouthful. This one he spat out, half chewed, onto the floor. "The middle is cold, and the bottom's burnt."

"You were late," I said, reaching for the plate. "I only just started reheating it. Let me fix it for you. The rest will be hotter now."

He swept the plate from my grasp. The rare porcelain hit the wood floor and shattered, sending meat, gravy, and chunks of potatoes and carrots flying.

I jumped to my feet, my heart pounding against my rib cage.

"So it's my fault?" he shouted, spittle flying from his mouth. "My fault? I give you everything. A roof over your stupid head. Food for yer lyin' trap. Clothes for yer skinny little frame. Even porcelain dinnerware." He was on his feet now, his anger making him seem tall.

I heard Hannah's faint cry. *Don't let him hear her.* From the corner of my eye, I could see the steady glow of her life, even through the mostly closed door of the cupboard.

"Maybe you don't deserve anything I give you!" He grabbed the neck of my dress and tugged, but the fabric didn't give. Instead, I was propelled forward, my head connecting with his chest. He shoved me back into the table, and it skidded several feet across the floor. The cups and utensils clattered to the ground. The sliced bread teetered on the edge.

Hannah let out a wail.

I bolted forward, thinking to somehow grab her and get outside, maybe leave her with a neighbor until Simon calmed down, but he was faster. Catching my hair in his fist, he pulled me back and yanked me around. I slid across the floor to slam my head against the solid oak door.

Hannah's cry grew louder.

"Shut up, shut up, shut up!" Simon screamed. His footsteps to the cupboard were heavy and determined.

Hannah cried harder.

Panic fueled me as I launched myself toward Simon. I reached him as he opened the cupboard door. Little Hannah was in her cradle, her face red and her mouth open. I saw two of her, my head still fuzzy from the blow. She took a breath and let out another scream.

"I said shut up," he growled.

I reached for him, but I was too late. His fist came down on Hannah.

The crying stopped.

His hand was ready for another punch, but I lashed out at him. Anything to stop him from hurting Hannah further. Maybe she was just stunned. Maybe I was imagining that the light around her had gone completely out.

"You leave her alone!" I screamed. "Or I'll tell! I'll tell everyone about the monster you are! And they'll believe me. Hannah hasn't been sick a day in her life. They'll know you're a murderer." It wasn't true. So many took ill and died. No one would think twice about Hannah.

"Whore!" Simon hit me on the side of the head. His next punch took me in the stomach with a blow that was all too familiar. Then I was on the floor and he was on top of me, fists pumping. I felt my teeth cave inward. Blood filled my mouth.

"You won't tell anyone nuthin'. Not ever again!" His hands went around my throat, blocking all the air. "I've seen you making eyes at Barker and even the pastor. Maybe you wonder what it'd be like to be with them. Maybe Hannah belongs to one of them. Eh? She certainly ain't mine."

I tried to shake my head, but his grip was too strong. My sight was foggy on the edges, a sure sign that I would soon pass out. I couldn't let that happen. There might be a chance for Hannah. Maybe the darkness I saw from the cupboard came only because of my own injuries.

Except that Simon's own body glow was so bright I could see it with my eyes closed. I could feel his rage, his sense of betrayal. I also saw an image of the farmer who had just come from England and was working the land two homesteads over. He had a twenty-year-old daughter with silky black hair. Simon was already planning my replacement.

My sight darkened. Before I passed out completely, the pressure on my throat eased. I tried to move, but my body refused to obey. Everything hurt. Worse than anything I'd ever known. When I finally pried my eyes open, I saw Simon, his pants around his knees, felt him pushing up my dress. My underclothes ripped. His weight pressed down on me.

His face was close to mine. He was breathing heavy, not with exertion now, but with arousal. "Just one thing left I've been wanting to try," he grated. A knife glinted next to my cheek. "Once, I almost . . . but I didn't. Don't need no potion for this."

He had prepared for this moment. Maybe not exactly like this, but he'd planned my murder. Maybe because he'd decided he didn't want me anymore, or because that new farmer's daughter might give him sons. He slid the knife down, and in a single motion, swiped it across my throat, cutting deeply. I gasped for breath, but none came. The blood welled.

Simon gave a deep laugh that sounded demented. His body trembled against me.

I felt strangely disconnected. I didn't care, not for me. Not with Hannah gone. I couldn't even feel or care about what he was doing.

Maybe I'd finally found my luck like the first Mrs. Brumbaugh.

Except it wasn't the end but only the beginning.

CHAPTER 2

BIRDS CHIRPED HAPPILY IN THE TREES. THE SUN FELT WARM ON my cheek but not on the rest of my face. A cool wind swept through, and the heat on my cheek wavered.

I had to get up. In the next room, Hannah might be awake and need me. I'd have to get Simon's breakfast before he'd finished with the livestock in the barn. That meant hauling the water, building the fire, gathering the eggs.

I stretched, slowly in case it was earlier than I thought and Simon was still in the bed.

Crackling leaves were the first indication that I wasn't where I thought I was. The warmth of the sun and the breeze I'd felt weren't coming from an open window at all.

My eyes flew open. Above me trees loomed, their leaves rustling in the gentle wind. I became aware of sticks and stones digging into my back. My breath came faster, my head rocked back and forth as I looked around, trying to determine where I was.

Nothing was familiar. I was in the middle of the woods, in a place I didn't recognize. Had I been hurt? What was I doing here? How long had I been lying on the ground?

Simon would be angry.

Hannah!

The thought bolted me to a sitting position. My sweet baby! I needed to get back to her. A glance down at myself showed me fully clothed, but the top of my dress was stained with something dark and stiff. Maybe blood. Where it had come from, I couldn't say, because I didn't appear to be hurt. Using a nearby tree, I pulled myself to my feet, feeling dizzy. Which way was home? I had to get back to Hannah.

I stumbled three steps before I saw her. My sweet baby, in her white, multilayered dress that I had worked so hard on during the weeks after her birth. The side of her face was caved in and an insect crawled over her darkened skin.

Memories came rushing back. Simon's fist crashing down on my precious Hannah. The beating, the knife slicing my throat, his weight on my body.

Hannah!

Collapsing to my knees, I began heaving violently. Over and over. Nothing came up. Not even yellow bile.

When the tortured spasms passed, I crawled to my baby and picked her up, cuddling her limp body next to my chest. Stench wafted up to me, bringing to mind a rotting calf I'd once found with its foot caught in a fence. A calf that had been missing for several weeks.

My mouth opened in a silent scream. I stared at the sky, shoulders heaving, clutching my baby.

My baby! My baby! Oh, sweet Hannah!

It was my fault. I should have left the second I found out I was expecting her. But my fear of Simon had frozen me in place. I'd found a journal tucked in a corner, belonging to his first wife. She wrote that he'd threatened to kill her if she ever tried to leave. She'd thought about killing herself.

I'd stayed, thinking that was the only way to save Hannah. To keep her alive until Simon died—he was already past fifty and had lived much longer than most men I'd known.

Yet I knew the truth. I, Ava O'Hare, had been afraid. Afraid of him finding me and the revenge he'd take. Afraid of how we would survive alone. Afraid of everything.

I killed her. It's all my fault.

The silent scream finally found voice, ripping out of my throat and piercing the quiet. My heart broke again and again as I relived the nightmare and my guilt. At last the screams became body-shaking sobs. All that was left was the deathly stillness of the little body in my arms and the pain that filled every portion of my soul.

I didn't know why I was still alive, and apparently unwounded. Had I imagined Simon's anticipation as he choked the breath from me? Had I imagined the hot slicing of the knife? Nothing made sense. Not how I was still alive or why Simon hadn't buried me so no one would discover his depravity.

Yet in the end, none of that really mattered. I didn't care about anything but Hannah.

Time passed. A day. Two. Or maybe three. I didn't know. Twice I slept, still holding Hannah's empty shell, immune to the smell. I wanted to die. Knew that I would eventually without food and water. But I only grew stronger. I felt no hunger, no physical pain. Though I didn't put anything in my mouth, I felt the taste of leaves on my tongue.

The third time I awoke, the agony of Hannah's death had burned to a hard ball in the pit of my stomach. Numbness had taken its place.

Still holding her, I stood and began walking. I didn't know where I was, but I couldn't stay in that place anymore. Trees filled my sight in every direction, giving me no sign of which way to go. In the glimpses of sky between the trees, the sun angled across the peaceful blue expanse, telling me I was heading east. I trudged on. At last I came to a river.

I knew that river. Following it, I eventually came to a section of our property. Simon hadn't shown much creativity in where he'd dumped us, but it was unlikely that our bodies would be found until he started a search. Had anyone even noticed I was missing? Simon had allowed me no friends, and only Mrs. Adamson would question my disappearance when I didn't deliver her embroidery.

If Simon planned to marry the new farmer's daughter, he'd have to report my death, or have someone find my body.

Except that I wasn't dead. I still couldn't figure out why.

The sun told me it was midday, and Simon should be out in the fields. I found a shovel in our barn and began moving again along the river, still heading east, still carrying Hannah. Walking along this river was one of the few freedoms I'd had, and I had wandered far past our property on the rare days when Simon was out of town and my prolonged absence wouldn't be missed.

I stopped at a place some distance from the river, still on our property, where the river widened and a large, gnarled oak tree stood watch as it had for dozens of years. I'd once entertained the thought of tying a rope to its lower branches and fashioning a swing for Hannah.

It was near this tree I buried her now. I dug a deep hole, lining it with a bed of leaves, and wrapped her in my petticoat before placing her inside. "Sleep in peace, my sweet Hannah," I whispered. Sobs once again shook my body as I filled in the hole, though I believed she was at rest.

My fault. My fault.

I could disappear now, take on a new identity. At thirty, I was old, but I was still strong. Any work I could find would be better than my life with Simon.

With Simon, who would now remarry. Another wife, more babies, more deaths.

Those would be my fault too.

That's why he didn't bury me, I thought. *He wanted someone to find us. He'd blame the murders on some fugitive or indigent, and he'd be free to abuse another woman.*

My tears dried. Clutching the shovel, I began walking.

CHAPTER 3

I WAITED UNTIL LATE IN THE AFTERNOON IN CASE SIMON appeared for the noon meal. But apparently, he'd eaten in town. Maybe even visited the brothel. I didn't care. He'd return eventually.

The kitchen looked as if a storm had come through. Dirty, food-caked dishes lay everywhere, the floor had mud tracks and scattered feathers and bones from the chicken Simon had apparently remembered how to kill and cook. There was no fire in the grate or water in the barrel. No fresh bread or butter. He hadn't replaced me yet.

I went to work, first going to the barn where I fed the hungry chickens, catching one to cook for dinner. While I waited for the water to boil so I could begin cleaning off the feathers, I hauled more water to heat for a bath. After spicing the chicken and adding potatoes and vegetables from the bin in the closet, I bathed, washing my long hair and changing into my best Sunday dress that I kept in the cedar chest in Hannah's room.

I needed clean undergarments, and those were in the bedroom I'd shared with Simon, which was as big a mess as the kitchen. There I found what I needed, as well as discarded clothing on the floor that was definitely not mine. My other everyday dress was missing.

The third bedroom looked the same as always, crammed full of farming equipment and Simon's sales manifests. In the top drawer of the old desk, next to several big horse pills, I found the small black bottle of liquid and carried it carefully to the kitchen, setting it on my worktable. I began cleaning the floor as the chicken sizzled in the copper kettle over the fire. The aroma was heady, but I had no real appetite. I thought of the tree and my sweet Hannah. Perhaps I should have dug the grave large enough for me.

The kitchen looked almost normal before I felt him coming. Down the road as usual on Old Bob. Without looking out the window, I picked up a bowl and ladled steaming chicken stew into it, setting it on the table in the place where I normally sat. Then I got another bowl for Simon.

I sat and picked up my spoon. The broth tasted as good as it smelled, probably the best I'd ever made.

The door burst open. Simon stopped and stared as he saw me, his jaw going slack. I smiled, knowing the emotion wouldn't reach my eyes. "Good evening, Simon.

I've made you dinner. It's hot and ready." I stared at him, my gaze not wavering.

He swallowed noisily, the blood seeping from his face. His muddy eyes looked as big as the pit I'd dug for our daughter's grave. He crossed himself and blinked.

"Come on, Simon. Why don't you sit and eat? I'm sorry, I haven't been around, but I'm back now." I stood and motioned for him to take his place.

He backed away, not out the door, but toward the window. "You . . . how . . . I . . ."

I laughed. "What's wrong, Simon? You look like you've seen a ghost. Come on, eat. You'll see your daughter soon. I know how much you love her." I walked over to the door, shutting it.

He still made no move toward the table.

I picked up a knife. "Sit," I ordered.

He scurried to the table and picked up his spoon, his eyes still fixed on me in horror.

I sliced one of the dry biscuits I'd made to go with the stew. There hadn't been time to make bread or butter, but the biscuits would taste good soaked in stew broth. "I'm going to make more pot roast tomorrow," I said, "if we have any meat left from the butchering. You remember the last time we had pot roast, don't you?"

He was gulping down the stew now, though it had to be too hot for such rapid consumption.

I laid the knife down and joined him at the table. "How long has it been?" I pressed. "The last pot roast. The one that was too cold."

He swallowed again noisily. "But you're . . ."

"What?" I smiled. "I'm what, Simon?"

"You're dead." He swallowed the food in his mouth, his spoon clutched tightly in his gnarled hand. "I saw you . . . I . . ."

"You saw what, Simon?" When he didn't reply, I added, "I'm obviously not dead, as you can see. Isn't the stew delicious? I made it just the way you like it."

He nodded, his thick neck bobbing like the chicken I'd beheaded hours earlier. He lowered his eyes, spooning in the broth and chunks of chicken with the same desperation as before. I sipped my own stew, the flavors exploding in my mouth, reminding me that I still had no answer.

"How long would you say I've been gone?" I asked. "You looked so surprised to see me. I can't really remember what happened. It's all a blur." I tilted my head and waited to see if he'd detect the lie. I always could.

With the comment, more color seeped into his face. "T-two weeks," he said.

"What happened?"

He stared at me for several seconds before gulping more stew as if he hadn't eaten during all the time I'd been gone. I didn't interrupt him, but let him spoon it all down and cram in the biscuit without once dipping it into the broth. He tipped the bowl to his mouth and slurped up the rest of the liquid.

"Would you like some more?"

He shook his head. "N-no." This time it was difficult for him to push out the word.

I stood and retrieved the small black bottle, setting it on the table near his bowl. "Last time you made me take two spoonfuls. You've just taken four. You're larger, so I thought it might take more. I hope I didn't give you too much."

He tried to speak, but it came out a jumbled, unintelligible mess. I smiled and finished my stew without saying a word. Then I arose, taking our dishes to the sink. But these I wouldn't be washing. I would never wash dishes again. I picked up the knife from the worktable and brought it back to Simon. I rubbed the side of the blade against his cheek. My mind screamed at me to plunge it into his heart, to cut off his hand or his manhood, but I wouldn't be rushed.

I drew the blade lightly over his throat, just enough to bring a few beads of blood. "Remember this?" I asked. I could see that he did. He remembered it all. And like me, he had no idea how I'd survived. I could feel his emotions as I always had this past year: his fear, his shame, his anger. Even now he wished he could move his limbs so he could kill me again.

And Hannah.

A sob shook me and I turned away, stepping out of his sight so he wouldn't see my pain. The knife clattered to the floor. I felt nearly blinded, agonized, with grief. How could I go on without her, especially knowing it was my fault?

I couldn't, of course, and that was why I was still here.

With the tongs, I pulled out one of the smaller logs from the fireplace, placing it under the table. Then I heaped on the piles of clothes I'd gathered: Simon's work clothes, the rest of mine, and even those left from Simon's prostitute. I didn't look at the monster that was my husband until the table was burning.

"No more," I said to Simon, whose eyes glittered with fear and hatred. "No more dead babies. Or dead wives. No more prostitutes. No more cheating or lies. It's over. You built this house with your own hands, and now you will see it destroyed by the freak you created. By me."

Fire licked at his shoe.

I left the kitchen, going back to Hannah's room. In the cedar chest that had once been my mother's, I swept up the tin box that held my most dear memories. Hannah's first little outfit, barely outgrown, the stuffed bear my mother had made for me as a child that I had planned to share with Hannah. The gold necklace that had belonged to the mother of my first love, Gabriel, a gift from her wealthy parents before she'd run away to marry Gabriel's father. She'd died when Gabriel was only ten, and he'd given me the necklace when I was sixteen, along with a rose that had long since dried and was crumbling. These treasures were all I had left of those I loved.

I slumped to the floor. Hannah's cradle was still in the kitchen cupboard where I'd left it last, but I felt close to her here. *I love you Hannah. I'll be with you soon.*

Something inside, a slice of sanity that remained,

screamed at me to get away. Another part of me cried out that I should have been more humane, even to Simon. I should have at least knocked him unconscious before setting the fire. As it was, he wouldn't be able to cry or scream, but he'd feel himself burning. When he'd given the potion to me, I had felt everything he'd done to my body.

During the afternoon planning, I purposely hadn't thought about any of the good times we had shared together, but they came now: a dance we had attended two months after our marriage, the time our crops had sold for twice what we'd expected, the day he had brought home the porcelain dinnerware.

I was doomed. Maybe by taking revenge, I'd made a pact with the devil himself.

I sensed Simon then. I felt the flames as they spread up his clothes in a deceptively gentle rush before sinking in and biting deep. I experienced his suffering, his regret— not regret that he'd hurt me, but regret that he hadn't done a better job of killing me.

I was burning—consumed by fire. No, *he* was burning. The flames hadn't yet reached the nursery, but in my misery, I'd forgotten we were connected, that I would feel his terror and anguish as if they were my own.

Greedy fire. Horrific agony. So much torture I didn't think I'd live long enough to feel actual flames on my own skin. I brought my hands to my head, clamping down, pushing him away.

All at once the agony stopped and I was aware of my

surroundings again, though I knew he wasn't yet dead. I still had an awareness of the glow that signaled his life, but I'd somehow separated myself from his pain.

I clung to my tin more tightly. Shattering glass echoed throughout the house. The glass Simon had been so proud of when he'd had it put in before any of the neighbors.

Smoke curled into the room, quickly becoming huge billows of gray. I began coughing. I could already feel the heat from the fire. For the first time since laying my baby in her grave, I was scared. Scared to feel the flames again. The agony.

Shame filled me. I couldn't even die right.

Clutching the tin, I scrambled to my feet and ran for the window.

CHAPTER 4

I FELL OUTSIDE, CUTTING MYSELF ON THE BROKEN GLASS. THEN I rolled away, my lungs gasping for breath. I made it as far as the dirt road in front of the house, and there I stood numbly, watching the house burn . . . and burn . . . and burn. Smoke gathered in a cloud, visible in the summer evening.

I was a coward. I'd been able to avenge my daughter's death, and the babies before her, but I hadn't been able to join her. Even now, I trembled as I thought about the flames eating my flesh.

A movement from the edge of my vision startled me. At first I thought it was Simon, somehow freed from the potion's spell and rising like a phoenix from the fire, but two faces came into sight from around the side of the house, a man and a woman.

The man saw me and began to run in my direction.

I cringed away from him as he reached out, but he let his arm drop without touching me.

"Are you all right?" he asked in an accent that sounded both lyrical and familiar.

My eyes flew up to meet those of the most handsome man I'd ever seen. His face was cleanly shaven, his blond hair slightly long but neat, and his well-built figure was set off by stylish clothing like the kind I'd only seen from afar at Mrs. Adamson's. He looked upset, but I knew his anger wasn't directed at me.

"Are you all right?" he repeated.

I shook my head, unable to speak. He reached for me again, but I stumbled away from him.

"Stop. You're scaring her." The woman was somehow on my other side, though I hadn't seen her move, and she was breathtakingly beautiful. Her thick mass of brown hair was artfully pinned on top of her head, her face was delicate but not at all pale, her dark eyelashes were the longest I'd ever seen. Uncaring of her own fine apparel, she enfolded me with her arms. "You're Ava, aren't you?" When I nodded, she continued, her accent matching that of the man. "Good. Then we have come in time."

It's proper English, I thought. Not like the language spoken by the new farmer and his family, but the educated kind.

"Come. It's not safe here," the woman continued. "We're too close to the house. It'll all burn before the neighbors get enough water to help."

That's right. The neighbors would see the smoke.

Simon was disagreeable enough that they wouldn't be quick to check on his property, but they would eventually come. I felt more than a little satisfaction knowing they would be too late to save Simon.

"Hurry now," the woman urged, propelling me several feet. She was strong for her slight stature.

I found my voice. "You don't understand. I killed him. *I* started the fire." When they didn't react, I added, "On purpose."

It felt good to let it out. Let them deliver me to the lawmen. I would take my punishment, welcome it even. Especially if it stopped this horrible longing for Hannah. The numbness had faded, and I didn't want to feel any more pain.

The man gazed at me, compassion radiating from his very blue eyes. "He was an awful man. We both know that."

Something clicked inside me. *He knows!* Somehow the man knew what Simon had been.

"He killed my baby," the words came tumbling from my mouth and more: the lost babies, the numerous times he'd forced himself on me, waking in the woods, burying Hannah, the potion. "I don't care what they do to me. I deserve it. Just when it's over, can you bury me with my baby?"

Tears came to the woman's eyes. "I'm sorry we were so late," she said, her voice like soothing music. "So sorry. We had no idea of course. We've not seen you since you were a child." The woman looked hardly older than I did, so I found that difficult to believe, but I was in too much pain to really care.

"I'm going to see my baby now," I said, glancing beyond the fire in the direction of the tree and the grave.

"Now is not the time," the woman insisted. To the man, she added, "There will be questions if we don't get her out of here before they come." She motioned toward the horizon where already we could see dust above the road that signaled our neighbors' approach.

I glanced between the strangers. Something was odd here. Even the glow surrounding them was dimmer than with most people, closer to the aura of the animals. And I couldn't feel the customary jumble of emotions that emanated from most people. It was as if they were . . . *blocking.* The thought startled me. *Why would I think that?* They were sympathetic, I felt that much—or maybe I only saw it in their faces.

The man's hand touched my shoulder. "Please, come with us. We have been looking for you these past weeks. We want to help."

For a startling moment, I could see into his soul. Feel him as if he were a part of me. It went far deeper than the emotions I'd experienced even from Simon. Not only did the man want to help, he wanted me. Not as a man wanted a woman, but as a father wanted his child. "Who are you?" I whispered.

"I'm Wymon Tilmock, and this is my wife, Eva. We're . . . you might say we're distant relatives on your mother's side. In fact, your name, Ava, is a variation of Eva's."

Eva smiled, looking more beautiful than ever. "Please, will you come with us? We'll explain everything. You need to trust us."

I nodded and let them lead me to a wagon I hadn't noticed before. Halfway there, my legs gave out and Wymon picked me up, cradling me like an infant. My mind felt wild with grief, but somehow, this close to him, I could more easily bear the burden because I felt as if he shared my grief. He laid me in the back of their wagon and pulled a blanket over me despite the warmth of the evening.

The woman sat beside me instead of up with her husband. As she gave me a drink of water, I knew without her saying anything that she planned to hide me with the blanket when we passed our neighbors. I was too tired to protest.

They were wrong about the neighbors coming to help so soon—I'd been wrong. The cloud was nothing more than Cuthbert Mander and his lawless gang, coming to clean up on our misfortune. Eva pulled the blanket over my face just as I glimpsed the five men atop their horses, spreading out to surround the wagon.

We rolled to a stop, and I knew five muskets were pointed in our direction.

"What we got here? Cuthbert asked. His voice was close, so he must have dismounted. The blanket was ripped off me, and I stared up into Cuthbert's lean face, his long dark hair hanging in lank cords to his shoulders.

"She's been hurt," Eva said, lifting my arm where I'd

been cut going out the window. The bleeding had already ceased, but red smeared the length of my arm.

Cuthbert's eyes fixed on me as they always did when I'd had the misfortune of seeing him at public gatherings. I couldn't help thinking of the suspicious deaths that littered his trail.

"Get out," Cuthbert ordered.

"Please," Eva said. "We need to get her to a doctor."

"Sorry," Cuthbert said with a smile that clearly said he wasn't sorry at all. "We can't let you go warning people about the fire. Not until we're done taking what we want. We need traveling funds."

"You are welcome to anything you find," Wymon said. "We won't stop you."

Cuthbert snorted. "Yeah, I'll make sure of that." He motioned and one of his men tossed him some rope. I clutched the tin from my cedar chest, surprised that it was somehow still in my hands.

Wymon pulled a satchel of coins from inside his vest. "Here's more than you'll ever need. Just let us go."

Cuthbert snatched the purse from his hand. "Don't mind if I do. Just fer that, I might let you ride away. In fact, you and your woman can go right now. But not"— he raised his musket, pointing at Wymon's chest—"with our Mrs. High-and-Mighty Brumbaugh." He held my gaze so I would know exactly what he meant. "You think I ain't good enough, don't you? Got so you won't even say good day to a gentleman."

My ignoring Cuthbert had been because of Simon's

jealousy, of course, so maybe Simon would get his revenge on me from the grave.

"Get her out, boys," Cuthbert ordered "I'm going to have me a little fun." Rough hands seized my arms, pulling me from the wagon. Eva shifted to a crouch, but she didn't try to stop them. I hadn't expected to live long, but facing Cuthbert like this was too much. Better to die by a bullet. My muscles bunched in preparation.

The second my feet hit the ground, I lunged toward Cuthbert, but the hands of his goons held me tight.

Cuthbert grinned at my desperation. "Let's get her into the trees in case those God-fearing neighbors decide they need to overlook Simon's uncharitable nature and do their Christian duty." To Wymon, he added. "You got thirty seconds to make yerself scarce or I start shootin'."

"Aw, you really lettin' her go too?" one of Cuthbert's rotten-toothed accomplices thumbed at Eva. "She's a pretty one."

"Shut yer trap," Cuthbert retorted.

Panic filled me. Wymon and Eva had no choice but to leave, if they wanted to live. They couldn't risk their lives. Distant relatives or no, they didn't even know me.

The next instant everything changed. Moving so fast my eyes could barely follow, Eva leapt from the wagon, kicking two of our assailants and somehow flattening both men. Before I could take a breath, she landed on her feet and tore into a third man, whipping around to pound him in the face. Wymon was moving as well, obviously skilled though not nearly as fast as Eva. He knocked Cuthbert's musket from his hand, and they began exchanging blows.

"Look out!" I shouted as the fifth member of the gang brought his rifle around to aim at Wymon. I jumped, grabbing at the gun. But Eva and Wymon were already next to me, knocking the man unconscious before he could pull the trigger.

Eva looked at Wymon. "You'll have to take their memories. It's better that her neighbors don't know she's still alive. Hurry—we are about to have more company." She glanced out over the road where another dust cloud hovered.

Wymon knelt down between two of the men, reaching out to touch both their faces. In seconds, he finished with the men and moved on to the third and fourth.

I stared at Eva in fascinated horror. "Who are you? *What* are you?" I'd never seen a woman move like that before, much less one who looked like Eva. And a man who believed he could remove memories with a simple touch? It was unbelievable, though a part of me wished he could take away the past year of my life.

Except that would erase Hannah, and I couldn't let myself forget her. Not ever.

Eva smiled, apparently unruffled by the fight or by her husband's supposed ability. "I'm your tenth great-grandmother. I'm Unbounded—Renegade Unbounded, to be exact. And since you are not dead, apparently, so are you."

PART TWO

Fifty Years Later

September 1795 - Savannah, Georgia

Lemonade and Love

CHAPTER 5

I SMILED DOWN AT THE FRESH LEMONADE MARTHA HAD brought on a silver tray. My fingers closed around the tall, cool glass, and I raised it, saluting Locke MacAulay, the blond-haired woman opposite me. "To your parents."

Locke smiled. "Yes, to my parents."

I sipped the sweet liquid. After my rescue fifty years ago, Eva and Wymon Tilmock had brought me here to Savannah, Georgia, where they had trained me and taught me the ways of the Unbounded, or the Unboundaried, if you wanted to be more correct. Humans whose active Unbounded gene caused them to Change and become part of a rare breed, usually between the thirtieth and thirty-first birthdays. Old injuries healed, barren women gave birth, a husband's knife had no permanent power.

Well, provided a future Unbounded lived long enough to Change.

Wymon had shared my ability of sensing and had

become closer than my own father, but Eva's combat training had given me the confidence I'd desperately needed. Never again would I be a helpless victim—to anyone.

Both Wymon and Eva were gone now, their lives cut short in an ongoing battle with our enemy the Emporium just two years after the close of the Revolutionary War. Their sacrifice had prevented renewed confrontations with England, but I still desperately missed them. I had lost myself in those first years after Hannah's death. They had brought me back from despair and taught me to live again, taught me to understand and accept the Change that made me nearly immortal with a lifespan of two thousand years.

Now I worked with Locke, their daughter and a fellow Renegade, who was my ninth great-grandmother but more like a sister than anything else. Our current goal was to free America from the curse of slavery, even as the slave trade ramped up with the demand brought on by the invention of the cotton gin. We would succeed, but it would take time because the Emporium Unbounded had their own agenda, and the mortals' greed had blinded them to the evils of slavery.

Locke's eyes lifted across the green expanse of grass where we sat at a table in the shade of a tree. It was late afternoon in September and not nearly as hot as it had been a few weeks earlier. "Looks like you have more petitioners," she said, her voice sounding more Scottish like her late mortal husband than her English parents.

I turned to see Samuel, our butler, his ever-calm face standing out darkly against his white suit, gliding across the expanse of lawn with a man in tow. The man walked steadily at the butler's side, without hunching his shoulders or averting his eyes as many petitioners did. Something about the way he walked was familiar.

A slight movement in the trees to my left registered on my senses. I knew it was Ritter Langton, who had been brought to us two decades ago, shortly after his Change, by Tenika Vasco, the second-in-command of our Renegades in New York. Tenika had been afraid Ritter's single-minded recklessness would get him killed in their frequent encounters with the Emporium. She'd hoped Eva and Locke could train him, and that somehow along the way Wymon and I could temper the anger he harbored at the brutal murders of his mortal family. In the decade since Wymon's death, I didn't feel I'd made much progress.

Ritter's movement had been purposeful, to let me know he was there watching, just in case. I couldn't feel his anger from this distance, but it was still there. I knew because anger had consumed me in much the same way. It made him both vicious and reckless. I was glad he was on our side.

As I refocused on the approaching stranger, shock flooded me. When Samuel reached the table, he bowed, "A mister Gabriel Smithson to see you, Miss O'Hare."

I nodded, scarcely seeing Samuel's face. I couldn't take my eyes off the newcomer, who was hardly more than a boy of perhaps twenty. Sixty-three years melted away as if they had never been. I was seventeen and he was sixteen, holding my hand as we cried together after my father announced my upcoming marriage to Simon.

No, it couldn't be the boy who had loved me, though he looked exactly like him. I'd turned eighty-one this year, though I had physically aged only one year in the past fifty, and my Gabriel would be eighty. He was probably long dead.

The young Gabriel's eyes went to Locke's deeply plunging neckline where the swell of her breasts stood out against the single roll of blond hair over her left shoulder. He looked away, his face reddening. "Please, Miss," he said to me, "I come to ask the favor of a loan. I will pay it back. I am a hard worker. I'll make my farm a success."

"The blight hit your farm?" This close, I could now detect differences from my Gabriel. The brown eyes were slightly darker, and the blond hair lighter and a bit wavy.

He hesitated at my words, and I opened my mind, reaching out to his. Many had come to me for help in the past years, and most of them had been sincere in their claims. A few had thought to deceive me, to use my kindness to their advantage. I wouldn't delve into all his thoughts, but this way most of his emotions were readily apparent. I would know if he lied.

"No," he said finally. "My father gambled our savings away and took out a loan against the farm. But he's gone now and my grandfather will be leaving the farm to me. If I can keep it from the bank."

His sincerity was clear, but I focused on the brief glimpse I saw of his grandfather in his thoughts. "Who is your grandfather? Where is he from?" Ten years after my Change, I'd checked up on Gabriel from a distance, wanting to know what had happened to him. Perhaps wondering if there was room for him in my life. I'd found him still in Virginia, married with four strapping sons. I was glad he'd had a life, that he'd found a way to go on, even if I couldn't seem to. I'd already known in my heart that there couldn't be any future for us because I was no longer the girl who would be happy as a farmer's wife, and he would never be anything but a farmer.

Gabriel smiled and love emanated from him. "From Williamsburg, Virginia originally. He and my dad and my uncles came here before I was born. But he's all I have left now, and I guess I'm all he has. I'm his namesake, and I'm proud to bear it."

"I have family from Williamsburg. Who were his parents?" A few more questions and I knew without a doubt that fate had once again crossed my life with the boy of my youth. "Is he well?" I asked finally. There was a catch in my voice that made Locke gaze at me more intensely.

Gabriel didn't seem to notice my emotion, his eyes now studying the ice in my lemonade. He must think it a huge waste of money, a curious luxury, but he couldn't know that Unbounded had advanced technology that

made ice a simple matter. "Not so much these days," he
said, meeting my gaze once more. "He's mostly bedridden
and he doesn't see well at all, though his mind is still
strong. But I plan to marry soon, and I pray that will ease
his burdens." His smiled faded. "That is, if I can . . . I . . ."

I knew what that meant. He wanted to be able to
support a wife before plunging into matrimony. From
where I sat now, he seemed too young to marry, but
mortal lives were short, so they only did what they should.

"You *will* be married." I looked at Samuel, who was
still standing, enjoying the shade. "Please bring me a
purse. And will you have Martha find my tin box? She'll
know what I mean."

"Of course," Samuel bowed. I trusted him with all
the running of the house, and like our other workers, he
was content. It was a fine line we walked, Locke and I,
treating our slaves with respect and trying to work within
the system to free them, while at the same time making
the cotton plantation support itself. Too often we'd had
to use the funds Locke's parents had left us to keep the
business afloat or to protect our friends.

When Samuel returned with the tin, he had Gabriel
sign the customary promise note, while I removed the
necklace that had belonged to Gabriel's mother. Without
unwrapping it from its handkerchief, I slipped it into the
purse of coins Samuel had also brought. "Don't open this
until you get back to your grandfather," I said to Gabriel.

"Thank you from the bottom of my heart." Gabriel
bowed to me and then to Locke before turning to stride

across the lawn. Even in his humble clothes he looked far more confident than when he'd arrived.

"What was *that* about?" Locke asked, arching a brow.

"I knew his grandfather as a girl."

"I see." She knew there was more, but I wasn't ready to share. I didn't know if I would ever love anyone the way I had Gabriel, but I had a lot of years to figure it out.

TWO DAYS LATER, I WAS IN THE LIBRARY WHEN SAMUEL APPEARED. "Someone to see you, Miss O'Hare."

"Who is it?" I looked up from the letter I was writing.

"Gabriel Smithson."

"Show him in here, please." What could he want with me so soon? I hoped it wasn't bad news. Perhaps he'd come to tell me his grandfather was dead.

The thought brought me to my feet, so I was standing when young Gabriel entered. His face was drawn, his eyes filled with pain. "What is it?" I asked. My heart thumped loudly in my chest.

"My grandfather is dying. I'm sorry, but . . . he's asking for you. He won't say why. I expect . . . maybe he wants to thank you."

I called for a carriage and went at once. The farmhouse was larger than I expected, and far more masculine. Gabriel's wife had evidently been dead a long time. I was shown to his room, where I found a frail, wizened figure in a large bed, the light—or life force, as I'd learned it was called—around him faded and weak. As I sat in the chair by the bed, he opened his eyes. Warmth shot through me. He *was* my Gabriel. There was no mistaking the eyes, despite the white haze clouding them.

His gaze shifted to his grandson. "Please, give us a moment."

When the boy was gone, Gabriel took my hand. "Ava." The word sounded like a sigh. "I knew it was you the moment I saw the necklace. But how? You haven't changed a bit."

I had Changed—and far more than he'd ever suspect. "Your eyes are old," I said. "You must be seeing a memory."

"I see well enough." A pause and then, "Ava, I never stopped loving you."

There was no sense in pretending. "Nor I, you."

He smiled at that. "Keep watch over my boy, will you?"

"I will."

PART THREE

Fifty Years Later

April 1845 - Natchez, Mississippi

Free at Last

CHAPTER 6

WHEN BETSY SIGNALED FROM THE BACK HALLWAY NEAR THE hotel dining room, her dark face was flushed, her eyes wild. My jaw hardened as I let the newest letter from Gabriel's second great-grandson fall to my lap. Betsy obviously had found something in her investigation of the slave pens.

I nodded once, letting her know that I would meet her in my rooms. Slaves weren't allowed in the dining area of this upscale hotel, though they could help their owners in the privacy of their own rooms. Betsy had been free for a decade and living in the North for the past five years, but in this town, home to the second largest slave market, it was wise to keep up appearances. Drinking a final casual sip of my afternoon tea, I placed the porcelain cup on the delicate saucer, picked up my reticule, and arose.

"Miss!" A motion to my left had me shifting

imperceptibly into a better defensive position. Despite my layers of petticoats and skirts, no one in the dining room could be much danger, but I was always prepared. I touched the handle of a knife, hidden in the folds of my dress.

A man bent and picked up my letter that had fallen to the richly tiled floor, his muscles rippling under his tailcoat. I caught a glimpse of a red silk vest under the coat. "You dropped this." His eyes bore into me as he stood, and for a moment, I didn't breathe.

Ah, it's you, I thought.

I'd noticed him when I'd come into the dining room. I'd even felt regret that I wasn't in Natchez on some pleasure trip that might allow me to meet him. He had light blond hair with a high widow's peak, intelligent blue eyes, a square jaw, and a bold, confident manner. So confident that if my ability hadn't included being able to instantly identify Unbounded, I might have mistaken him for one of my kind.

He'd also noticed me, and the interest I'd sensed from him earlier was stronger now at close proximity. He handed me the letter, and our eyes held. It was difficult to tell his interest from my own, though I refrained from delving into his more private thoughts.

It's been too long. Too long since I'd let myself care for a man. Here I was acting like a young girl simply because a gentleman had been mannerly.

A really fine gentleman.

I blinked the thoughts away and accepted the letter.

"Thank you. I very much appreciate it. It would have been a great loss to me."

His smile was disarming. "I'm glad then. Though I daresay, I'm jealous of the man."

"Oh, really?" I couldn't stop amusement from seeping into my voice. "How do you know it's from a man?"

"The intentness in your gaze." He inclined his head, his grin still wide. "But he is far away, and I am here. I think it might be important to point this out."

That made me laugh. "Maybe so. I'll think on it."

"It would be my great fortune. I will be here a day or two." He gave a full bow that somehow seemed both to mock and to flatter me. "I won't keep you. I saw your girl wave to you. She looked . . . upset."

His concern for a mere slave intrigued me. "Yes, you are correct. Please, excuse me."

He bowed again, and I forced my curiosity about him to the back of my mind as I hurried out of the room and up the front staircase.

Betsy was waiting in my sitting room, terror for her sister and her family etched across her face. "I saw 'em! Looks like they only jest come t' town. Got 'em in the pen, out in the open, not inside. Like there's too many to fit. They be on the block t'morrow, if'n I guess right."

"Then we'll act tonight. Locke and I will get them out. And Ritter, of course. You must stay here. You've risked enough by traveling here on your own."

Betsy nodded. "I cain't see how sumpin' like this can happen. They was free and happy up North. We all was."

"You will be again." I set my reticule on the narrow wall table next to the door. "If you will, please go inform Locke and Ritter that we need to be ready to go before nightfall."

Betsy took two steps toward the door before she halted and turned around, flinging herself into my arms. "There was nowhere else t' go. I knew you'd help Frances. But don't go gettin' yo'self hurt. You's the only white angel I know."

I returned her exuberant hug. Betsy was my own physical age, and she'd grown up on my plantation in Savannah. She didn't seemed to notice that I hadn't aged while we'd lived together or in the five years since I sent her and her sister, a former slave from a neighboring plantation, north with their families.

"Don't you worry. It'll be all right." My drawl hid my real emotion. Inside I was furious. This wasn't the first time my former slaves had contacted me for help, but it was the first time an entire free family had been stolen from the North and brought back to be sold into slavery.

Since my recent return from England with Locke and Ritter, I'd been hearing more and more about such illegal events happening, and there was no way I was going to sit by and watch as my friends' lives were stolen. If I had my way, this particular slaver, Lucias Johansson, was going out of business—permanently.

Just that fast, Betsy curtsied and was gone. I began removing my skirt to prepare for the evening's adventures. I normally loved the gowns of the south, but my combat training had also taught me how impractical they were. I couldn't be encumbered by skirts tonight. The clock on the fireplace mantel told me I had plenty of time for my disguise.

Excitement rippled through me—my Unbounded genes kicking in. I was ready for action. I craved it. Though we'd recently had two skirmishes with the Emporium in New York City when their agents had tried to assassinate several key political leaders, for the most part I had been in the background. All Unbounded were gifted at something, but my sensing ability was a rare talent and none of our Renegade allies were willing to risk me. After determining the guilty parties, I'd been relegated to watching and waiting.

Neither of which I did well, even when necessary. Maybe it was something I'd learn in the next hundred years or so.

My eyes landed on the letter I'd been reading earlier, sticking partially out of my reticule. Miles Smithson, Gabriel's second great-grandson, had grown up to be a good man, and the money I'd spent educating first his father and then him had been well-employed. Miles had become an attorney-at-law in Alabama and hadn't needed my patronage for years, but I still enjoyed exchanging letters with him. Though I couldn't tell him the full extent of my life, he shared my views on nearly every political issue—especially those regarding slavery.

Of course he might not have had much chance to pursue other opinions. I'd been his family's benefactor since Gabriel senior's death, sending all his posterity to college. Because I was their benefactor, they'd had no choice but to listen to my views, and the more educated they became, the more they understood the world at large and the evils slavery represented.

I'd met Miles only once, when he was a young child. Though I'd promised Gabriel to look after his family, I'd satisfied my duty with letters from afar so that my unchanging appearance wouldn't be noted. Every now and then I made an appearance as some relative—a granddaughter or the granddaughter's niece. It was enough to fulfill my promise and to keep them safe from the Emporium, who would use them as collateral against me if they discovered an opportunity. The Emporium would be happy to capture a sensing Unbounded with an extended lifetime of childbearing in front of her.

At that thought, my stomach tensed. I had almost married again a decade ago, but for the fertile Unbounded, marrying always meant bearing children, and I couldn't. Not then. So I had let him go. I hadn't regretted my decision. Mostly. One advantage of living two thousand years was having plenty of time to change your mind.

Maybe I'd look Miles up on our way back to Georgia. He would be twenty-nine now, only a few years younger than I was, and he wouldn't remember my visit so long ago. I'd be interested in meeting a man who wrote an old lady—or someone he thought was an old lady—such witty and intelligent letters. I'd have to pretend to be an even younger relative than the granddaughter's niece he thought me to be, the woman he'd met as a child. Maybe a cousin this time. I'd have to research what I'd told him.

Humming under my breath, I turned into my bedroom to finish dressing.

LOCKE'S SMILE GREW WIDE AS SHE TOOK IN MY APPEARANCE. "YOU make a mighty pretty boy." She was also dressed as a man, and her blond hair was hidden under a hat like mine, but her disguise made her look in need of a good shave instead of a woman wearing a man's clothes. Nothing short of a miracle where the very female Locke was concerned.

Dragging my gaze from the mirror over the bureau, I scowled. "That noticeable, huh?"

Beside her, Ritter barked a laugh. "Your skin. It's not right. Not even close." He peered closer, a sardonic grin on his face. "Is that face powder mixed with coffee grounds?"

I groaned, though a part of me noted the laugh. Even after seventy years of working together, the laughs didn't come frequently enough. His anger still consumed him, but he was more careful now. Maybe in another fifty years he might understand that anger never brought our loved ones back. It only made us different from the people they had loved in life. Maybe we even risked becoming someone they wouldn't care to know.

"I was trying a new process," I said, "but I hadn't tested it yet." I usually did our operations in my dresses—accidentally touching people or pushing my way into their minds to study the sand stream of their thoughts. More often than not, my job was primarily to inform those gifted with other abilities which Emporium agents were Unbounded and which were mortal employees. Only when I was really lucky did I get to use my combat training. This only made me train all the harder because I didn't want to let anyone down if I did have to fight.

Locke opened her bag and began setting out containers on the bureau. "Well, the smell certainly screams *eau de l'homme*." She meant aroma of man, but the French words lost something in the translation.

Ritter folded his arms across the very wide expanse of his muscled chest. He looked dark, dangerous, and deadly. I sensed he wasn't offended by Locke's comment, his thoughts already far away. A flash of memory filled me: a dark-haired woman in a blue dress, her body severed in three. Ritter's former fiancée, who had been murdered with his family. Severing the body's three focal points—the brain, the heart, the reproductive organs—was one of only two ways Unbounded could be killed. That his fiancée wasn't likely to undergo the Change hadn't mattered to the Emporium. They had been gunning for Ritter, who, after reaching his thirtieth birthday, had Changed, and for his little sister, who had the possibility of Changing one day.

I wished I could convince Ritter that it wasn't his fault, but in the end I didn't think it would matter. His family and the woman he loved were still dead, along with Ritter's Unbounded ancestor who'd arrived barely in time to save him. It was a guilt he'd have to come to terms with or the two thousand years of his life would be long and lonely.

That loneliness I sometimes still felt in my own heart, and on those days, Locke and Ritter and my work weren't enough. I still longed for my Hannah, but I no longer blamed myself for her death, even though ultimately, through my youth and inexperience, I was responsible for it.

"So what's the plan tonight?" Locke asked, as she began fixing my face. She was older than me by more than four centuries but was content to let me lead. She just wanted to fight. Between her and Ritter, who shared her combat ability, I'd have to make sure they didn't have too much fun. Mortals broke easily, and while we wanted to stop the abuse of our friends, our ultimate goal was to protect mortals from the Emporium—and from themselves.

"We'll free Frances and her family from the holding pen," I said. "Then we'll track down Johansson and have a chat with him."

"So we aren't just going to wait until tomorrow to buy Frances's family? It might be better." We'd done it before, but the anticipation in Locke's voice belied her comment. She wanted to put an end to the slaver as much as I did.

"No," I said. "We're going to shut Johansson down."

CHAPTER 7

THE CLUSTER OF BUILDINGS AT THE FORKS OF THE ROAD WAS little more than a dirty prison camp. The sprawling market would sell up to five hundred slaves a day, most bought in Virginia and sold here in the Deep South to cotton plantation owners. Importing slaves from outside the US hadn't been legal for over forty years, but the domestic breeding and slave trade abounded. The profit was huge and even larger when the slaves weren't really slaves at all like Betsy's family.

Anger burned in me. We'd helped thousands of former slaves over the years, and our Renegade allies were active in politics, fighting to end slavery altogether, but the greed of humanity—and the Emporium, who had fingers in every large slaving company—meant that it would likely be years before the end came altogether.

One life at a time, I told myself.

Most of the slavers had marched their so-called property to Natchez like cattle, boating them only part of the way. Here they would be bathed, clothed, and then haggled over like a mule or a wagon. The indignity aside, being torn from their homes and loved ones was something they never got over.

I knew because I felt their emotions, and they were every bit as human—perhaps more so—as those who treated them like animals.

Rough wooden buildings partially circled the slave holding pen, the spaces between the buildings enclosed with wood fencing, tin scraps, or whatever was at hand. A large gate led into a courtyard. Inside the buildings, slave men and women and children were kept at night and bargained over during the day. But Betsy had seen Frances and her family in the courtyard with others, constructing makeshift tents or simply collapsing on the ground. That told me the market was unusually full, but the coming summer did mean higher profits, so it wasn't surprising.

We investigated the entire area from the outside and formulated a plan, noting the positions of the few patrolling guards. In the fading evening light many of the exhausted slaves in the courtyard resembled sacks of flour lumped on the ground. Evening came early in April and could be deathly cold, though tonight it was still relatively mild. I hoped the good weather would hold.

A child's cry cut through the night. A child who by morning might never see his mother again.

"Wait for the signal," I told the others. I was going inside to find Frances.

Locke and Ritter nodded, fanning out along the perimeter. I didn't have to tell them to watch for the patrol. Locke and Ritter both knew their job, and I'd signal with the pistol I carried in my holster under my coat if things got out of control.

Getting inside shouldn't be a problem. I carried a crate of white cotton shirts that matched those the slavers distributed, and while I was older than most delivery boys, I knew how to get through. I approached the two guards at the gate entrance, my eyes down on the ground.

"What you got there?" With the squeak of a leather boot, one of the guards stepped in front of me. He reeked more of *eau de l'homme* than I'd smelled on any man since Simon had grunted over my body after a full day of work in the fields. His long brown hair looked greasy enough to oil my gun.

"More shirts. They need 'em before morning. Gotta get them Negroes up to snuff."

"Who they for?" asked his partner. His hair fell into his mean eyes, and a vertical scar ran down the center of his cheek from his eye to his jaw, looking awfully similar to the fake one Locke had fashioned across my cheek. I hoped he didn't expect me to trade war stories.

"Oh, it's that tall dude. Should be in the courtyard. Mister, uh . . ." I was gambling a little, but there seemed to be too many slaves in the courtyard to belong only to Johansson, and for now I didn't want to be remembered in connection with him since I planned to steal Frances and her family away from here. Reaching out, I used my proximity to push into the long-haired guard's mind. There his thoughts ran in a stream that resembled sand angling from the top right of my vision and vanishing near my lower left, each grain representing a thought, and not always a conscious one. I saw almost immediately what I needed. "Mister Armstead," I said.

"He ain't that tall." This from the first man, who was rather short.

I shrugged, not meeting his eyes. "Everybody's tall to me."

He barked a laugh and puffed out his chest. "That's true enough."

"You'll find Armstead's Negroes that way." The mean-eyed fellow threw out an arm in the opposite direction I wanted to go. Oh well.

I took a step forward. "Thank you."

"Wait." Hard fingers gripped my shoulder. Mean-eyes, of course. "Don't you got somethin' for us? You know the rules. It's after hours."

I pulled a bottle of gin from under the shirts. "Right. Almost forgot." They took the bottle, laughing greedily, and didn't stop me from hurrying away.

Before long I was weaving around the clumps of people, many dead to the world after their gruesome march, their dark skin blending into the night. Every so often a sob reached my ears, but for the most part an eery silence reined. A silence of despair and hopelessness.

I ducked around a tent that tonight was being used as a bathhouse. Several guards were peeping in, watching a group of slave women through large gaps in the cloth. Some women used their bodies as shields for others as they bathed. I burned with anger. I could take out all the guards but not before they raised an alarm. I angled away from the tent.

Somewhere a deep mournful voice was singing, words in a language passed down by their fathers. I'd learned several dialects, but this one wasn't familiar, and I understood only a few words. The notes caught at me, begging for freedom, for escape. I pushed on.

I found Frances and her family in a group beyond one of the smaller buildings. She sat holding her daughter, Mabel, a child of ten, who was wrapped in a thin blanket. Tears marked Frances's face as she rocked back and forth soundlessly.

Her husband, James, lay on a tarp, his arms spread protectively over their two teenage boys' huddled forms, giving the children what warmth he could. James was gaunt and looked miserable. He had to be exhausted, but his eyes were open and searching the sky. Searching for what?

I didn't know.

I approached slowly. Fear blossomed in Frances's eyes as she spotted me. "Don't worry," I said, in my own voice. "I have something for you."

"They give us clothes already," she said.

James sat up, abruptly becoming aware of my presence.

His fists clenched. He was wearing the white shirt, plain pants, and sturdy shoes of a slave about to be sold.

I glanced around, fearing that some of the other slaves nearby would hear. There was little hope of privacy. I had to get closer. James moved as I did, clearly ready to protect his wife.

I went to my knees at her side. "It's me, Ava O'Hare."

Frances's eyes widened, and she motioned for James to squat down with us. "Thank de blessed Lawd," Frances said. "I knew ya'd come."

I didn't tell her that we almost hadn't made it in time. If Betsy hadn't sold everything she owned and sent a rider to me with a message to meet her here, if she hadn't been able to find out that the slaver Johansson was heading to Natchez, and if we hadn't ridden hard to beat them here, everything would have worked out differently. My anger burned again. Too many ifs.

"My baby," Frances said. "She burnin' with fever. James carried her most all de way from de North. I cain't lose her."

"You won't. But we have to move closer to that building back there. Next to it there's a length of wood fence. James, wake the boys and tell them to go there. But have them circle around. We can't risk drawing attention." I flicked my eyes in the right direction. "Go slow. Don't call attention to yourself. You know how the guards are." They wouldn't shoot unless they had to, because they considered the Negroes valuable livestock, but killing one that was trying to escape would bring about less guilt than putting down an old horse.

"Yes, Miss." James's eyes met mine, hope replacing his former desolation. "Thank ye fer comin'."

"Hurry," I said. Some of the sleepers around us were waking now, and though we'd been quiet, their eyes were watchful.

I arose and said louder to Frances in my practiced male voice, "Come with me. I have medicine to dose the child. Mister Johansson won't be happy if he can't get a sale tomorrow. If you're lucky, you'll go together. But only if she's better."

A sob caught in Frances's throat at the words that we both knew were truth—or would have been if I hadn't come. But we'd gone only a few paces when Frances whispered. "What 'bout de others?"

"Others?"

"More'n sixty-five of us, I think."

I stepped closer to her, accidentally bumping her in my shock. "Sixty-five? Taken from the North?"

"'Bout forty from de North. We was met partway by others come from Virginia. And dat man what brought de others—" She gave me a frightened look, her eyes glistening in the darkness. "I never saw de like. I think he de real boss man. Put me in mind of Massa Ritter. But meaner."

Ritter would correct her if he'd heard Frances use that title. He wasn't anyone's master, he'd say, but some habits were hard to break, and Frances wasn't about to change now. Her description bothered me, because Unbounded were different from other people, but to people without my gift, it came across as striking beauty and confidence. In a rich drawing room where everyone looked their best, it wasn't as noticeable, but in a setting like this, where so many men were missing teeth, had scars, or were withered by the sun, Unbounded always stood out.

"De others," Frances said into the silence. "They has chillens."

More children. My mind raced. *One thing at a time. Think about the others after you free Frances.*

"You!" a shout came from across the courtyard.

Frances stiffened. "Let me do the talking," I said. Not that she'd speak anyway; she looked too frightened. Even if I had to fight my way out, I trusted that Ritter and Locke would be ready to back me up.

A man came striding across the sea of captives, those who were awake cringing away from him and his two companions. His life force glowed dimmer than everyone else's in the area, signaling a blocked mind.

That wasn't all my ability confirmed. Mortals could also block, those who learned how, but this man was definitely Unbounded, and that meant the Emporium was here.

CHAPTER 8

I WOULD HAVE GUESSED THAT HE WAS UNBOUNDED EVEN without my ability by the way he carried himself. As if he owned not only the Forks of the Road but all of Mississippi. Emporium Unbounded saw themselves as gods, and all mortals as little more than slaves to be used and discarded as desired. If they had their way, this place would someday see white flesh mixed in with the black. Even if combat wasn't his ability, this Unbounded was likely trained, and the double pistols at his sides certainly weren't for looks.

Yet as long as he didn't share my ability and couldn't tell that I was Unbounded, I still had an advantage. The two mortals accompanying him had bright life forces, but they carried rifles, useless in close fighting. They would not be a concern unless I let down my guard. I reached into my crate and began moving objects.

"What's going on here?" the Unbounded demanded. I briefly met his stare before looking down like any subservient would. He wasn't an Unbounded I'd ever met or one we had listed in our files. He also hadn't seemed to mark me as Unbounded, so he didn't share my particular ability. "I am employed by the city of Natchez. As you know, we can't risk an outbreak of disease, which is why we have the Forks set up away from town. I am examining this child. She might be contagious."

"You're a doctor?"

"Only an assistant." I let a little derision slip into my voice, telling everyone within range know that I considered treating "livestock" beneath even an assistant.

He gazed down into the crate I carried, but instead of the white shirts, the top items were now bottles of chemicals and powders. "You do not have permission to remove them from the courtyard." Arrogance dripped from the words.

"That won't be necessary. Are you Lucias Johansson?"

"Nah. He's John Cardiff," said one of the henchmen. "Johansson works for him. These Negroes are his property."

When Cardiff didn't refute him, I said, "I need space to check this child." I pointed to a place some ten feet away from a length of wood fencing. Not where Ritter and Locke waited, but it would have to do.

Cardiff's gaze fell on Mabel, and I took the opportunity to study him. Dark eyes framed by thick black lashes. A head of dark hair that was slightly wavy and looked freshly washed. A narrow, recently shaven, face that would have been compellingly attractive except for the cruel set of his jaw. Clean clothes that fit his figure well and not so much hinted at but screamed wealth.

I wanted to stab my knife into his heart.

He pointed a finger at Frances. "Put the child down over there and get back with the others. The *assistant* here will bring back the whelp if it survives."

Ignoring Frances's swift intake of breath, Cardiff jerked his hand, and one of his goons jabbed his rifle into her, keeping well away from Mabel. Frances stumbled forward. At the place I'd indicated, she laid Mabel down, tucking the thin blanket around her small figure.

Frances stared at me, her eyes pleading. "Please, Massa, keep my babe safe." I knew what she was saying, for me to save Mabel and the rest of her family, even if I couldn't come back for her.

"Git!" said the man with the rifle at her back. "I see you back here, and I'll put a bullet through yer head!"

Frances fled. Without another word, the Unbounded and his companions turned and stalked away.

Now what? I felt Mabel's forehead. She moaned and her eyes opened with a fluttering.

"Shush now," I said. "It'll be okay."

"Who are you?" Her brow furrowed in concentration.

"I'm a friend of your Aunt Betsy."

"They took my book," she murmured, tears filling her voice. "Said Niggurs like me can't read. It was my only book."

"I'll get you another one. I promise."

I sent my mind out, reaching for Ritter and Locke. I hoped they were close enough. There. A life force near the fence. Ritter. And he was even more angry than usual. I felt the emotion, though not the reason.

Making sure no one watched me, I whistled. Seconds later, Ritter knelt by the fence.

"What about the guards?" I asked.

"They won't bother us. Where's Frances?"

"I'll have to go back for her."

"Scoot the child closer."

I heard a sawing noise as he worked at the bottom pole. I held up a bottle, pretending to examine its contents, but in reality, I was searching for watching eyes. "There's a man over there paying us a little too much attention," I whispered. "You're in enough shadow that he won't be able to see you, but he'll certainly notice if I push her through the fence."

The sawing stopped briefly. "You'd better have a talk with him."

I bent closer to Mabel and whispered. "This nice gentleman is a friend. He's going to take you to your daddy. Don't make any noise. Understand?"

She nodded, the fear in her eyes tying a knot in my throat.

"If you can't get Frances out at the original location," Ritter said, "meet me at the rendezvous. We'll formulate another plan."

Giving Mabel a comforting pat, I stood and walked

toward the slave who'd kept glancing in our direction, the only man awake in a group of huddled people. He was a big man with a prominent forehead and arms that went on forever. But like James, he was gaunt and appeared exhausted.

"You sick?" I asked. "I work for the city. We can't have sickness spreading to the town."

"No, Massa, I ain't sick." His voice was higher than I expected and docile.

I saw a rag sticking out of his pants and the slight darkness of a stain below the knee. "Roll up your pants."

He blinked. "Ain't nothin' wrong."

"I'll help you. Please."

He blinked in surprise at my words. Still, with great reluctance the big man rolled up his pant leg. The rag he'd tied around his calf was soaked with blood.

"I'm going to have to look at it."

The knots were too tight to untie, and he made no objection when I took scissors from my crate and cut it off. A gaping wound met my efforts. "This needs stitching." I looked around and grabbed a stick from the dirt, handing it to him. "Bite down on this. Sorry, but it's going to hurt." I'd seen men take fever and die from lesser wounds.

I splashed alcohol around the wound and began stitching. I wasn't a healer, but every Renegade learned to patch people up. To the man's credit, he didn't utter a peep, though rivulets of sweat rolled down his face. When I had finished with fifteen neat stitches, I used clean bandages to wrap it, then I handed him a pill from one of the bottles. "Take this. It'll make sure you don't get a fever."

He swallowed it without question. The drug was one that our Renegade healers had invented for mortal use, though we estimated that it would be another hundred years before mortal technology began to catch up. We'd helped fund studies involving mold, but there was only so much we could do without making our existence known. The slow-release antibiotic would stay in the man's system for a week—hopefully long enough. If the night weather didn't turn warmer soon, or if he wasn't given a blanket, he still might not survive.

I glanced back to where I'd left Mabel, but she was gone. "Musta gone back to her momma," the big man said, seeing my gaze.

"Guess she's feeling better. Look, in this many days"—I held up two hands and then one more—"these threads have to come out. The swelling will have gone down. All you do is cut off the knot and pull it out. One of the women should be able to do it for you."

He nodded. "Fifteen days."

I had underestimated him. Over the years I'd made sure the slaves on my plantation could count and read, and I'd given secret lessons to their families who lived nearby, but many slave owners felt doing so was dangerous to their superiority. "That's right. Fifteen days."

It took a few more moments to extract myself from his exuberant thanks, but the more time that passed without alarms being raised, the more likelihood that Ritter and Locke had managed to get James and the children free. Now if I could do the same for Frances, we'd be in the clear.

I didn't fool myself that Johansson wouldn't eventually notice five missing "slaves," and Cardiff was even less likely to let it slide. But my plans for disrupting Johansson's entire operation had to wait now that there was an Emporium agent in charge. We'd need more Renegade agents and deeper intel on their operation before we moved on them, because in all probability, this was only a small percentage of his business, and we would need to bring it all down to save even more people.

Tenika Vasco of the New York Renegades was descended from Angolan Unbounded, and she'd be more than happy to pose as a slave to infiltrate his operation. Her ability was called hypnosuggestion, and she could talk any but the most resistant to coming around to her way of thinking. Plus, she was a strong soldier, so she'd be safe enough if we kept an eye on her. I didn't like the idea of delaying anything, especially in light of the other people stolen from the North, but that couldn't be helped. Unless I could come up with another plan—and fast.

My thoughts scattered when I realized Frances wasn't waiting where I'd first found her. The tarp was still there, but the tattered bag of belongings was not. Anxiously, I searched the area. Had she found her way to the original escape point?

I leaned over and touched a huddled form, and a man uncurled to look at me. "The woman who was here with her family, a sick little girl. Did you see where she went?"

"No, Massa." When I nodded my thanks, he curled back up and closed his eyes.

"I see her go," a little boy spoke up, rising with a blanket wrapped around his thin shoulders. "With my momma. De boss man take 'em. He havin' a party and need some workers. Her girl wasn't with her."

"He chose Miss Frances?" I knew slavers claimed they could barely tell one slave from another, but it was odd that he'd chosen her when he knew I would be bringing back her child.

"No, she jest follow de others that was taken."

Getting out one way or the other—I had to admire Frances's ingenuity. She must have expected me to leave with Mabel and figured that following the other slaves out of the pen was her only chance to join her family. But escaping on her own put her at higher risk of being caught. I had to get to her before she made the attempt.

I nodded at the child and turned away.

"Massa," he asked, "is my momma comin' back?" He looked frightened as he bent in on himself.

"I think so." For all the good it would do him tomorrow. He looked about Mabel's age and according to law that was old enough for separation.

Swallowing the bitter lump in my throat, I hurried to the wide gate and escaped. Relief filled me as I left the hopelessness and anguish behind.

A whistled signal drew me to the shadows near the rendezvous point, where Ritter waited. In his arms, he cradled Mabel, now wrapped in an additional blanket from our supplies, her face partially covered so no one could see her color.

At the question in his eyes, I shook my head. "Frances is with an Unbounded I met earlier in the courtyard. Name's Cardiff, and apparently Johansson works for him. He's got to be Emporium. We don't have much time." If we were going to save her, I meant, but I wouldn't voice it aloud because of the child, who might not be asleep.

He nodded. "I'll go."

"No. You'd better get her to Locke. She needs attention." I was strong and quick, but Ritter could move faster than any combat Unbounded I'd met, even Eva when she'd been alive. "I'll track down Frances."

The muscles in his jaw worked. Clearly, Ritter wanted to protest but didn't because he knew I was right. I was also his leader, and he knew how to follow a leader he believed in. It was why I could trust him with my life.

He gave a sharp nod. "I'll meet you when I'm finished."

CHAPTER 9

RITTER VANISHED INTO THE NIGHT TO CATCH UP WITH LOCKE and the others, while I exchanged my crate for an oversized bag of weapons and disguises. I had to be prepared for anything. It was barely past the normal dinner hour, but darkness lay heavily on the cold streets.

After a little asking around, I located Cardiff's residence. In typical Emporium fashion—and Renegade as well—he apparently owned a two-story, red-brick house on the south edge of town, using it only when he was here on business. No wonder he needed additional slaves for his event. No doubt he would be entertaining other slavers and local leaders, and the staff who normally kept his house wouldn't be enough for a large event.

Cardiff's house was set back from the road, with a large space for carriage parking, as though he entertained often. A cobblestone walkway, huge white columns, and a second-floor veranda over the entry testified of his wealth and privilege. Bright lights burned from every window, making the house gleam like an evil jack-o'-lantern on All Hallows' Eve, contrasting sharply with the happy, playful music that floated on the cool night air.

Couples had already begun arriving at the house, dressed in their finest clothing. A stableboy directed the drivers where to park after delivering their wealthy cargo, and three drivers already stood in a group near one of the parked carriages, smoking and mumbling in low voices.

I skirted the house, pausing only to look into the windows. I saw white servants dressed in uniforms, arranging platters of food. No slaves there. Apparently Cardiff didn't like his slaves to have direct contact with his guests. I'd have better luck around back.

Sure enough, the kitchens at the rear of the house were alive with activity. A dozen women, their dark faces lean and unsmiling, hurried about their business. Such a contrast from my plantation where laughter often rose over the clatter of pots and pans. Most of the women wore the standard clothing issued by slavers before a sale, but a few wore uniforms and seemed to be directing the others.

None of the women were Frances. Had she already tried to run away? If so, she could be lying in a ditch somewhere, and I was risking her family and myself for nothing by looking for her. I pushed the thoughts to a corner of my mind with the other dark thoughts that haunted my past.

I was debating whether to go in through the back door when a single scream pierced the night, barely distinguishable under the music. It cut off instantly, but the sound had come from the direction of the stables. I ran, keeping to the shadows. Pausing near the barn's partially open double doors, I stashed my bags into some bushes and pushed out my thoughts. No life forces glowed near the entrance, but there were numerous life forces of animals. Deeper inside, I located people. Two, maybe, or three if two of them were very close together. They were deep enough inside the structure that the distance made it difficult to distinguish.

I slid inside, checking my pistol but knowing using it would be a last resort.

The inside of the barn was dim except for a glow at the end of a row of horse stalls. I moved stealthily past the stalls, aware of the animals watching me. I sent out a calming emotion, which generally worked with both animals and mortals. Not so well with Unbounded since they usually blocked their minds.

At the end of the stalls, I reached an open area, dimly illuminated by the light cast from a lantern that was hanging on a nail near a mound of flattened straw. A white male with a worn hat pulled low over his eyes had his arms around a woman with dark skin. She was weeping. Her back was toward me, but I could see her clothing was torn and disheveled, her hair full of straw. Her emotions told me she'd been violated.

Frances!

I launched myself at them, tearing the woman from the man's grasp and throwing my fist into his face, even as a part of my brain registered that the woman wasn't Frances after all.

Pain exploded in my cheek as the man lashed out at me. I'd almost expected Cardiff when I'd first heard the scream, but this man wasn't Unbounded and he dressed like a common slaver. Maybe Johansson then? But wouldn't he be over at his boss's party?

I ducked his next punch, and spun, landing a kick on his thigh that made him cry out. I slammed him twice more, then blocked one jab and took another on the shoulder. Not a hard hit, and it put me into a good position. I pulled back for the finishing blow.

He rushed me, his heavier weight giving him advantage as he knocked me to the straw-carpeted ground. I twisted free as we hit, my hat flying and taking my brown wig with it.

I struck hard before he could manage to pin me. Something in his face gave, and blood spurted between us. I jumped to my feet while he was still on his knees and pressed forward, punching hard and taking another blow, so I could whip around and put him in a headlock. My chin knocked his hat to the ground.

"Move and you die," I growled, pressing my knife against his throat.

"Stop!" the woman shouted. "Stop!"

I looked to my side to see her grabbing a pitch fork, then twirling it so the prongs pointed at my head.

"What?" I said, not relinquishing my hold. "I'm trying to save you!"

The woman jabbed the pitchfork closer. "He saved me!" she said at the same moment the man asked, "*You're trying to save her?*"

I craned my neck to see the man's face. His eyes, now unhidden by his hat, stared back at me, bright blue and familiar. "You!" I whispered, my hold loosening. Gone were the expensive clothes, and he'd definitely done something to fake that hair sprouting from his face because he'd been clean-shaven in the hotel dining room only a few hours ago.

"You seem to have me at a disadvantage," he said, his voice teasing as it had been at the hotel, as though the entire brawl had amused him. "Whom do I have the pleasure of addressing?"

I was relieved he didn't recognize me, though my hat was gone and my blond hair, pinned tightly to my head, was obviously more abundant than that of a typical male. Before I could respond, I became aware of another life force behind several bales of hay. Two life forces, I had thought when I'd entered the barn, but the man and woman had been too close and I should have counted them separately. The other life force was lying motionless but still burning strong.

The man's eyes flicked over to the bale, following my stare. "I see you located the real perpetrator."

I blinked because he couldn't possibly know that I could sense the unconscious man behind the hay.

Could he? Then I spied a boot emerging from behind the bale; it had to be what the man thought had drawn my attention.

"I assume that means there's a man attached to that boot," I said, still using a deep voice that I hoped would continue to hide my identity despite the loss of my hat and wig. "All right. I'm going to step back now."

"Please do," he said dryly. To the woman, he added, "I think you can put that down now."

She nodded, her eyes bulging slightly, and lowered the pitchfork but didn't drop it entirely. Who could blame her?

In a swift move, I released the man and stood, still gripping the knife just in case, placing him between me and the pitchfork. He arose, removed a handkerchief from his pocket, and began wiping the blood from his face. He was taller than I was, though not by much, but he had a good thirty pounds on me, at least. Even with the disguise, he was attractive, and I didn't like the way something in me reacted to him.

"Who are you?" I asked.

One brow arched. "Who are you?"

Mortals were so tedious at times. I hoped I wouldn't have to knock them both out and remove their memories before I could continue looking for Frances. "You first," I said, pulling out my pistol, though I had no intention of using it and alerting those in the house to my presence.

"Hold it," he said, his hands out in front of him. "I am here only because I heard Lucias Johansson illegally enslaved free Negroes. I plan to stop him, so I talked to a few people I know, found out where he was, and followed him to the house. I was waiting for my contacts when he took a liking to this woman"—he dipped his head respectfully in her direction—"and I had to take action." To her, he added. "I'm sorry I wasn't able to stop him sooner." He was telling the truth on both accounts, I sensed.

"Then we are essentially on the same side." I put away the gun.

The woman gave a sob, her face crumpling. "I want to go home to my family." Finally, she let go of the pitchfork.

"Are you from the North?" I asked. She sounded younger than I'd first thought. Not a woman, really, but a girl. It was hard to tell sometimes when children often worked in the fields under the hot sun. Whatever her former occupation, she was both pretty and curvaceous, which was probably why Johansson had targeted her.

She shook her head. "Petersburg."

Virginia. A slave, ripped from her family. Not illegally. Her emotions were all over the place, and I had to block them before the despair made me desperate.

The man averted his gaze, taking a step in my direction and reaching out a hand. "You can call me Smith." For the first time he was telling me an untruth, but as I wasn't about to share my identity, I didn't hold it against him. If I needed, I could get it from his thoughts, but more pressing matters demanded my attention.

Ignoring his outstretched hand and the way his smile

made my heart trip harder in my chest, I stepped around the bale of hay to look at the sprawled man. His pants were on, but sagging around his hips, his untucked shirt hiding most of him. He was obviously out for the count.

"So this is Johansson," I mused. He was dressed for a party. Not nearly as nicely as his more dangerous boss, but he clearly wasn't hurting for cash. No wonder, if he was abducting people from the North.

"My plan," Smith came up beside me, "was to have him arrested tonight, and when I learned about the party, I thought the more witnesses the better. But after this"— his head indicated the inert figure—"I may be the one who ends up in jail." He meant because the slave girl was Johansson's property, and if he wanted to molest her, it was his business in most men's eyes. Not in Smith's, though. I warmed a little more toward him and mentally cursed the fact that we'd run into each other like this instead of tomorrow at the hotel.

"He'll never remember you." I stepped across Johansson's body and squatted on his other side where I could still keep an eye on Smith and the girl. "Make sure no one is coming," I told Smith. Finding a liquor flask in Johansson's pocket, I unscrewed the cap and began splashing him with the contents. No one else was approaching, of course, or I'd sense a new life force, but I didn't want Smith to see what I was going to do next.

Smith obeyed me with that amused glint in his eyes, one that for some reason made me want to jump into his mind and discover his secrets. But I didn't invade people without a reason, especially good people, and I believed he was honorable.

Placing my hand on Johansson's head, I pushed into his mind. Unconscious thoughts were much less volatile than conscious ones. No sand stream of rushing thoughts, just a placid lake. I dove into it. Down, down—until I saw bubbles of thoughts. Not everyone's unconscious state represented as a lake, but most did, and I was glad he was typical.

Stepping aside from an oncoming bubble, I began searching for the one that held memory of this night. There. Dragging the girl to the barn, his body burning with anticipation, the girl's struggle heightening his lust. Her soft, warm flesh as he felt her breasts through the cloth and pushed aside her skirts. Her scream as he pushed her down and forced her legs apart. Then outrage as he was yanked to his feet, his lust not yet fully satisfied.

I plucked the entire bubble, pulling it to me until it disappeared. I didn't know or care where it went, but for him it no longer existed. I took the next one, too, where, after a few furious blows, Smith's fist plunged him into blackness.

Disgusted, I opened my eyes to see the girl watching me. "I'm sorry," I whispered, for her ears only.

A heavy single tear dripped from her eye and skidded down her cheek. "Not the first time. I had a baby once."

I saw in her thoughts the rest she didn't say, that she'd only been twelve and her mulatto son had died at birth.

I wanted to castrate Johansson right then, and every other male slave owner for good measure. Or take all his memories so that he'd be as helpless as a baby. Only Frances stopped me from taking the time, because I'd seen her in his mind, along with the rest when they arrived with Cardiff. She was in the house and that meant, one way or the other, I had to go inside and free her.

I arose. "We need you to keep quiet about our being here," I said, keeping my voice gentle. "Get back to the house. Not a word."

Her eyes fell to Johansson. "He'll kill me when he wakes."

"He won't remember, I swear to you. I have this." I reached inside my jacket and down my shirt, pulling out the small talisman nestled between my breasts. It had been carved back in 1755 by the oldest slave on the Savannah plantation. At the time, I'd been with Wymon and Eva for ten years. Ten years since I'd murdered Simon, and my nightmares had disrupted the household. The slave told me it was African magic and that it would make the nightmares stop. They did stop, and though I was sure it was more because of his kindness than any magic, I'd carried the talisman with me on missions ever since.

The girl's soft gasp told me she believed in magic. This would be more understandable to her than my own ability, which I supposed could be viewed as a magic of sorts instead of an inborn skill.

"Go on," I said. She nodded and hurried into the darkness past Smith. I stood as he abandoned his watch and strode in my direction. He carried a dark bag I hadn't seen before.

"A little alcohol isn't going to stop Johansson from remembering what I did to him," he said. "And if I don't go into that party and give my people the signal when he finally wakes from his sweet dreams, he won't be arrested and the people he kidnapped will be sold as slaves."

"If you clean up, he won't recognize you." I almost added, "I didn't," but stopped myself. "But at this point, I'm not sure you should do anything. Johansson isn't calling the shots anymore, if he ever was. Some man called Cardiff is in charge."

"The man who owns this place." He shrugged, his expression hardening. "Doesn't matter. If he knows that Johansson has been abducting free people, he should be arrested as well."

His eager righteousness was admirable, but he knew nothing of the Emporium and their viciousness. If they couldn't free their agent by bribery or force, they'd simply fake a death and move him elsewhere. A shot through the head might hurt Cardiff temporarily, but he'd awake to do more damage within days.

"You don't understand," I said. "Cardiff is dangerous. You stay away from him. He's *my* problem."

Smith's eyes regarded me unwaveringly. Even in the dim light, I could see their color, but I didn't recognize his expression, and for once, his emotions, though I could feel them, were unclear. My heartbeat increased.

"All right," he said finally. "You can have Cardiff

while I'll take on this clown." He thumbed down at Johansson. "I'll go in the house and make sure it's all set up." He dropped his bag and began unbuttoning his shirt.

"What are you doing?" I asked, as it dropped to the ground.

"Well, I can't go in looking like this."

He had a nice wide chest, covered with curly blond hair that beckoned to be touched. I didn't avert my gaze. Unbounded weren't concerned with nudity the way most mortals were. Something about living two thousand years and fighting in close combat often made it necessary for us to disrobe in front of our comrades, regardless of gender. I'd seen Ritter and many others in various stages of dress without reaction.

I was reacting now.

Okay, maybe it wasn't only the idea of having children that stopped my last relationship. Maybe it ended because I didn't have these feelings. I had cared for my suitor, had enjoyed his kisses, but I'd never wanted to lose myself in him. Never wanted to tell him about my past or my true self. I'd begun to wonder if Simon had forever ruined the part of me that made me a woman.

Except at the moment, that part was working overtime. I stood there shocked, whether because that kind of emotion had returned at all or because it was so powerful, I couldn't decide.

Smith pulled on a white silk shirt and began removing his boots. "Maybe you ought to keep watch. I won't be a minute." Again his voice was teasing, as though it didn't bother him that another man was staring at him as he dressed. Maybe he liked men in that way. But, no, I'd felt his attraction to me earlier.

Remember Frances, I told myself, stepping across Johansson, who, as if by signal, jerked. Not conscious yet, but it wouldn't be long.

I stopped to get my hat and wig, and by the time I reached the dark corridor between the horse stalls, my mind was working on a plan. My own clothing would need to be adjusted in order to get me inside the house undetected by Cardiff. Or maybe a different disguise altogether. He'd probably remember the physician's assistant with the scar. I had everything I needed in one of my bags.

I told myself I was going in for Frances, but I knew it was also for Smith. He might be man enough to take down Johansson, but I'd barely broken a sweat immobilizing him, and that meant Cardiff could easily kill Smith and his contacts. I wished Ritter at least were here, but hopefully the surprise on my side would allow me to handle a lone Emporium agent.

If there was only one.

Smith looked like a new man as he approached me in a burgundy tailcoat with a deep V opening that revealed his shirt and a dark cravat that matched the snug pants. Only his face looked odd with spots of the face paint that he was attempting to scrub off with his bloody handkerchief.

"I will let you know what happens," he said. "But tell me, is all this off my face?"

"No. Here." I pointed to my own face to show him where. "I'm going inside with you."

His eyes fell over my clothes. "I went to a lot of trouble to obtain an invitation, but they won't let you in like that, even if I vouch for you."

"I have other clothes. No, not there—you're missing it." I pulled out my own handkerchief and scrubbed off his cheek near his ear. This close he was even more compelling. "There." I gave him my handkerchief, feeling heated under his stare.

"You really intend to accompany me?"

"I have supplies outside. Just give me a few minutes."

"All right. But I must tell you that you are losing something." His hand went to my face and pinched, pulling off a large piece of my fake scar.

Oh, no. The piece kept coming. When he'd hit me earlier, it must have broken lose. The next thing I knew his other hand was on my chin and the realistic beard stubble Locke had worked so hard on came away.

Realization changed his expression to one of surprise. "Why you're . . . not a man at all!" He laughed, a glad sound that was unexpected in this dark place. "The woman from the hotel! I thought you seemed familiar. Your eyes. I've never seen gray that color before."

My cover was blown, but maybe I didn't need it anymore. Maybe in this case no disguise was the best disguise. Without responding, I turned and started toward the barn doors. Steps from behind told me he intended to come along.

I retrieved my bag, and we went back inside the barn, though not past the stalls this time. Rummaging inside the bag, I pushed a canteen filled with water at him. "You still have blood on your forehead."

It probably said something about his character that, though I could sense he urgently wanted to, he didn't once look my way as I traded my pants and shirt for a blush rose gown with a pointed waist and sloping shoulders. It had been packed tightly in one of my bags, but the material was impervious to wrinkles, or impervious enough not to attract notice. The neckline showed a good deal more cleavage than my usual choice, but left me freedom to fight. I didn't use a corset, of course, as that would have hindered movement. The gown had been specifically designed in England by our Renegade allies to hide weapons—mostly knives and a short sword, of which I was rather proud.

Brushing out my hair, I swept it up into something that would be appropriate for a party. I used a solution to wipe off the rest of my disguise, and my small mirror revealed that I hadn't escaped my fight with Smith unscathed. Under where the fake scar had been, my chin sported a large bruise that was fading fast, and a cut on my lip was knitting itself back together. I had other bruises on my body, but only the one on my shoulder showed slightly. A little face paint would hide all the damage well enough, especially if I let another fifteen minutes pass. Before the hour was out, I'd be completely healed.

I mentally checked on Johansson, then hurried toward the barn door where Smith waited. "Time to leave. He'll be awake any minute."

Smith's eyes widened, and it did something inside me to feel the tug of his desire as he regarded my new self. "I have just one question," he said, his voice strangely husky.

"I might answer." I thought he would ask my identity, or how I'd become involved with abolitionists—none of which I could tell him.

"Where did you learn to fight like that?"

Ah, now I detected a bit of wounded pride. I laughed. "Around."

I tried to move past him, but he remained motionless, his eyes still locked on my face. "Your bruise. It's gone."

"You just can't see it. It's dark." We had left the lantern with Johansson at the other end of the barn, but Smith was apparently seeing enough.

His gaze dropped to the cut on my lip, though he couldn't possibly see it under the red I'd painted there. My Unbounded genes boiled, demanding that I take what I wanted. What I'd been thinking of since the moment I'd seen his chest. Two steps would be all I'd need to get closer to him. I wouldn't have to raise myself far to meet his lips.

He dragged his eyes back to mine, and they echoed the passion that had sprung between us, heavy and aching.

I was lost. I hadn't expected this reaction in myself. Yes, the Unbounded gene was driven to survival, and I'd learned to control simple urges, but this was different.

No, this was a mistake. I stepped past him. "Johansson's waking."

"But—"

"Hurry."

"Who are you?" he asked, his voice still rough.

"You can call me Ava."

CHAPTER 10

I DON'T KNOW WHY I TOLD HIM MY REAL NAME, NOT THAT it mattered. Only those closest to me knew it now. Everyone else was dead. *As this mortal will be,* I told myself, *before you age another year.* Getting attached was never without risks and consequences.

I needed to focus on Frances.

We walked around to the front of the house. Several servants stared at us as we strode up the walk, but Smith winked at them and gave me a heated look that they couldn't misinterpret. I laughed. At least my new persona gave Smith a reason to be skulking around Cardiff's house. They would likely assume we had arrived earlier but had taken the opportunity for a little sport before going inside.

At the door, Smith handed the white butler an invitation. So many life forces were already present, glowing in my mind as bright as the oil lanterns placed to enhance the gas lighting installed in the house. We were ushered into a large parlor where no expense had been spared. The evidence of opulence was everywhere, from the handmade lace tablecloths to the rare foods on the banquet table. I could see no life forces blocking my mental searches, and the resulting jumble of emotions and thoughts was insane. So many in this room were angry, ambitious, and eager.

The mental cacophony would have overwhelmed me years ago, but now I cataloged, assessed, and blocked the people who were of no concern. As I'd seen before, only white servants were present in this room. Their master was nowhere to be seen.

"Is that ice cream?" Smith asked.

I sensed he loved the stuff. "So it appears." I gave him a level stare and he colored slightly. "Are your friends here?"

He nodded. "I've given them the signal. They'll act when Johansson arrives."

I followed his eyes to the side of the room holding the refreshment table. A man with a sheriff's badge stood with four other men. Not many against an Unbounded. Unless they were trained by someone like Locke or Ritter.

Where was Cardiff?

I pushed out my thoughts, searching for both Cardiff and Frances. I wished my ability weren't limited by distance, but I had to work with what I was given. I moved across the room, and Smith went with me. Eyes followed us, a customary occurrence. Mortals saw the undisguised me as far more than beautiful. Striking, perhaps. Compelling. It no longer fazed me—except Smith's sudden reluctance to leave my side, which could get him killed.

"Attend to your friends," I said. "I have my own agenda."

He gave me a wink. "I'll go talk with them, but I'm not finished with you, Miss Ava. Don't forget that I know where you are staying."

So much promise and confidence in his voice. He must have enjoyed the benefits of a good education, and I wondered what he did for a profession. Perhaps some kind of law enforcement. If he survived this night, I might find out.

Something in me shifted at that thought. If Smith died, it would be at the hands of Cardiff because I had failed. I needed backup if I wanted to have more than a chance of getting Smith and Frances out of here in one piece. Not to mention all the party guests. Ritter should arrive soon, unless he and Locke had encountered difficulties. I prayed that they hadn't.

Refusing a drink proffered by a servant, I slipped into the hallway, acting as if I knew where I was going. One servant stared at me as she passed with a new platter of ice cream, but I ignored her.

I reached the kitchen, but I couldn't find Frances, not even in alcoves and corners that I hadn't been able to see from the outside. Near the fireplace, the girl Smith had rescued in the barn looked up at me and then away again quickly, as though hoping not to be noticed. That made two of us, though she couldn't possibly recognize me in my present dress.

I stopped one of the slaves, whose clothing told me she'd come from the Forks of the Road. "I'm looking for Frances. Do you know where she is?"

She shook her head. "Maybe upstairs. We was told to make up rooms for the guests."

"Thank you." With the size of this group, it made sense that some of the guests would be staying. I only hoped Cardiff didn't make an appearance before I found her.

I'd only gone a few feet down the hall when a side door banged open, and there was Johansson, looking more confused than angry. He had a cut on his forehead, which he'd tried unsuccessfully to clean, instead smearing his face with blood.

"You there!" he growled at the servant who had passed me earlier with the ice cream platter. "I need attention." His eyes met mine as several white servants clustered around him, one with a basket of supplies.

I turned, feeling his eyes digging into me, and made my way down the hall to warn Smith about his arrival and to ask him to hold off on confronting Johansson until I found Frances. As I entered the parlor, Cardiff loomed before me. I recognized him instantly, though his clothing was considerably more elegant than it had been at the Forks of the Road.

His attention immediately fell to me, and a smile slashed across his handsome face, this time minus the cruelty. He bowed without apparent recognition. "Good evening. I am John Cardiff, your host. I am delighted to meet you Miss . . ."

"Mrs. Smith," I said, with a curtsy. "Frances Smith. The pleasure is mine. I am a visitor to your city. I came with my husband, who is probably over by the ice cream." I let admiration creep into my tone at the mention of the treat, a sentiment I was far from feeling.

"I am glad he is enjoying himself." He took my hand, though I had not offered, bringing it to his lips without releasing my eyes. "As this is not my usual residence and I come here only on business, fate must be smiling upon me to have our paths cross this enchanting evening. I trust you found what you were looking for?" He was asking my reason for wandering around his house, which showed that despite his glib words, he was suspicious of everyone. As he should be.

I was.

"Indeed," I replied. "I had a mishap with your ice cream, but it has been resolved." I touched my bare neck and his eyes greedily followed the motion before slipping lower. Maybe it wouldn't be so hard to trap this Emporium agent despite his caution—as long as he was alone. A little distraction would give me ample opportunity.

Besides craving for power and a blatant contempt for mortal life, another way Emporium Unbounded were not like Renegades was in their view of family. For Unbounded, intimacy always meant having children, as the Unbounded gene sought reproduction, and children meant the responsibility of checking up on them and their descendants for six generations to see if any posterity underwent the Change. Or for much longer if new Unbounded blood entered the family line. Renegades guarded family and relationships fiercely. We didn't dally. We loved with all we were until death, or we stayed apart. It was our way.

The Emporium was more like the parasitic cuckoo, planting their offspring where someone else would have to deal with the consequences until the child came of age. In their disregard for mortals, they viewed them as incubators and nannies to increase their own strength. In that light, a dalliance with a married woman was often most practical for their intentions. No one to kill or to pay off. No responsibility.

"Excuse me." I inclined my head and moved away, a little too fast for courtesy, but wise because my survival instincts were pushing me to attack this dangerous enemy. That had to wait until I found Frances.

I sidled up to Smith, who looked more pleased to see me than he should. "Johansson's here," I murmured, "but so is Cardiff, and I still haven't found the person I'm looking for."

"Oh?" His brow arched again in a way that for some unknown reason made my chest ache. "I didn't know you were looking for someone."

"I am. That's why I need you to hold off. I have to make sure she's safe."

His eyes went past me. "Too late." His voice held an apology.

There in the doorway to the parlor stood Johansson, looking like a man completely out of his element. Unlike Cardiff, he would be more comfortable with the servants rather than among this group of Natchez elite, regardless of his finery. The men Smith had pointed out earlier had already begun talking to him. I moved closer to hear what they were saying.

"What I'm saying is that we have proof that you have abducted free Negroes from the North," said the man with the badge. "Do you deny this?"

Johansson's already ruddy face grew more flushed. "I most certainly do. Tell me, where are my accusers?"

"Here." Smith stepped forward, pulling out a paper. "I have an official complaint drawn up by Wellison and Durham, attorneys at law, who have evidence to support the accusation."

"I . . . well . . . that ain't possible," blustered Johansson. Guilt radiated from him like a foul stench but was overshadowed by anger. "I am a respected businessman. I have paperwork for all my slaves."

"Then you won't mind presenting it," Smith said with a little smirk. "But the complaint involves more than your current batch of slaves. Wellison and Durham would like to investigate your files for evidence of past abuses."

Wellison and Durham—why did that name seem familiar?

Cardiff stepped close to Smith and took the paper, perusing it briefly before crumpling it in his hand. "This is preposterous! Johansson works for me and to accuse him is to accuse me. My reputation is indisputable. You have only to query the governor of Virginia to ascertain whether or not this case has merit."

Interesting. That meant the Emporium had someone in the governor's office, if not the governor himself, who was Unbounded or working for them. When this was over, I would make it a point to find out who and eliminate them. For now it meant that forged papers would likely come from the governor's office and Johansson would walk away free.

The sheriff hesitated, holding his handcuffs uncertainly. Smith glared at him. "You can't wait. Miss Amelia Mitchell, a respected plantation owner in Georgia, has lodged a complaint in a legal manner. Let these men present proof of their ownership immediately if they have any."

My stomach did a little twist. Amelia Mitchell. Oh, yes, I knew that name—too well—but what I didn't know is how Smith had heard it. He believed he was telling the truth, I sensed, but he couldn't be unless . . . *Oh, no.*

There was only one way I could think of that would explain both his involvement and my immediate attraction to him. No wonder Wellison and Durham seemed so familiar.

"You come to my home as a guest and dare question me?" Cardiff put a hand on his hip, though I couldn't see the pistols that had been there earlier.

Smith's frown deepened. "If that's what it takes. I believe the law will prevail."

Cardiff's hand went to a bulge in his coat, which was probably exactly what I thought it was. I stepped in front of Smith, wishing I had known of his connections before we entered this house. I might have played the game differently.

"He is only saying that Mr. Johansson must have worked to deceive everyone," I said. To the sheriff, I added, "Johansson does have free Negroes in his possession. I know this because I paid for their release and sent them to the North myself. They must be freed. That is why I am here tonight."

A collective gasp went up from the guests. A complaint by someone not present held little weight compared to a live witness, especially a white, obviously well-to-do witness. I was acutely aware of Smith behind me, whose shock was greater than anyone's.

I didn't dare look away from Cardiff's narrowed eyes. I'd given him a way out, a way to put the blame on Johansson. But would he take it? Forty slaves and a look into past sales meant a considerable sum, but even if they uncovered hundreds of violations, this setback would mean relatively nothing to him. He had centuries to amass untold wealth.

His nostrils flared and anger briefly exploded from his

mind, then disappeared just as suddenly as he controlled himself. I suspected the anger meant he wasn't going to end this peacefully, but what remained to be discovered was if I could beat him. The Emporium were known for breeding combat Unbounded, and if that was his ability, my focus would be more a question of holding out until Ritter arrived than beating Cardiff myself. I had prepared for something like this confrontation the entire past century, but he might have also.

Outside, a sudden wind rattled the windows. An unnatural wind. The concentration on Cardiff's face was unmistakable.

Maybe my chances of besting him weren't so bad after all.

CHAPTER 11

EVEN AS I HAD THE THOUGHT, THE STORM OUTSIDE GREW stronger. People stared at each other in confusion and worry. Two women and three men hurried to the windows. Murmurs started, and at least one woman fainted and had to be carried to a couch. Only Cardiff smiled, his eyes holding mine, his face arrogant and self-assured.

Assured as I was when I took someone's memories or felt their emotions.

"Perhaps," Cardiff said to the sheriff, "it would be wise to take this up another day. It appears there is a severe storm gathering." As if to punctuate his words, the entire house shook.

I alone realized that it wasn't just a chance storm. I'd heard of an Emporium agent with the ability to manipulate wind. He had caused us many deaths over the years, but we'd never identified the Unbounded with the gift.

Until now.

"Like the tornado five years ago!" a woman cried out. "Oh, dear. I have to get home to the children!" She grabbed her husband's hand and hurried out of the parlor, heading toward the entryway.

Amusement filled Cardiff's eyes. "I think it would be wise if we all secured our homes."

Smith moved around me and lunged toward Johansson. "He'll be coming with us, then."

A sword suddenly blocked his way. "I think not." Cardiff's smile mocked us. I hadn't seen him grab the sword, but I wasn't surprised he had one. All Unbounded carried them close these days.

"Mr. Cardiff is right," said the sheriff, retreating with his companions toward the entry. "We can deal with Mr. Johansson later. If it's anything like that tornado five years ago, we have far more important things to concern us."

More important than a stolen life, he meant. Because after all, the people I was trying to free were considered only a subspecies, while a tornado might kill whites. His implication made me furious despite the very real threat Cardiff represented.

The house rattled again more violently as guests hurried toward the entryway, many without pausing for their outerwear. I knew why. The tornado of 1840 had come just as suddenly, and more than three hundred lives had been lost, with numerous boats, plantations, and dwellings destroyed. The total deaths in reality were rumored to have been much higher because slave deaths often went unreported.

Smith retreated from the sword but returned immediately with a poker he'd grabbed from the fireplace. Johansson cowered behind Cardiff. "Now, now," said the sheriff, "we will settle this later."

I had to admire Smith's courage, even though he was ultimately not a match for Cardiff.

From outside there was a huge crash and several women closest to me screamed and tried to force their way into the growing crowd spilling from the parlor into the entryway. At the same time, slave women flooded in from the back hallway where I'd gone looking for Frances earlier. Their eyes were wide with terror, and a few of the younger ones sobbed. I spied Frances among them and gladness spread through me. I would take her to her family, and tomorrow Smith and I could worry about the others.

"What do we do, Massa?" a slave asked Johansson.

"Git out of here!" Johansson spat. A stream of curses followed as he lashed out at the nearest woman, who shrank away from him.

In the midst of the slaves, I spotted the girl from the barn at the same time she saw Smith. Keeping as far from Johansson as she could, she ran toward us. "Please, the servants say we're goin' t' die!"

Smith had already begun moving toward her when

Cardiff leapt forward, his sword singing through the air. Time seemed to slow as I turned, watching it slice with amazing precision.

Smith! I thought.

My own short sword was abruptly in my hands, and I moved to counter, even as the sword struck the slave girl. The blade sliced through her neck, coming out the other side. She took another step before her head rolled off her shoulders and her body collapsed. Her life force vanished.

Horrified screams echoed from both the whites and the slaves.

"Get back to the kitchens!" Cardiff shouted at the slaves. "Go, you filthy, blood-sucking wretches! You belong to me, and if you don't leave now I'll slaughter the lot of you!"

The crowd of whites looked toward the sheriff and his men, but we all knew there wasn't a court in the land that would convict Cardiff, especially if his Virginia contacts could provide evidence that the girl had been in cahoots with abolitionists.

With a great swelling, the slaves and the guests fled from both sides of the room, until only Cardiff, Johansson, Smith, and I remained. Several heartbeats passed as the wind howled and banged at the windows.

Cardiff smiled and raised his sword toward Smith.

This time I was there first, blocking him, move for move. He was good, but I'd been trained by better. His attention was also on the wind, as he controlled and manipulated it.

"Renegade," he said with a sneer.

I smiled. "Took you long enough to figure it out."

His only answer was a knife that sailed toward Smith where he grappled with Johansson. The knife dug into Smith's shoulder and he cried out. Johansson took the opportunity to scurry away, but Smith tripped him with the poker and jumped on him, fists pumping.

Cardiff laughed, and outside the storm grew louder. He fumbled for another weapon inside the folds of his coat, but this time I stopped him with my own throwing knife. I'd always been rather good, but I missed his throat by several inches, partially embedding the knife instead in his upper chest. Not a fatal wound, unfortunately, but one that would slow him down.

He swiped at the knife, pulling it out, then attacked with fervency, as though determined to beat me back with sheer determination and the larger size of his sword. But he was tiring. I just had to play it out long enough to let his wounds and his efforts with the storm weaken him further. From the corner of my eye, I could see that Smith was on top of Johansson, tying his hands behind his back. In a moment he'd be free to help me with Cardiff.

Or maybe to get in the way.

From the back hallway, I sensed another life force approaching the parlor. Reaching out, I saw Frances—and that she gripped a heavy cast iron frying pan in her stiff hands. I needed to end this dance before either she or Smith were hurt.

"Hold!" Cardiff sidestepped my lunge. "Truce," he said. "I let you and this mortal go free. I'll also stop the wind." Not stupid, he had come to the same conclusion I had about his likelihood of beating me.

I gave a very unladylike snort. "That's assuming I believe you, which I don't." With a series of furious blows, I had him scrambling backwards. "And assuming this *mortal* means something to me, which he doesn't." This I said so he wouldn't waste energy killing Smith. The sentiments, though not typically Renegade, should be close enough to his own to be believed.

"Then the whole town dies!" Cardiff shouted.

Wind exploded the windows, punching into the room and stealing my breath. The doors banged open and then shut and open again. The pins ripped from my hair, throwing the strands across my vision. My skirts billowed and wrapped around my legs. Pictures flew off the wall, lanterns fell over, food sailed through the air. The wind screamed and howled liked damned souls in hell, and I had to fight not to clap my hands over my ears.

Yet I noticed the flames from the oil lamps blew out before they could light anything on fire and the heavier furniture stayed in place. Whatever else he did, Cardiff planned on saving his house.

I glanced toward Smith and saw with relief that he was holding his own. Relief because I did care very much about him; I'd been caring about him and his family for over a hundred years.

The violent turbulence eased slightly as Cardiff again went for the weapon in his coat. I was faster. Despite the wind, my pistol rang out, the ball flying true and clear to carve a hole in his forehead. He toppled forward, missing Smith and Johansson by a few inches.

Instantly, the wind ceased.

I reached out mentally, searching for Frances. She was still in the hallway, frightened and hugging the ground, if the glow from her life force was any indicator, but she was not in any pain.

Dropping the pistol, I stepped closer to Cardiff, raising my sword in both hands. *Never again.* He was too dangerous to let regenerate.

"What are you doing!" Smith yelled, jumping to his feet and grabbing my hands. "He's already dead."

"No, he's not!" I shouted. "And if I *don't* do this, you and everyone in this town will be dead before the week is over."

"What are you talking about?" His face was close to mine, his eyes disbelieving.

"The wind—listen! It's gone. It was him! I know you don't understand it, but believe me when I say he was responsible. He's not going to sit back while we take what he sees as his property. He'll make sure everyone pays. In fact, your sheriff and his friends are already as good as dead if I don't do this. Now let me go!"

Horror filled Smith's face. Whether because he

believed me, or because he decided I was crazy, I wasn't sure. He released me and stepped back. I brought the sword down hard, slicing through Cardiff's neck and severing it. Blood spilled onto the ground. One focus point to go and he'd never be coming back.

As I moved into position, my foot sent his head rolling to a nearby couch, where the slave girl's head had been wedged by the wind. My stomach roiled. It was my fault she was dead. Mine and Smith's. If we had never gone to the barn, she might still be alive.

I raised the sword again, but in the next instant hands were taking it from me. Ritter. I recognized his emotions of fury and regret—surface emotions he let me see.

"I'll take it from here," he said in my ear. Now his surface emotions were gone, tucked behind the block in his mind with the rest that was buried too deeply for me to ever glimpse. Maybe I never wanted to.

I relinquished the sword because cutting through a man's torso was far more difficult and Ritter was better equipped than I was, both in strength and weaponry. "What took you so long?" I said.

"Ran into a minor complication with some other slavers. Locke is still finishing up." His eyes took in the room. "Not as complicated as here, it appears."

I shrugged. "I found Frances."

Finally a hint of a smile. "Never doubted that you would. Who's he?" He jerked his head at Smith.

"An ally of sorts. Don't kill him." This last I said only half-jokingly.

"Maybe you'd better get him out of here then." Ritter sounded deadly serious. I laughed.

Smith was hauling Johansson to his feet as we talked. I sensed he wasn't happy about my exchange with Ritter, but sometimes with Ritter it was better safe than sorry. Because if Ritter thought for even a second that Smith was a danger, he would kill him without thinking twice about it.

"Stay here," Smith said to Johansson, shoving the man into a chair. Then he turned to me. "This must be the guy from your letter." His gaze flicked over Ritter, his eyes hard.

"Letter?" I had no idea what Smith was talking about.

His tone relaxed and the hint of amusement was back, which impressed me quite a bit with Ritter still glaring in his direction. "My competition," Smith explained. "The man who wrote that letter you were reading so intently at the hotel."

"Oh, that letter." I wanted to laugh at the absurdity. "No, this is a colleague of mine. We work, uh, in the Underground Railroad together. About the letter. There's something—"

At that moment Johansson jumped to his feet and ran for one of the windows, throwing himself through it. With an exclamation, Smith sprang after him.

I sighed. "Well, go on," I told Ritter, nodding at Cardiff's body.

"Hadn't you better go after them?"

"Johansson's hands are tied. Smith should be able to

take care of himself." The words didn't exactly match my feelings about him, but Cardiff was too dangerous to ignore. As the leader of our little band of Renegades, my duty was clear: I had to take care of him now.

I readied the black bag from the supplies Ritter had brought, while he made sure Cardiff was permanently dead. Afterward, I went to find Frances. It took time convincing her the danger was past and to pry the frying pan from her hand, but that was just as well. When I returned with her to the parlor, Cardiff's remains were already packed away. Ritter had also found a blanket and placed it over the slave woman, her head lying where it would have been in life. Sometimes he surprised me.

Blood stained the floor and the scent was overwhelming, but my stomach didn't heave. A tight numbness had filled me, which was almost as bad because it reminded me of my baby. Of losing Wymon and Eva. How many times would I have to battle evil in my very long lifetime? And if I didn't fight it, who would? As long as the Emporium existed, Renegades were the only force standing between them and the enslavement of all mortals, regardless of the color of their skin.

"I'll make them pay for what they did to her," Ritter's voice grated against my ears.

He thought he was referring to the dead girl, but I knew he really meant it for the woman he was to have married. He carried her ring and those of his mother and little sister on a gold chain around his neck. He was never without it.

"Don't blame yourself," I told him. "Neither of us could have stopped it." I let a few seconds go by before adding, "And we both know that death is not the worst thing a person can suffer." Saying it somehow eased the numb feeling in my chest.

He didn't reply, and I had no idea if the words had helped him, but I would keep at it. Someday I would get through. And someday he would find another reason besides revenge to give his life purpose. I knew because I was finally ready to find another reason for myself.

Smith came in then, the proper way through the door, pushing a bruised Johansson in front of him. Smith bent momentarily to peek under the blanket at the slave girl, his mouth set grimly. I wanted to tell him it wasn't really his fault, but I knew it wouldn't help.

"I need to take Johansson to the sheriff," Smith said, "but I have no idea what I'm going to say about Cardiff." His chin jerked toward the black bag at Ritter's feet, which looked more like a bundle of laundry than the remains of a man, though clearly Smith deduced the contents. The bag wouldn't leak, but the blood already on the floor and the disarray caused by the wind made the place gruesome.

"There isn't going to be any reporting of anything," I said. "Cardiff was one of ours"—so to speak—"and he's our responsibility. The local authorities wouldn't have been able to hold him long anyway." It wasn't the time to explain the politics of Unbounded to him, or how they manipulated the mortal world.

Smith regarded me for several quiet seconds. "Okay, I can live with that. What about him?" He glanced over at where Johansson stared dejectedly at the blood-stained floor. "He saw it all. I still need to take him in so I can free some of the people he's taken. But he's bound to talk."

"He's coming with us," Ritter said.

I nodded. "And his so-called cargo. All of it."

Smith stared, and Johansson looked unnerved. "You can't do that!" Johansson growled. "They're mine."

"Not anymore," I said. "You lost that right—if it ever was one—the minute you began abducting free people."

"They ain't people!" he roared.

I nodded at Ritter, and with a blurred motion, he crossed the room and slammed Johansson against the wall, a knife at his throat.

I moved closer until my face was near Johansson's. "Listen and listen good. I'm only going to say this once. They are people, and you will never own or sell another one again. Ever. I will know if you do, just as I know about the many times you've abused and forced yourself on their women, and the fact that your own grandmother was a slave."

He gasped at that and pulled away from me into Ritter's knife. Three beads of blood sprang up along the edge of the blade. "If you so much as raise another hand against a Negro for any reason," I continued, "I'm sending Ritter here after you. Now where are your papers for the people you've got up at the Forks of the Road? You're going to set every man, woman, and child free, or

I will kill you myself. Like I did Cardiff. But without the bullet. And far more slowly."

He nodded, eyes wild, his entire body shaking. Ritter released him with a hint of disappointment.

"Time to leave," I announced.

"My family?" Frances asked.

I smiled. "They're waiting for you on the boat."

Without apparent effort, Ritter hefted the black bag like so much garbage, his stare still pinning Johansson to the wall. Then he grabbed Johansson and pushed him in the direction of the entryway.

"The boat will only fit twenty more," he said over his shoulder.

"So we'll need another boat." That was a problem I could handle.

"I'll get the others from the kitchen and meet you out front." Frances hurried from the room.

"What about my client?" Smith asked when we were alone.

Client. His training was showing. I laughed. "You mean Amelia?"

"Yeeesss." The reply was hesitant.

For a moment we stood staring at each other in the ruined parlor. My eyes drank in his battered face, the rumpled clothes stained with blood. Now that I knew who he was, I didn't know why I hadn't recognized him immediately. Every word and action shouted his identity. The attraction we'd felt in the barn resumed with force: his and mine, our emotions twining together. The feelings rushed through me, singing in my veins and threatening to block out all rational thought.

He was still waiting for further explanation.

"That woman who was just here is Frances," I said. "Miles, I came for her because of Amelia."

Smith stared, his battered face puzzled. "You know my name."

Miles Smithson to be exact. If I hadn't already deduced it, his thoughts were practically yelling it at me now. "Yes. I also know you're an attorney with Wellison and Durham. But now it's your turn to answer a question. How did you know to come here?"

He rubbed a hand across his chin, wincing as he touched a bruise. "Amelia wrote a letter saying she was leaving Savannah to come here to free Frances and her family. She was worried about making it in time, and Alabama is closer and the mail arrived fast. I thought I might get here in time if she couldn't. I pulled a few strings so it would all be legal just in case Johansson had fake papers."

I *had* told Miles about Frances in my last letter, written and mailed on the trail to Mississippi. I knew he would share my outrage, but never had I imagined that he would abandon his busy practice to travel here to help me.

"I knew where she stayed the last time she was here . . ." he began again, and then stopped. "Wait, are you with her? Is she at the hotel?"

I heard the hope and understood that despite his

attraction for me, he'd give me up forever if that was the only way he could meet Amelia. She meant a lot to him. More than she should. Knowing this made me want to tell him what his letters had meant to an old lady who wasn't really old at all.

"She'll be on the boat." What else could I say? He wouldn't understand if I said that Amelia Mitchell was the name I'd made up for him and his siblings, an alias like a dozen others I'd used over the past century.

"So what is your real name?"

"Ava O'Hare."

He stared. "O'Hare. You're related to Amelia then. O'Hare was her mother's maiden name."

"Something like that."

"No wonder you seem so familiar." He closed the space between us with several long strides. "Wait. The cut on your face, from your fight with Cardiff. It's healing."

I nodded. "It is."

He studied me for a long moment, again waiting. He did that well—waiting. I could feel Ritter's impatience outside the front door. He should have left already to retrieve Johansson's papers, but I'd never get him to leave me alone with an unknown, not after what had happened tonight.

"There isn't time for that conversation," I said. "Are you coming with us to the boat?"

"Absolutely. This has been the most fun I've had since law school."

I knew it wasn't really for me that he was coming, but

for Amelia, and that only added to my anticipation. "If this is fun, you're as crazy as I am."

He smiled. "No one is that crazy."

He hadn't met Locke yet or the rest of the Renegades.

I turned to go, but his hand grabbed mine. "Is there time for this? Because I've been waiting it seems my whole life." He leaned forward and kissed me.

I'd been waiting a lot longer. He'd taken years to become the man whose letters had first intrigued and then called to me. I kissed him back, opening my mind and letting some of the emotion run back to him. He wouldn't understand what it was, but it might get his mind off the other me that he couldn't wait to meet.

"There's always time for this," I said.

PART FOUR

Present Day - Kansas City, Kansas

The Greatest Revenge

CHAPTER 12

"**M**ILES STAYED EVEN AFTER LEARNING THE TRUTH," I TOLD Erin Radkey in the hospital cafeteria, rubbing my finger against an ice-cold glass of lemonade. "We were married in less than a week, and he worked with us after that. Well, Locke went back to England to be with her son and to keep an eye on their descendants, but Ritter and I stayed, and our little band of Renegades grew. Ritter also kept track of Johansson until he was killed in a logging accident a few years later. Not long after, we began patrolling the West Coast as the territories were organized. We lost a lot of good people, but we did a lot of good and kept the Emporium from taking over the States."

"I wish I could have met Miles." Erin put her elbows on the table and leaned forward. Her hair, once burned to stubble, was several inches long now. Only a week had passed since her Change, and I claimed three centuries, but we looked more like sisters than women separated by four generations. In actuality, Erin was my fourth great-granddaughter.

"I wish you could have met him too."

Erin was silent for a long moment. "Do you miss him?"

My heart squeezed just a little when she asked. Miles was the first man I'd loved as a wife, but not the last. I'd outlived several mortal spouses and given birth to half a dozen children. Despite how hard it always was to lose them, I wasn't against loving again. "I will always miss him, but we had a good life, and our posterity"—I reached across the table and took her hand—"has made me proud."

It had been too long since someone in my family line had Changed, and Erin and her younger brother, Jace, had given me new purpose. I believed Erin's sensing ability would far outreach my own, and her dedication to her duty as a guardian of humanity would do more to help our cause than anything else we'd done in the past century. Jace would need a lot more experience before he'd come into his full usefulness as a combat Unbounded, but that he'd Changed at all bordered on miraculous. I felt rich with their presence. Even Chris, their older mortal brother, had joined our Renegade cell, bringing his two motherless children with him. We would have to bury them long before we were ready to let them go, but they made the battle worth fighting.

Erin took a long pull of her lemonade; I hadn't yet

been able to teach her that it was best sipped. "You've done it then," she said.

"What's that?"

"When Chris told me his wife had been murdered by the Emporium, I told him the greatest revenge we have is to go about our lives, raising our children, and finding happiness wherever we can." Erin's gray eyes held mine. "Ava, you've done that. Gabriel is gone, and so are Miles and your children, but you went on, found a life, and you were happy." Her smile faltered. "For a while, after we almost lost everyone, I didn't really believe it was possible to be happy while the Emporium exists, but now with Ritter—"

She didn't have to say more. I understood. She had hope. "He's different now," I told her.

Erin smiled a secret smile that told me something had passed between them. Maybe something good. But I'd have to wait to find out because Ritter was on his way now to our location. I wondered if she felt him yet, or if she needed more time to develop her new ability.

Ritter strode into the nearly deserted cafeteria, followed by our Unbounded healer Dimitri Sidorov, who was as close to a co-leader as I'd ever had. He'd been alive for a thousand years, and we'd been working together well over a century. Shorter than Ritter by a head, he was every bit as wide, and he exuded an almost animal attractiveness.

He could kill or heal with a touch, but he was also one of the kindest men I'd ever known.

"The room is ready," Dimitri said. "They will begin to prepare your father as soon as your operation is underway."

Erin's momentary surprise at seeing them told me she had been concentrating too hard on me to sense them coming. She jumped to her feet, her lemonade forgotten. "I'm ready." After a bloody clash with the Emporium, her father needed a heart, and she was determined to be the donor. Only one focus point, so she'd survive and generate a new one. I couldn't blame her for wanting to save his life.

Ritter stepped closer to Erin, though they didn't touch, and emotion between them flared, too strong for their mental shields to hide altogether. Ritter was still a killing machine and the best tactical leader I'd ever worked with, but Erin had turned his life upside down this past week. I believed he'd finally found what I'd wanted for him, something more than revenge to live for. I knew that frightened him even more than he hated the Emporium, but it was a risk he took because he loved my granddaughter.

Together they strode toward the doorway. Ritter was showing Erin a new pistol he'd arranged for her, the gift a mating ritual understood only by combat Unbounded and tolerated by the rest of us. Erin didn't yet have a clue; she'd think the weapon came from our general arsenal.

She also didn't know, and he'd never think to tell her, that it was a temporary goodbye, a placeholder until he returned from London. No way was I getting in the middle of that. They would have to work it out for themselves.

As we followed them, Dimitri's hand brushed mine. I met his dark eyes, my breath catching in my throat. He was my best friend, and it had been a long time since I'd felt that way about a man, the first time for a man who was also Unbounded.

Soon I would have a decision to make.

Maybe it was time for a little more of the living kind of revenge.

MORTAL BROTHER

AN UNBOUNDED NOVELLA

To all my mortal readers, who wish secretly to be Unbounded. We can still be Renegades!

CHAPTER 1

THE ARMED MEN CRAWLING ALL OVER MY PLANE WERE THE first indication that something wasn't right. Well, it wasn't exactly my plane, but I was a Renegade, and it belonged to our group, even if I was mortal and wouldn't live two thousand years like my Unbounded comrades. Besides, I was the only one who could fly the plane, so I considered it mine.

I'd thought taking care of the plane in this little out-of-the-way airstrip in the Mexican jungle while my friends looked into an attack on the medical lab we funded here was little more than babysitting duty, something to keep me away from the real action. Safe. More than a bit irritating, but if staying behind meant staying alive, I'd deal with the irritation for my two children, who had been through more than any children should since their mother's murder two months earlier.

I'd nearly lost them, too, yesterday when the Emporium had attacked our stronghold in Oregon. One of our men *had* died, so being safe wasn't all that bad.

Except now I'd bet the men trying to get inside that plane weren't doing it for my welfare.

"More coffee?" asked Diego Molina, the young Mexican who, along with his father, ran the airstrip. He put his hand on the pot of bad coffee sitting on the small table between us—the third pot since my arrival several hours ago. The coffee and the stale biscuits made me wonder if they were trying to poison me or simply weren't used to entertaining. If it hadn't been for the delicious smells coming from the attached kitchen and a promised dinner, I would have already retreated to the privacy—and comfort—of the plane.

"He is probably sick of that swill," a young woman said, appearing from the kitchen for the first time. She set a sweating can of beer in front of me and smiled. It was the first I'd seen of anyone besides the two men since my arrival. She wore tight, American-style jeans and a light blue tank top that hugged her small curves. She looked barely out of her teens and pretty in a dark, exotic way, with long black hair and eyes that were almost too large in her narrow face.

Ignoring the can, I jumped to my feet and strode to the small open window, stopping to draw out a pair of binoculars from my backpack of survival gear so I could see better. Across the wide expanse of dirt that sepa-rated this small building from where my plane sat, the strangers were inspecting the underbelly of the plane, presumably trying to find another way inside besides the locked door. That wasn't happening any time soon. Only our Renegades knew the combination to the hatches, and there was a handprint reader for added security. While they could eventually break the codes or drill through the mechanism, it would take time.

"What are they doing to my plane?" My hand went to my pistol, which suddenly seemed inadequate protection against the half dozen men. Rough men, who looked prepared to do whatever it took to achieve their goal, if the rifles slung over their shoulders were any indication.

Diego followed me to the window, his Adam's apple bobbing as he swallowed nervously. "I don't know," he said, his accent thicker than ever. Turning, he rattled off something in quick Spanish to his father, César, who still sat at the table.

The two men exchanged more rapid conversation, and then the older man stood and clumped to the outer door, pulling it open. A short time later, he was in the sedan he'd picked me up in and was speeding toward the plane. The men stopped banging on the lower hatch when they saw him coming. They clustered as they waited, and I thought it a promising sign when none of them attacked him as he climbed from the car.

The goodwill didn't last. We were too far away to hear anything said, but the violent gesturing told me the newcomers were angry. The pistol one of them waved around also spoke loudly of their intentions. Diego's father nodded and lifted his hands in an obvious plea for them to wait. Then he returned to his car and drove back across the dirt.

When César arrived, his wide, sun-darkened face was even darker with anger as he exchanged more words with his son. Diego looked the picture of a wounded child who had done something he knew he shouldn't have.

The girl's head yanked back and forth between them as she followed the conversation, the flush rising on her face making her more compelling. She spoke to the men, and Diego answered her sharply. I was beginning to regret that I hadn't paid more attention to learning real world Spanish. I just hadn't needed it in my hometown of Kansas City.

"What is it?" I demanded.

César pointed at his son. "Diego mahk dee deal wid bandeets. Day loose men. Day are wanting plane or keel us." His disgust was obvious, but his English was even more heavily accented than his son's, and I had no idea what he was saying.

"What?" I asked.

"Bandits want your plane," the girl said. "Diego made a deal with them, and they want it because the deal didn't work out. They will kill us if we don't give it to them."

"No way." I slid my pistol from its holster, glad my Renegade training meant I carried extra magazines and more target practice in a month than most mortals had in an entire lifetime. "They are *not* taking my plane."

Cost aside, the plane was our way of rushing back

a cure we desperately needed for the husband of Stella Davis, one of our Unbounded Renegades. Bronson was dying of a rare autoimmune disease, and our lab here in the Mexican jungle had reported a breakthrough with a cure. But two days ago, the lab had been razed to the ground, and my team was tracking our scientists that we believed had escaped with the research. I wasn't about to let my people down, especially after what had happened at our stronghold yesterday. It was more than just the life we'd lost. Far more.

"You no understand," Diego shouted, punching his fist in the air. "Your friends keel their men. They no leave. They will keel you."

I pointed my gun at him. "What deal did you make?"

No one answered for a long moment. Then the girl said, "They were supposed to rob your friends."

That almost made me laugh. Against my younger siblings, Erin and Jace, and the experienced Renegades with them, an entire army of mortal bandits wouldn't have stood a chance. Unbounded can't be killed, not in the normal way. Head and heart and reproductive organs had to be completely separated. No two sections could remain attached or they would fully regenerate. Unique abilities made Unbounded even more powerful, but of course, these people knew nothing of Unbounded.

"You sold us out?" I spat at Diego. I was going to kill him! We'd paid them a small fortune to land here and to park the plane while we finished our business. The weaponry alone that we carried would have been attractive to any militant group, but I'd expected some honor in dealing with César, who I understood had worked with our Renegades in the past. Apparently, his son was greedy.

The girl was still studying me. "All the men who attacked your friends in that big vehicle died, except two who were tied up."

Big surprise there. "Just give them back their money," I said to Diego.

He shook his head violently. "No. They want more. They want the plane."

"Geeve me key," César ordered, holding out his big hand, palm up.

I backed away. "There is no key. It's numbers, and I won't give them to you."

"Then you die!" Diego growled. "One man against all them. You no succeed."

"You have guns," I jerked my head at the two rifles standing against the wall. "We can take them together. Or drive them away."

"No! No!" César shouted. He glanced out the window where the bandits were still gathered in a clump near a blue truck. "Day keel you! We no help or day keel us too."

As if they could hear us, the bandits began piling into their truck.

Above all, I had to hold the plane. Not just for Stella's husband, but for our team. The Renegades were all that stood between humanity and enslavement by the Emporium Unbounded, who considered themselves gods to the expendable mortals. The Emporium had murdered my wife and tried to kill the rest of my family to further their agenda. They'd tried to abduct my children for their breeding experiments. Now they were here in Mexico and were most certainly behind the attack on our labs.

The plane was our way to safety. There was only one choice.

I lunged for the girl, grabbing her and pulling her against me, my gun pressed into her side. "You will help me fight. You made a deal with us, and you won't break it. Now pick up those guns, or I'll kill her."

I must have sounded convincing because both men, nodding energetically, started for their guns. Suddenly, it didn't seem wise to be in the same room with them. "I'll watch the back door. When they come, I'd better hear shooting."

With that, I dragged the girl into the kitchen. It was a small place with only one narrow window opposite a black potbellied stove that looked like something from a frontier movie. Shutting the door to the other room, I shoved her into a chair. "Don't move."

She watched me, seemingly more curious than afraid. "You a good shot?"

"I guess we'll see." I wished I were wearing my body armor.

I slipped a picture from the pocket of my white T-shirt. My young children stared up at me, Spencer's thin face covered in freckles and Kathy's blue eyes looking so much like her mother's. They were in hiding with the rest of our Renegades until we regrouped after the Emporium attack. Safe for now, but as long as the Emporium existed, they would always be in danger. I slipped the photograph back into place.

My watch said that only two minutes had passed when the shooting began. I stepped to the back door, almost expecting the girl to bolt, but she remained sitting. As I opened the door a crack, a man came around the edge of the house. I fired, and he crumpled.

I felt sick. All the practice in the world hadn't prepared me for actually taking a man's life. I was a pilot by profession, not a killer. Not Unbounded. Just a regular guy, who chose to work with the Renegades in order to protect my children, to make the world a safer place. That might sound noble, but I'd seen what the Emporium had to offer, and there was nothing noble about fighting them. I fought simply because it was the only way humanity would survive.

Except these men weren't semi-immortal Emporium agents. They were mortal.

A movement inside had me turning my gun back toward the girl, but she already had a pistol in her hand. For a several seconds, we stared at each other while the *boom* of rifles came from the next room and from outside. I couldn't shoot her. She was innocent.

She whirled from me abruptly, breaking the window with her gun and firing at someone outside. I blinked, almost surprised to still be alive. More men were coming around the house, and I fired again and again. So did the girl. The faces ducked out of sight.

"Is there a way onto the roof?" I asked.

She started to shake her head, but then nodded. "You can use the window and climb. You will have to do it from outside. I will cover you."

If we made it out alive I'd have to ask her where she learned to speak such great English. Her words were accented, attractively so, but completely understandable.

Should I trust her? She could just let them kill me.

"Why are you helping me?" I asked.

Her chin lifted and for a moment she was fiercely beautiful. "Because those men killed my husband."

It was good enough for me.

CHAPTER 2

"Take this." With one hand, she pushed a high-backed chair at me. "To help you climb."

Letting off a few shots, I sprinted outside to the window and threw down the chair. I vaulted onto the windowsill and from there onto the low roof. Much easier than I'd thought, thanks to our grueling training sessions with Ritter, our combat Unbounded, who was like Rambo times thirty. He and my sister Erin made a perfect couple, though she didn't know it yet.

Shots followed my progress, telling me the girl had fulfilled her promise. I squat-walked across the roof, shoving in a new magazine. Two men were dead out front and, with the one I'd shot, that meant only three more left.

Close to the edge, I got down on my stomach and pulled myself along with my elbows. I picked off two men hiding behind their blue truck before they realized I was above them. The remaining man scrambled for cover, but a shot rang out and he fell before moving two feet.

The girl walked into view below me, still holding her pistol. I wondered if she was happy with her revenge, or if it made her feel as empty as I was feeling. I moved to the edge of the roof and lowered myself down, jumping the last few feet as Diego and César burst from the house. I tensed, but neither tried to shoot me. They were talking a mile a minute again in Spanish. After the words slowed, together they began carrying bodies and tossing them into the back of the battered truck.

I lifted my brow and looked at the girl.

"They want to move them and the truck away from here," she said, "and then they want to hide. They are afraid the rest will come."

I groaned. "There's more?"

A hint of a smile touched her lips. "Not too many. We are lucky they hijacked the van that was here before they sent their men after your friends. Some of the bandits drove it to their hideout. That was why only six came for the plane."

In a rush, the dread was back. "They hijacked the van?" This was bad news. Very bad news.

Two of our allies, Tenika Vasco and Irwin Stafford, also Renegade Unbounded, had met the plane to take into custody the eleven Emporium agents we'd captured yesterday during the attack in Oregon. Each of our captives was Unbounded and, though temporarily dead or heavily sedated, would heal sooner or later. They were being transported to our prison compound here in Mexico where they would be reformed or stand trial for their crimes against humanity.

Or at least that had been the plan before the van had been hijacked.

The girl frowned as her brother and father passed us carrying another dead bandit. "I'm sorry, but they are saying that the bandits were bragging about killing the driver."

I clenched my fists, my mind searching for options. I hadn't been at the plane when Tenika and Irwin had arrived in the gray van and loaded the Emporium agents, but I'd watched them through my binoculars while Diego was arranging his "vedy good coffee," and Jace had filled me in by sat phone on the details before they'd left. He'd been excited because Irwin had been famous in Australia for wrestling alligators before he'd faked his death to hide that he wasn't aging. He had been assigned to Mexico until his face was forgotten by the rest of the world.

Tenika, on the other hand, was here from New York City, delivering her own Emporium prisoners. She had agreed to help Irwin, who was shorthanded at the prison, transport our captives because she knew we were pressed to find our scientists. I'd met the Angolan woman several times and had a great respect for her.

The bandits wouldn't know how to permanently kill

Tenika and Irwin, but they could put them out long enough to allow the Emporium captives to regenerate, and the Emporium definitely *would* kill or capture my allies.

I had to do something.

If I were Unbounded and had an ability, I might be able to track them myself, but as it was I would have to depend on technology. All Renegades had embedded nanochips in their bodies, programmed to prevent their immune system from rejecting them. The chips emitted a constantly changing pattern, traceable only by someone using the same set of algorithms that would take even a technopath months to decode—and by then the algorithms would have changed yet again. If Tenika and Irwin weren't already too deep in the jungle, I should be able to track them. The captives had also been injected with tracking devices.

Still gripping my gun, I strode away from the building, heading across the wide expanse of dirt for the plane. Reaching into my pocket for my sat phone, I put in the password and made the call to Ava O'Hare, our cell leader. She was also my fourth great-grandmother, and three hundred years old, though physically she was thirty-seven, a year younger than I was.

She answered immediately, which told me she was waiting for news. "Hey, Chris."

"We've got a problem. I need you to track our captives and Tenika Vasco."

A brief pause. "On it. I'm contacting the New York

cell now to have them check for Tenika's codes. What's up?"

"Bandits tried to take the plane. They didn't succeed, but I learned they grabbed Tenika and the guy from the prison compound a few hours ago. The bandits were probably looking for weapons and money, but if they've dumped the bodies . . ." I didn't have to finish. Ava knew better than I did what the Emporium agents were capable of if they recovered before our people did.

"Okay," she said, "I can't locate any of the captives' signals." Which had to mean the tracking chips had been deactivated or that they were under cover of the jungle and the overhead satellites couldn't locate them. I was betting on the trees.

After a few seconds, Ava added, "They can't find Tenika's signal either." No hiding the worry in her voice. "Marco's on the line with the prison compound now about Irwin." Marco was one of our former black ops mortal employees, and we'd left him and two others like him to help Ava protect Stella Davis, her husband, and my children.

Several seconds of silence and then I asked, "How is Bronson?"

"Not good."

"And Stella?" Stella Davis had paid a huge price at yesterday's battle—loss of the baby she was carrying. With Bronson on his deathbed, it was a horrible turn of events. We all knew she had wanted their child more than she'd wanted anything in her two centuries of life.

If Bronson died, their chances of having another child would be over forever.

I owed Stella. I would always owe her. She'd made the choice to fight, to save my children. When this was all over, I'd go home to them because of her sacrifice. I was determined to bring her the cure Bronson needed the minute the others tracked down our missing scientists.

"Okay, we found Irwin's signal," Ava said. "Pinpointing now."

I'd reached the stairs to the plane and began climbing, opening the door with the combination and my hand on the reader.

"He's only a few miles northwest of your position," Ava said in my ear. "Way too far for Ritter and Erin and the others to get to him, even if I could call them back. You'll have to go after him and see what happened. Could be the bandits just took the van and weapons and dumped the rest. They could all be nearby."

I didn't blame Ava for wanting the best-case scenario. I hadn't been on many ops—okay, I really hadn't been involved at all except for flying. All the fighting was left to the experienced mortals or the semi-immortal Unbounded. When Erin and Jace had been little, I'd taken care of them. Now that they had Changed, the roles were reversed. That took a lot of getting used to on my part because deep down I was still their protective older brother.

"I'll get supplies," I said, sealing the plane door behind me and striding down the aisle to the storage compartments located in the small kitchen at the back left side of the plane.

"Grab sedatives and extra curequick." She hesitated before adding, "Better take one of Ritter's bags."

I already had one in my hands. Ritter's bags contained everything a soldier could need in a battle: an assault rifle, extra ammo, several handguns, radios and earbuds, a change of clothes, and even a few grenades. I was stuffing the curequick into it now, along with food rations that Unbounded wouldn't need. They could absorb nutrients from the world around them, which I had to admit made me envious at times. A soldier who didn't need to eat but whose energy was continuously renewed was infinitely better in combat. No need to find or carry water. No worrying about how long a campaign might take.

But there were no Unbounded here, only me, and I was going after our people.

"I'm sending the coordinates to your phone," Ava said. "Let me know the minute you have eyes on them. Go slowly when you get close. The bandits may still be there or could have left a guard."

"Will do."

Hanging up, I stuffed a second water bladder into the bulging shoulder bag and began shedding my clothes, exchanging my jeans and T-shirt for a bulletproof vest and jungle camouflage. It was muggy here and hot, even in mid-November, at least it would be until night fell, but anything to keep me safe and unnoticed was worth it. The concern in Ava's voice had me jumpy, but I was glad she hadn't pointed out the fact that I could be killed. I was already made aware of that every day working with my siblings.

CHAPTER 3

As I resealed the plane, the blue truck revved and left the building, heading not toward the plane but down the dirt road that bordered part of the runway. César's sedan followed. So much for my plan of taking the blue truck at least part of the way. The nearly three miles to Irwin's location wouldn't take me long to cover on foot, but every second could mean greater problems for Tenika and Irwin. I started toward the road.

I couldn't help but think of my children. I joined the Renegades to make a difference, to find justice for my wife, Lorrie, and because only the Renegades understood what happened to rip our lives apart. I believed in this fight and would give all I could to it, but ultimately my children had to be my first priority. It was comforting to know I wasn't the only one who felt Kathy and Spencer were important. The children weren't really just mine anymore, but a part of our larger family of Renegades, something they desperately needed after losing their mother.

A high, whiny sound of a motorbike cut off that vein of thought, and I turned around, grabbing the assault rifle hanging over my shoulder. It was a small bike, the kind that most American men would laugh at and refuse to own. I eased my finger off the trigger when I realized that riding it was the girl from earlier.

She came to a stop next to me. "You will go after your friends?"

I nodded.

"I can take you."

"Just give me the bike. I'll bring it back or pay you for it."

She shook her head. "I want to come. They killed my husband."

"Don't you understand? They don't care about you! You can't make a difference against them."

"We made a difference back there," she retorted. "And you are only one. Together we are stronger."

"Give me the keys."

In answer, she turned off the bike and put the keys down the front of her shirt, giving me a compelling glimpse of cleavage.

I was tempted to throw her off the bike and take the keys, but I wasn't that kind of man, and I didn't have time to convince her. Besides, she *had* helped me back at the building.

"You can go partway," I said. "Then you let me go on alone to check on my friends. I can't have you putting them in danger. Deal?"

She wanted to protest, but apparently something in my eyes convinced her I wouldn't bend. Nodding, she scooted back on the bike, fished out the keys, and handed them to me.

I blinked in surprise, both at her trust and the fact that she would let me drive. Not something the women in my current life would even think about offering willingly. *Maybe I'm living in the wrong country,* I thought.

"No, you drive," I said. "I'll keep a lookout."

Her eyes widened in a way that made me feel strangely protective. She'd been married and was a widow, so maybe she wasn't as young as I'd first thought. A woman, not a girl. She was certainly beautiful, even if in a way that was completely opposite to my blond-haired, blue-eyed wife.

Lorrie. I wondered if the pain would always come whenever I thought of her.

Looping the assault rifle over my head, I pulled out a pistol instead. We were off, the air once again filled with the whiny complaint of the small engine. But it drove well on the dirt road and, if it didn't alert every bandit in Mexico with the sound, we would get there in minutes.

I became acutely aware of my left arm draped loosely about the woman's waist. I didn't even know her name. She had a pistol tucked into the back of her tight jeans. No holster.

"Okay, stop here," I yelled in her ear a few minutes

later. She eased to the side of the road and turned off the engine. The abrupt quiet sounded almost loud.

"Wait here," I said. "I'll come for you when it's safe. Or you can go back to the house and wait for me."

Her mouth pursed in a scowl and her dark eyes narrowed, but she nodded. "I'll wait here."

I hurried away, straight into the woods, when really I needed to go further along the road. I couldn't have her following me. After a minute, I altered my direction, ran hard for stretch, then began my real approach. Slowly now. Careful. Eyes searching.

I could hear nothing but the occasional cry of a bird; whatever had happened here had frightened away the animals. My chest felt tight. I checked the GPS. Irwin should be just up ahead a few yards off the road.

Even more cautiously, I crept forward. I didn't know what I'd do if the bandits were still there, but if they were, I wasn't about to leave Irwin with them, Ava's orders or no.

The trees were thinning now, and I scanned the area carefully. *There,* I thought. I could see an arm poking out from under a bush. I circled around, trying to locate any attackers, but no one else seemed to be anywhere near here. Just to be certain, I hunkered down and waited, my heartbeat slowing as I breathed deeply.

After five minutes, I was convinced the bandits had abandoned Irwin to the animals, which thankfully hadn't yet appeared. I rose and pushed my way through the brush, looking under the lush greenery to see if I could locate Tenika as well. But there were enough breaks in the trees overhead that if she'd been nearby, Ava would have been able to locate her using the satellite.

I pulled Irwin from under the bush. The blond man was drenched in fresh blood. He'd been shot in the chest and again in his leg, where shards of bone jutted from his blood-soaked jeans. He had no heartbeat, but already the wounds were beginning to heal, and the curequick in my bag would help him regenerate even faster. I injected the substance around each wound and then sat back on my heels. Nothing left but to report the bad news to Ava.

She answered before my first ring finished. "Hello?"

"I found Irwin, but no sign of Tenika yet."

"What's his condition?"

"Not too bad. He bled out from a chest wound. Heart stopped beating, but they missed hitting it directly at least."

"No head wound?"

"No. But his leg's pretty badly busted up. I can see bone."

"With the curequick he should regain consciousness soon. See if he can tell you anything. How much did you give him?"

"Two syringes. One near each wound."

"Wait five minutes and give him two more. Meanwhile, search the area for clues."

"Okay, but they've taken everything of value from him—guns, phone, the van. You'll need to let his people know."

"We figured as much. They're waiting to hear from us."

I broke the connection, wondering what she expected me to find. I'd been training with the Renegades for two months now, but we hadn't covered tracking in a foreign jungle. Or if they had, I'd been taking care of the kids that day.

I walked around, noting the torn leaves and signs of a struggle. Tire marks showed where they'd been forced off the dirt road. At some point Tenika and Irwin must have left the van. One thing was certain, they hadn't been defeated easily.

I followed the tire marks of the van through the jungle foliage, trying to determine where it met back up with the road, if it did at all. Some distance away from Irwin, another smaller road appeared, deep under a canopy of trees. Near this, I found four more bodies, heaped on each other like refuse.

"Hello," I said. These were our captives. Or some of them.

They still had no pulse, but they didn't look worse than when they'd left our plane. All the blood on them was long dried and their wounds on their way to full healing. The bandits must have thought them dead. But why had they kept the other seven? Maybe because they'd started breathing again. If they had only taken those who were alive, it could mean they kept Tenika as well.

All our Emporium captives had been heavily drugged, but in another day, or maybe by morning, their bodies would have cleared the drugs from their systems. I needed to find them before then.

But how?

A movement in the trees sent me scuttling backward, my gun drawn. Sweat dripped from my hairline down the back of my neck as I wondered if the bandits or one of the less-damaged Emporium agents had returned to consciousness.

CHAPTER 4

"DON'T SHOOT!" CAME A FEMALE VOICE. "IT'S ME, MARISA."
I had no idea who Marisa was, but the slamming in my chest abated slightly as my heart decided I wasn't in immediate danger. "Come out!"

The woman who'd brought me here emerged from the brush onto the small road, her blue tank top contrasting noticeably with the dark green jungle decor. Her pistol was in her hands, though it was pointing at the ground—for the moment.

Okay, so I did know her, and I wasn't really that surprised to see her. I stepped out from my tree. "I thought I told you to stay with the bike."

One delicate shoulder lifted in a shrug. "I did. It's just over on the main road. I walked it here."

I couldn't really blame her for disobeying when I'd planned to disregard my own orders and fight the bandits if I had to in order to save Tenika and Irwin, but it unnerved me all the same. If anything happened to her, I'd feel responsible.

Marisa hesitated several long seconds before taking a few steps and squatting down to stare at the captives. "They're dead. Who are they? Why do they have that . . ." She struggled to find the word. "Metal bracelet."

"Shackles." I shook my head, knowing she'd never believe how dangerous they still were. "I'll come back for them later, but first . . ." I delved in my bag for more of the drug that had been especially prepared to sedate Unbounded. I couldn't kill them with it; in fact, an overdose would only buy me a few more hours. As I injected the drug, the woman stared at me as if I'd left my brain back at the plane, which maybe I had.

"Come on," I said roughly.

She followed me through the brush back to where I'd left Irwin. I knelt down and began giving him another dose of curequick. Afterward, I checked his neck for a pulse, my fingers looking white against his deeply tanned skin. A faint beat awarded my effort. It wouldn't be long now.

"He's dead," she said, disgust lacing her voice. "Can't you see that? What did you give him? It's different than what you gave the others. The needle is bigger."

"Since you're so good at observation, can you tell me what happened here? I'm looking for the woman that was with him."

"You mean the black one with all the long braids?"

"How did you know?" Because Marisa definitely hadn't been introduced.

"You're not the only one who has binoculars." With another uneasy glance at Irwin, she stood and began looking around, studying the signs of the struggle as I had. After a time, she sighed. "There's not much to see. They were pushed off the road, and they took cover behind the van. I see many empty shells."

"Shells. Right." I hadn't even noticed.

She cocked her head, her voice devoid of emotion. "I'm sure they have her. They always need women, so they'll want to keep her. She might have a chance to run away after they have their fun."

"They'd keep her alive?"

"For a while at least. If she doesn't fight too much." The emotionlessness tone was emphasized by a deadness in her beautiful eyes, and I wondered what else they'd done to her when they killed her husband.

I forced myself instead to think about Tenika. If she was with the bandits, it might be a good thing. Her talent was hypnosuggestion, which she used in her cover job as a psychologist. If the bandits listened to her, she might be able to convince them to let her go and to turn over the Emporium captives. The bandits wouldn't know to muzzle her unless one of the agents somehow regained consciousness.

"Tell me about the bandits," I said, settling in the vegetation a couple feet away from Irwin. "What's their gig?"

"Gig?"

"How do they survive?"

She sank down in the soft grass beside me, on the side away from Irwin. "Stealing, drugs, anything really. Some groups deal in slavery—mostly capturing the native Maya." She wrinkled her nose as if she'd caught a whiff of something nasty. "They take whole family groups, make them work for them."

"What kind of drugs?"

She shrugged. "All of it. I don't know."

The drugs made me feel uneasy, but I didn't know why it would trigger my alarms more than kidnapping. "Do you know where they live?"

Marisa frowned, staring at me with a worried crease between her eyebrows. "No." After a few seconds of hesitation, she added, "My husband found their place, the same bandits who did this. That's why they killed him."

"How long ago?"

"Two months." Her flared nostrils and clenched jaw told me that it still felt like yesterday.

Two months, the same amount of time Lorrie had been gone. "You should go home to your father and brother—or wherever they are."

"They can't protect me. They expect me to stay and cook for them, but I won't. I have an uncle who owns a ranch outside of Palenque. My mother's brother. I lived with him and his American wife when I was little after my mother died. I will go to him when this is over." Her gaze dropped.

I wanted to ask how old she was, but it wasn't something I felt I could do. "I'm sorry."

She shrugged. "Who is in the picture? The one you took out of your pocket earlier?"

I felt for it and passed it to her. "My children, Kathy and Spencer."

A smile chased the sadness from Marisa's face. "Oh, they are so nice. They don't look much like you, except the blond hair."

"Kathy takes after her mother. Believe it or not, when I was young, I had those same freckles that are torturing my son's face."

She laughed. "Then he'll be as handsome as you when he is a man." She lowered her eyelashes, peering at me from under them. She was flirting, but I didn't mind. It had been a long time since I'd noticed any woman flirting with me, though Lorrie had claimed many of the clients I'd ferried around had flirted like mad.

"And your wife? Do you have a picture of her?"

I did, but I had stopped carrying the photograph because it hurt too much. "She's dead," I said. "Two months ago. Killed by those men back there." I jerked my head in the direction of the Emporium captives. It wasn't those same men, of course, but others from the same group.

Her eyes opened fully now, and I could see they glistened with moisture. "That's why you killed them. I understand."

"Not me. I wish it had been."

She nodded. "That, too, I can under—"

A gasp from my other side cut off her words. I leapt to my feet and hurried to Irwin. He had a knife in his hand and sliced at me, his eyes rolling back and forth wildly

Marisa shrieked and jumped up, pulling her pistol with one hand and crossing herself with the other. Her mouth spilled long strings of Spanish. Cursing or prayers, I couldn't tell which.

"Stop!" I said, raising my hands in front of Irwin to show I was unarmed. "I'm a Renegade. Part of Ava's group. I'm here to help you."

He calmed immediately, despite Marisa's pistol and her continued flow of words. "All right," he said in a thick Australian accent. He shifted his body slightly, grimacing with the pain. "Fill me in."

"Marisa," I barked, "put that down!" I glared at her until some sanity returned to her eyes and her weapon lowered.

I turned back to Irwin and explained what had happened in a few short sentences. "I think they have Tenika," I finished.

"That's my bet. We'll have to go after them." He attempted to sit but gave up as his body convulsed in pain.

"You aren't going anywhere. Here. Let me help." I dragged him to a tree and propped his back against it. He panted through gritted teeth, his forehead furrowed with agony.

"You don't understand," Irwin said as the pain eased.

"Those bandits will wake up our prisoners with their drugs—they're quite proficient at knocking people out and waking them for interrogation. Once they discover the Emporium will pay to get those guys back, they'll make a deal."

"The Emporium won't pay bandits. They'll just kill them." If it weren't for Tenika and losing the captives, I'd just leave them to it.

"Probably. Unless they think they can use them in the future." Irwin grimaced down at his leg. Already the shards were less noticeable as the new bone regrew and knitted itself back together.

"I have some pain killer," I offered. His body would get rid of it quickly as it did anything else, but given enough, he ought to experience some temporary relief. "I gave you a small amount already in the curequick, but I have some separate. Injectable."

Irwin waved the suggestion away. "Look, we have to go after them. We're shorthanded at the prison. It'll take hours before I can get someone here, and by then we might lose their trail."

"Trail? There is no trail. They got on a road, and from there we have no idea where they went." I glanced back at Marisa for confirmation. She'd fallen silent, but her face was frozen, her pistol in a death grip—thankfully pointed at the ground. I wasn't sure she even heard me. "They have several hours on us already."

"I *can* track them." He said it with such confidence that I had to smile.

All Unbounded were arrogant to a point, even my own siblings. I believed it was mostly because the gene demanded it. Changing was just that: a complete Change. From mortal to semi-immortal, aging only two years for every hundred that passed. No more submissive tendencies, no more willingness to remain on the sidelines. Those who Changed had only the best genes. They were stronger, faster, and even more intelligent than the average human, and their individual abilities increased their confidence and usefulness.

But sometimes it also meant they didn't recognize their limits.

"You can't do that while sitting here in these weeds," I told Irwin. "And you aren't going anywhere until morning without transportation. So unless you've got more tricks up your sleeve, it looks like I'm going to have to start down that road without you and just pray I find Tenika before it's too late."

Irwin's mouth, still tight with pain, quirked up. "You'll go after her then."

"Do I have another choice?"

He shook his head. "No. But just so we're clear, I can track them. Even sitting in these weeds."

"How? You want me to carry you?" Judging by his pallor, he wouldn't even make it several yards on Marisa's motorcycle.

"Him." Irwin's eyes went past both me and Marisa, who also turned.

Amber eyes stared out at us from the midst of a large jungle bush, verdant with huge, deep green leaves. I had barely a glimpse of tawny fur and black spots before Marisa raised her gun and fired.

CHAPTER 5

THE EYES VANISHED AS MARISA JUMPED BACKWARD INTO MY arms. Her slender body trembled.

"Take that gun from her!" Irwin ordered. "She scared him!"

Marisa whirled on Irwin. "Scared him! You're dead— or were. And that's a-a jaguar!"

"So?" Irwin frowned. "Woman, you might have just ruined our one chance."

Then I understood. Irwin's ability was to communicate with animals, or at least some of them, and I was willing to bet that creature knew more about this jungle than any of us.

I took Marisa's gun, removed the magazine, and handed it back to her. "No more shooting. Got it?"

She glared at me as she had when I'd left her with the bike, but she eventually nodded.

Irwin had shut his eyes, whether to try to communicate

with the animal or in pain, I couldn't tell. After a long minute, his eyes snapped open. "Go wait on the road. I'll call you when it's safe. Hurry, both of you!"

I grabbed Marisa's hand. "Come on!"

"You crazy?" she asked, her accent intensifying with her emotion. "He's hurt. That creature came because of the blood. He'll kill him again!" She stopped speaking, mouth slightly agape as the incongruity of her statement hit her.

"Irwin knows what he's doing. Half the world grew up on this guy wrestling alligators."

"What?" She crinkled her nose in a way that was becoming familiar and, if I wanted to admit it, rather attractive.

"Never mind."

She looked behind us, letting me drag her through the jungle foliage. We hadn't yet made it to the road when she tugged against me. "Look."

I stopped and saw that the jaguar was approaching Irwin, who held out a cupped hand. We waited, holding our breath as the creature reached him and pushed his face into the hand, nuzzling it. Soon Irwin was scratching the animal's neck.

Marisa was mumbling in Spanish and crossing herself again. I had to admit to a decided urge to begin mumbling to myself in some kind of foreign language because I didn't have words to describe this. It seemed only a few seconds passed until the jaguar pushed once more against Irwin's hand and bounded away into the forest.

"You can come back now," Irwin called, motioning to us.

We took no time in returning. "All right, mates," he said with a cheerful grin that almost hid his pain, "this is what's going to happen. My furry, four-legged friend—try saying that fast three times—knows where the bandits are, and he'll take you there. But he says to lose the motorbike. Won't be any use where you're going." Irwin frowned at Marisa. "And he doesn't want her to come along."

I had no intention of taking Marisa. "You're sure he knows the right group of bandits?"

"Yes. There's another group nearby, but their scent isn't here. You can trust him." Irwin gave a self-conscious smirk. "Well, as far as you can trust any wild animal."

So not at all. "Okay," I said.

"You can't be serious." Marisa stared at me aghast. "That thing will kill you."

"No, he won't," Irwin said. "I told him not to." To me, he added, thumbing in the direction where I had found the dead Emporium agents, "There's a smaller road over there. Just start on that, and he'll let you know when you need to veer off. He'll only show himself to get you to change direction or if you aren't going the right way. However, it's already near four, and it'll be dark by six. Could be sooner the deeper you go. I think you might make it before dark if you push hard, but you might not. It's hard to tell time and distance with animals."

"That's okay. I have everything I need." I hefted my bag. "I should take you back to the plane first."

He gave me another of his grins. "I'll be okay hanging out here for a few hours. If you're not back by morning, I'm coming after you."

He'd probably feel almost normal by then. "I already reported finding you," I said. "We're in contact with your people at the prison. That's how I found you."

"Good. I don't want them wasting time coming after me. Better they focus on getting a team together to back you up."

Or to do the job if I failed, he meant. "Take this." I gave him an extra pistol. "Just in case."

"The animals won't bother me," he said in that annoyingly confident tone. I decided I was beginning to hate his Aussie accent.

"It's for the two-legged kind." I turned and started through the forest. Marisa stumbled after me. From the corner of my eye, I got the merest glimpse of the jaguar up ahead, moving in the direction of the small road.

I waited until we reached it to talk to Marisa. "You heard what he said. You can't come. Besides, it'll be another few hours before he'll be well enough to travel. Then you can use the bike to take him back to your place. Take care of him until he can defend himself or until someone comes for him."

Marisa stared, backing away from me. "He is a ghost. I cannot. I—"

"Please," I said.

Without waiting for her reply, I turned and started jogging down the road. She didn't follow, which I took as a good sign.

I knew I had to make a choice about reporting to Ava what I was doing. If I didn't, it'd be grounds for expulsion from the Renegades, and I didn't want that. But I also couldn't have her ordering me back to the plane. Because if I had to wait for backup to search for Tenika, that might mean losing the captives altogether or at the very least a delay in bringing the cure to Bronson once our people tracked it down.

In the end, my conscience won out. I waited for a break in the trees overhead before slowing to a walk and dialing.

"Where are you?" Ava asked.

"I'm following a jaguar."

"What?" The amusement in her voice told me I'd caught her off guard. Good to know my young granny wasn't beyond surprise.

I gave her a quick rundown. "Irwin says his friends won't be able to get backup till morning and that the bandits have the ability of waking our Emporium friends."

"Chris, you know how dangerous this is."

I couldn't stifle my flare of anger. "What I know is that Stella didn't stop to consider her welfare when she protected my kids yesterday. I want all of this cleared up before Erin and the others get back with Bronson's medication."

She was silent for the space of a few heartbeats. "Okay, but reconnaissance only. Use good judgment. Follow our protocols. Report when you can."

The mark of a good leader was knowing when to back down, to let those under you take responsibility for their actions. I knew she didn't want me going, but she also knew I was going anyway.

"Will do," I said.

"Oh, and Chris."

"Yes?"

"Remember you have two very important reasons to come home."

Her words were quiet, but they might as well have been shouted from a loudspeaker. Or delivered with a drop kick to the gut. As if she had to remind me about Kathy and Spencer.

"I always remember that," I said quietly.

"Good." A faint click in my ear told me she'd hung up. I tucked away the phone and started jogging again.

I'd only gone five more minutes along the road when a low growl called my attention to the right. "I must be crazy," I mumbled, catching a glimpse of the jaguar's tawny coat with its black spots. My kids would be amazed when they heard this story—if I survived.

I had every intention of doing so.

I angled through the jungle, jumping over shorter bushes and circumventing the larger ones and the trees. I tried to maintain a good pace, keeping in mind that I really needed to find the bandits' encampment before dark. Hopefully, that also meant I'd arrive before they got around to waking up any of the Emporium captives.

When a stitch appeared in my side, I slowed down a notch, realizing that we were angling slightly upwards now. I heard what had to be a howler monkey, numerous bird calls, and the scream of another large cat. There were many creatures I never saw but only heard scurrying away—and not for my sake, but because of my guide. I was glad now for our rigorous training schedule because I would never have been able to keep up this pace two months ago.

The thought was like a knife turning in my stomach. Two months ago, Lorrie had been alive. Such a short time and yet it felt like years with all that I'd been through.

After thirty minutes of pushing through the foliage, I stumbled to a halt, my hand going to a tree for support. I had no idea how close an eye the jaguar kept on me, but he'd realize soon enough that I'd stopped moving. Mostly I needed to relocate my water to a more accessible position, allowing me to take more frequent sips without stopping. Having no way of knowing how much further I had to go, I'd better prepare for the worst. While checking my GPS, I downed a ration bar to keep up my strength. We'd gone mostly in a straight line since leaving the small road, though we'd recently taken a sharp turn around a raised bit of land.

My eyes wandered over the terrain. There was no evidence of human habitation. I might be standing on a spot that no human had ever stood on before. It was beautiful—no, gorgeous. Trees filled my vision, their green so bright and lush that it made something inside me ache. Why hadn't I brought Lorrie here before she died? Why had I been so preoccupied with making a living that I hadn't realized the best years of my life were already ticking away?

Stifling the urge to scream out my loss, I slapped at the back of my neck, squashing a mosquito that I hoped didn't carry some deadly virus. Maybe it was okay that I hadn't brought Lorrie here after all. She hated roughing it. A hotel in Paris would have been better. I should have sprung for that. Pastries, long walks along the Seine. A visit to the Eiffel Tower and to the Louvre to see the Mona Lisa.

I pulled back on my pack. *Hope you're watching for me,* I told the jaguar.

I'd taken only two steps when a faint voice called out my name. I stopped, listening. Nothing.

My imagination.

No, there it was again. Definite crying. Screaming. Female.

I hurried back the way I had come.

CHAPTER 6

PULLING MY NINE MIL, I DROPPED MY PACK AS I RAN, MENTALLY cursing at the delay. I had a sinking feeling I knew who the woman was, but I didn't know who—or what—was making her scream. I didn't even know how she knew my name, though thinking about it now, I had introduced myself to her family back at their place.

Every day I worked with women who were tougher and stronger than I was, most of whom had centuries of experience. I was mortal, the older brother who was more fragile than his younger siblings. They always wanted to protect me. So it was an odd sensation to be hurtling through the trees with the hope of rescuing a woman. Of knowing I was the only one who *could* rescue her.

I didn't even want to think about being too late.

Seemingly long minutes later, I spotted Marisa through the trees, waving a big stick in her hand. Twenty feet in front of her, partially hidden by the trees, a jaguar looked ready to pounce. Without thinking, I sprinted through the remaining foliage, bursting out between her and the creature.

"Hey!" I shouted.

The animal yowled, sounding worse than a dozen tomcats fighting in an alley.

Marisa gasped. "He's going to kill me!"

I took aim with the gun. I had no way of knowing if this was the animal I had been following or a new one on the scene. Either way, I'd be sorry if I had to shoot it. The creature screeched again, its amber eyes digging twin holes through me. Should I fire the pistol into the air? If this was my guide, I might scare him off completely. Or he might decide I would behave better inside his stomach. A pistol shot might also alert the bandits of my approach, if they were near.

With a flick of his tail, the jaguar pounced—but into the forest instead of at me. For several long seconds, I contemplated my survival. Then I started after him. With a cry of dismay, Marisa scrambled after me.

I whirled on her. "I told you to stay behind. What, do I have to tie you up? Are you determined to get yourself killed?"

Or maybe she was working for the bandits. But no, she'd helped me kill them.

"Look," I said more calmly. "I have to keep going. Good people will die if I don't."

She glared at me. "You going to leave me here?"

"Go back to Irwin."

"What about that *diablo*?" She glanced in the direction the jaguar had disappeared, her chest heaving in real terror. Devil. That was one Spanish word I knew.

Guilt waved through me. I shouldn't have accepted a ride on the motorcycle in the first place. If I hadn't, she wouldn't be anywhere near here. Even if that jaguar was the one I was following, it might return for a soft meal. I'd have to give up another gun, unless she still had hers and I could return her magazine. "You can't keep up."

"Try me." She pushed past me, leaping over the brush with a grace that reminded me of the jaguar.

She was right, of course. I couldn't leave her in this remote place any more than I could leave Tenika to face the bandits alone. I sprinted to catch up, pulling ahead of Marisa and leading her back to where I'd dropped my pack. The crushed leaves of the plants made the trail easy to follow. No wonder she'd been able to track me. Her eyes followed my movements as I picked up my pack, the tip of a red tongue wetting her lips. She was breathing even harder now, and I had trouble looking away from her heaving chest.

I offered her the water tube, and she took it gratefully, opening the end with a practice that told me she was familiar with hydration packs. She took two steady pulls and gave it back.

"Better wear this," I told her, pulling out a camouflage T-shirt. As much as I hated to cover her up, she was like a neon sign in that blue tank—and it was better to keep my mind on the op instead of on her curves.

She pulled it on with a little roll of her eyes, telling me she'd noticed my interest. Not meeting her eyes, I tossed a ration bar at her before taking off again. I couldn't see or hear the jaguar, and I hoped he hadn't abandoned us all together. If he had, it was going to be a long night.

We'd gone another twenty minutes in the same direction before I glimpsed the jaguar again to the left. "That's right, buddy," I murmured, turning in that direction. "Good boy."

"Can we walk for a moment?" Marisa asked.

So far she'd kept up, and if I was really truthful—which I didn't plan on being—I'd gone faster with her watching my progress. I could do with a rest myself.

"Okay," I said, passing her my water tube. "Do you have any idea how far away they might be?" The bandits had taken the van and had a few hours on us, but since they had to use the little road instead of cutting through the jungle, maybe we wouldn't get there too far behind them.

Marisa thought for a moment. "Not too far. They have come and gone to my father's place in maybe thirty minutes, and the road isn't good. It winds back and forth like a snake."

"Okay, we'd better start being more careful then." Irwin had estimated that we'd make it before dark, and the light was beginning to fail. We'd also run a good way, which maybe Irwin hadn't counted on. The last thing we needed was to accidentally run into the middle of their camp or alert their lookouts.

Now that I was thinking about lookouts, I wondered how I could make sure we didn't get picked off before we realized we were near the hideout. Unfortunately, I didn't speak jaguar like Irwin.

I held back a large leaf so it wouldn't smack Marisa in the face. She smiled her thanks, which made me remember how she looked in that blue tank. I shook the thoughts away. I was missing Lorrie, that's all. Couldn't blame a man for looking.

We hadn't hiked another fifteen minutes before the jaguar screamed ahead, much further away than I'd heard him before. There was a shout and the bark of an automatic rifle.

It looked like we'd found the bandits.

Something came at us fast, the foliage rippling like a wave. I grabbed Marisa and pulled her into the shelter of a bush. The jaguar sprang into view, landing in front of us with a deadly snarl. For several seconds he stared at us, then snarled viciously again before bounding away, disappearing the way we'd come.

I waited, the woman in my arms trembling, but no one came after the jaguar. "What happened?" she whispered.

"I think we've found the camp, and it looks like the bandits aren't crazy about chasing Irwin's friend."

"Crazy like you, you mean."

"Hey, don't knock what works."

"Don't knock?" She arched a brow.

"Never mind." She couldn't know I'd seen stranger things than an obedient jaguar since I'd joined the Renegades. My sister could sense emotions and thoughts, my brother could run almost faster than I could follow with my eyes and fight ten mortals without breaking a sweat. Stella could control three high-powered computers at once, processing more information than an army of nerds, and at the same time carry on an intelligent conversation with me.

"Who is she?" Marisa asked softly. "The woman who puts that expression on your face."

She was right, however much I didn't want to admit it. If anyone ever told me I'd be interested in another woman when my wife was only two months dead, I would have thought they were insane. Lorrie had been everything to me from the moment we met. Every day we'd been together, I'd known she was a ten on a scale where I hit maybe only a four or a five. Sometimes at night I'd watch her sleep until I couldn't stand not touching her, and then she'd awaken and we'd make love, and I knew that I would never stop loving her. I'd always prayed she wouldn't get up one morning and realize what a mistake she'd made in marrying me.

I wished Lorrie had been the one to survive that horrible day, my first encounter with the Emporium, but she hadn't, and Marisa was right that there was someone else: Stella, who was fighting for the life of her aging, mortal husband, Bronson. I'd be lying if I let myself believe that I was only here because of what she'd done for my children. I certainly wasn't risking my life for Bronson, though I liked the man well enough. No, I was here in this jungle because Stella's happiness meant more to me than almost anything, and she loved Bronson as much as I'd loved Lorrie.

"What's she like?" Marisa took my silence for agreement.

I closed my eyes, pushing back the images that threatened my control. Stella Davis was half Italian, half Japanese, with the drop-dead gorgeous looks men dreamed about—I know I had. She was also a talented technopath who could manipulate electronic information at a rate that wasn't conceivable to even most Unbounded, much less mortals. Yet it was her kindness, not her intellect or beauty, that had helped me keep things together during the dark days after Lorrie's murder, when at times I hadn't believed it possible to go on.

I couldn't pinpoint the moment my feelings for her had changed from gratitude to . . . something more, but not for a second did I fool myself that I had a chance with her. Not only because Bronson still lived but because I would die too soon, just like Bronson. Even with the cure for his disease. He was already in his seventies, and old age would eventually win out. No way would Stella be stupid enough to replace a mortal lover for another one who would leave her again.

"There is no woman," I said.

Marisa tilted her head, staring at me for a long moment. Then she asked, "What now?"

"We go slowly. I doubt the jaguar went into their camp, so that shot must have come from a lookout. Keep close." I eased forward, this time taking care not to leave a trail. I indicated for Marisa to do the same.

We heard the men before we saw them, and I eased behind a tree and glided along its leafy branches to the cover of another tree where two men came into view. They looked as brutal as the ones who'd tried to steal my plane. One was gesturing and the other laughing.

"Can you hear what they're saying?" I asked Marisa.

She shook her head. "I think maybe they talk about the jaguar."

"They may have more lookouts." We watched as the men finished their discussion, then one headed away, while the other shimmied up a tree.

"Only one lookout, I think," Marisa said. "He can see everything from up there."

We'd have to be sure he didn't see us before we took him out. I moved slowly around my tree until it was between me and the lookout bandit. "Looks like we've got a pretty good view of the camp," I whispered.

Marisa edged over to sit beside me. From where we sat, the ground angled downward slightly into a gentle valley, just large enough to accommodate one small, low-slung cabin, one large tent, several smaller tents, and an outdoor cooking area. There were also a couple motorcycles, a beat-up truck, a car, and the missing van, which looked decidedly worse than the last time I'd seen it.

The man who had been with the lookout disappeared into the big tent. I eased out my binoculars and had a closer look, but there was no one else in sight except two women who were cooking over a fire. They both appeared haggard and were wearing dirty clothing. The younger one was openly crying. Every now and then the older woman would stop working to offer comfort, her eyes glancing nervously toward the tent.

"She must have lost her man today," Marisa said, her voice dull and expressionless. "Or the one protecting her."

"What will happen to her?"

"Another will take his place. Women are in short supply." Again that dead tone that ripped at my heart. I remembered now when I'd heard it last: in my own voice after Lorrie had died and I'd been trying to figure out how to tell the kids.

Marisa had pushed so close that I could smell her sweat, but it didn't turn me off. In fact, I wanted to pull her closer and protect her. I wondered again how old she was, and if she would ever love another man or if she would mourn her husband until it was too late to matter.

Or was I thinking of Stella again?

A movement directed my attention away from Marisa to the tent below where a man was emerging. With him were two other bandits and one of the Emporium agents, hands still shackled, but awake. The agent was a large black man who had been shot in the hip, if I remembered correctly, then knocked unconscious by Ritter during the fighting yesterday. He had to be held upright by the men, his legs dragging behind him uselessly, also still shackled.

The Emporium agent was talking urgently as they pushed him to the ground several feet away from the women, and the first bandit pointed a gun at his face, barking something I couldn't hear. The agent fell silent. The other bandits grinned at his arrogant, angry face. If the captive was gifted in combat, it wouldn't be long before all the bandits were dead, shackles or no shackles. Their women would likely end up murdered as well.

The women began serving something in bowls to the bandits, who sat down to eat on a felled log that seemed intended for that purpose. The man with the gun waved away the proffered bowl and kept his weapon aimed at the Unbounded.

I lowered the binoculars. "I see only three men and two women, but there's no telling how many might be in the tents or cabin. And we're already losing the light. I'm thinking we should take out the guy in the tree and move in to see if we can learn more."

She shook her head. "They'll be sending someone to give him food. Let me see." I handed her the binoculars, and in the next second, she gave a swift intake of breath. The darkness was falling fast now, and I wasn't sure if I was imagining the paleness that seemed to creep into her dark skin.

"What's wrong?"

"Nothing." She pushed the binoculars back at me. "There will be at least one more in the tent with the woman and the others you seek, if they are here."

"We need to hit them before they realize what's coming. That guy down there is either their leader or he's taken over now that their leader is gone. He doesn't look stupid."

"No, he's far from that." Marisa's voice was strained, as though she could barely form the words.

Now I understood. "So he's the one."

She nodded, her jaw clenched so tightly it must hurt her face.

I put a hand on her shoulder. "You stay here. I'll get closer to the lookout. Don't worry. I'll wait to see if they feed him first. After I take care of him, I'm going down to look around. I have to see if Tenika and the others are here or if they've dumped them somewhere else."

If they had dumped them, what was I going to do? I couldn't risk my mission to take revenge for Marisa, however much I wanted to wipe that hurt from her face. I'd have to find the road they'd driven here on and back-track along it, hoping the wild animals hadn't beaten me to the bodies.

Still, some feeling told me they were in that tent. I had to know what was going on inside it sooner rather than later. Ritter had always taught us to follow our gut instincts, and that's what I planned on doing.

Before leaving, I typed out a message on my sat phone that would send automatically if I ever got into a clear spot where it could connect with the satellite. I knew Ava would have been tracking my implant, and I'd tried to walk in the open when possible, but the jungle was dense and I really didn't know if she'd be able to direct Irwin's friends to my location in the morning. Irwin might have to find another jaguar, and by then Tenika and the others could be anywhere.

No, I'm going to free them tonight.

I had to. Before it was too late.

CHAPTER 7

MARISA WAS RIGHT ABOUT WAITING ON THE LOOKOUT. One of the men soon came in search of him, not with food, but to relieve him. I debated taking them both out right there, but I needed more time to find Tenika—time I might lose if the lookout didn't return to camp on schedule. I let him go, hoping I wouldn't regret it later.

This lookout hadn't gone up the tree like the previous one, but was pacing in front of the tree. His movements were taut and angry, and I couldn't help wonder who he'd lost today. But I didn't feel sorry for him for long because he'd chosen a life that exploited others and fed on their misery.

I took out a tranque gun because I was still feeling sick over the other men I had killed. I'd loaded it with double the dose. Not enough to kill a man his size, but enough to make even an Unbounded sleep for a few hours. The bandits might be out as long as twenty.

I aimed carefully, using the scope. A dot of red appeared on his back, showing me where it would hit. I pulled it a bit higher. He stiffened as the needle entered the base of his neck, but he didn't have time to turn before he crumpled into the vegetation without a sound.

Slipping through the foliage, I pulled him over my shoulder and carried him some distance away, tucking him under a bush. They wouldn't find him until morning—if there were any bandits left to search. I didn't think animals would be a problem this close to the camp, but you never knew.

The thought made me stop for a minute, staring back at the bush. *You can't worry about him,* I told myself. *Find Tenika.* Of course, it really wasn't for her. It was for Stella. I had to finish up here and be ready to take that cure home to Bronson.

I moved through the trees, gradually and without sudden movements that might catch the eye. The darkness had closed in and I was relatively sure those around the cooking area couldn't see me because of the light from the fire.

The leader was seated across from the Emporium agent now, and they were talking earnestly. They offered him food, which took him several seconds to accept. I could imagine his disgust at the campfire cuisine— Emporium agents were notorious for their fine dining. People who didn't need to eat could afford to be very picky. But this captive couldn't afford to alienate the bandit before he got free or succeeded in awakening more of his people. So far he was still securely tied, and that showed a cunning on the part of the bandit, which didn't bode well for my overall mission but that was working in my favor at the moment. No way did I want that Unbounded freed.

The young woman again attempted to hand a bowl of food to the leader, and this time he took it. From my new position, I saw that the woman was pregnant, her belly jutting tellingly from her thin figure. This didn't stop the former lookout, who'd arrived at the camp, from slapping her on the bottom and making a comment that had her scurrying back to the older woman.

I should have killed him.

I needed to be careful about such feelings, though, because emotion tripped up the mind and caused mistakes. Besides, I didn't know the woman's loyalty. Maybe she was here by choice.

I sidled around to the back of the big rectangular tent the men had come from earlier. It wasn't the usual nylon kind you could buy at Costco or Walmart or any local camping store but was made of thick leather sewn together with leather strips. The tent reminded me of a sturdy Indian tepee in the shape of a large army tent. While the bottom edges of the leather were held to the ground with wooden stakes, the poles themselves were rebar cemented into the earth—so not a transitory structure. Obviously the tent was built to endure both time and tropical storms, and the tiny valley and trees gave it added protection.

It was still a tent, and it didn't take me long to find a gap in the leather. Inside, the space was dark except for the light coming from a stone fireplace set along one of the walls, complete with a makeshift chimney. In the corner closest to me, I could see lumps on the ground that were obviously the Emporium captives, laid out unceremoniously on the packed earth. A guard stood over them, though none appeared to be moving, except for the slight up and down motion of their chests.

Closer to the fireplace, a figure sat on a solitary chair, but the person's identity was blocked by a second guard standing in front of the chair. It had to be Tenika sitting there, and she appeared to be conscious. Beyond her was an uneven row of cots, complete with mosquito netting.

Three bandits out front, two in here, plus the two women. Not a lot, but the conscious Emporium Unbounded changed everything. I could use Tenika's help taking the camp, if she wasn't too badly wounded. That meant I had to start here. Quickly, before their leader made his deal and Tenika was put out of the picture.

The guard in front of Tenika leaned over and said something into her face. I caught a glimpse of her narrow braids as she tried to respond through the gag tied over her mouth. Her hands were also tied and one shoulder sported a white bandage stained with a copious amount of blood. The guard said something to his companion and grunted, making an obscene movement with his hips. They both laughed.

I leveled the tranque gun and sent a dart into the

guard next to Tenika. He crumpled. Before I could shoot again, the other guard ran over to her, talking fast and low. She lunged forward, bringing the chair she was tied to with her, and rammed her forehead into the guard. He brought his gun up, but she twirled and savagely smashed the legs of her chair into him. They both collapsed.

I was reaching for a knife to cut my way in when an exclamation behind me halted the motion. A fist slammed into the side of my face. As I fell against the tent, I caught sight of the first lookout, the one I should have taken out when I'd had the chance. His pants were partially unbuckled.

Just my luck I'd chosen the side of the tent near their latrine, though it was logical since the area behind the tent was the farthest from the middle of camp and the most private—exactly why I'd chosen it.

He knocked the tranque gun from my hand before I could pull the trigger, but I did the same to him before he had his pistol halfway out of his holster. In a flurry of fists, we clashed. He hit my shoulder, I got his chin. Blood spurted out his nose; my lip split. He attempted to use a dried branch to club me; I used the same branch to smash his knee. He was about my size and the meanness in his eyes testified of more kills than I could imagine, but I had been trained by the best.

He tried to step back and call out for help, but I punched him hard enough to steal his breath. I followed with a kick to his already damaged knee, then an elbow to the head. He managed to plant a fist in my stomach in a move that might have been fatal if he'd been holding a knife. But he wasn't and the punch opened him for a potentially devastating blow. I pulled back my fist.

"*Para!*" Metal jabbed into the back of my neck.

I turned to catch a glimpse of the older woman who had been at the fire. Her eyes were determined, her teeth gritted tight. Her scrawny chest heaved, her worn gray tank top barely covering her sagging breasts. "Okay!" I slowly began to raise my hands, waiting for the right moment. The moment when she relaxed slightly, sure that the worst was over.

I hoped it would happen fast because the guy I'd hammered was grinning now, his bloodied face looking gruesome. In a moment, his fists were going to seek retribution.

Maybe bandit women didn't relax their guard.

Wait, there it was. The barrel pulled slightly away, and the woman began speaking in that same rapid-fire Spanish that everyone seemed to use without taking a breath.

I stepped abruptly back and to the side, my hand darting out to wrench the gun from her. She tumbled forward with the motion—right into the fist of the lookout as he lashed out at me. She collapsed instantly. Not looking twice at the woman, the bandit dived for a gun in the foliage. Since I already had her gun in my hand, I shouldn't have cared, but pulling that trigger would be stupid if I wanted to keep my presence a secret from his companions. I jumped on top of him, knocking him flat.

I felt for the gun he'd been after—my tranque gun. My fingers closed on the trigger just as I heard a shout from behind.

Suddenly my head exploded in pain and the world went black.

CHAPTER 8

WHEN I AWOKE I LAY IN THE TENT NEAR TENIKA'S CHAIR. My eyes took several moments to focus and when they did, I almost wished I'd remained unconscious. This close to Tenika, I could see clearly what I hadn't been able to see before. Her dark face was a mess, as though someone had used it for a punching bag. The rag around her mouth was tied so tightly that her jaw was forced open. Not only had she apparently been shot in the shoulder, but her other arm had an open knife wound extending at least ten inches. Already congealing now.

Something wasn't right about that wound. These men used guns, and in hand-to-hand combat her skill would have far exceeded theirs. I suspected the cut had been inflicted after her capture, perhaps for torture. But torturing a gagged woman wouldn't be very productive, and if the gag was off she would have talked them into releasing her. Somehow the cut and the gag were related, but my mind was too foggy to connect the dots.

Tenika didn't meet my gaze but stared at someone behind me. I twisted to see who, and my body protested the movement in a hundred places that hadn't been hurt before I'd lost consciousness. Probably the lookout exacting his revenge while I was unconscious. I was lucky they hadn't let him kill me.

I really should have tranqued him in the woods.

As I rolled into the new position, I kept my hands first to my sides and then behind my back so they wouldn't see them and remember that they hadn't tied me up when I was unconscious. The guard I'd tranqued in the tent was still out and should be until morning without interference, and the man Tenika had butted with her head was also sprawled on the ground, his eyes shut. The bandit leader—who looked bigger up close—was standing with the lookout bandit I'd fought and the black Emporium captive who was awake. The captive was still tied and a gun was pointed in his direction, but he clearly found amusement in my predicament.

"I told you they'd send people after me," he said. "The only way to stop them is to let me contact my people and get out of here. We'll take the woman so you won't have to deal with her lying tongue. You saw how dangerous it was earlier." His words were jittery, and I wondered how many drugs they had shot him with to counter our sedative. "And look, that cut you made? You can see it's healing just like I said it would. Her face too."

"Shut up!" the leader growled in heavily accented English. "He cood be your friend and not hers."

"I am here for him." I gave the scowling black captive a smile. "Hey, dude, sorry the rescue didn't go as planned."

"Renegade scum," he muttered. He took a step forward, but the bandit leader stopped him with a jab of his gun.

So the captive must recognize me from the Emporium files, or maybe from when they'd held me prisoner after murdering my wife. Anger flooded me, though I knew this Emporium Unbounded wasn't directly responsible for Lorrie's death. He was only a drone in the Emporium army.

I shook my head, which instead of clearing my thoughts only made it pound that much harder. "Look," I said to the bandit leader. "If you deal with him, you will all be killed. That's a guarantee. He's not human like we are, and they don't care about humans. My people were taking him to a prison for his crimes."

"You shut up too!" The bandit growled. He paced a few steps, then paused and blurted out a stream of Spanish at his companion.

I shifted again, and pain blurred my vision for a few seconds, causing me to curl in on myself. Had the bastard broken my rib? But it was that position that allowed me to see Tenika's hands moving, her wrists tied to the armrests but her fingers free. Was that sign language? I wracked my brain. Wait. The movements resembled the signals Ritter drilled into us for ops, which I didn't usually pay much attention to, knowing that because of the kids and their need for me as a pilot, he would never let me put those skills to use in real life. But it was hard not to have some of it sink in. Tenika wanted me to free her. *Only two of them. Two of us,* she signed.

I had to give it to the Unbounded. They refused to give up easily, but then two bandits with guns probably didn't seem like much of a challenge to someone who couldn't be killed by a bullet. My mortality aside, she was right. We should be able to do something and, even damaged as we were, together we would be a match for them.

As the two men rattled off more high-velocity Spanish, the Emporium captive trying to insert a word or two during any pause, I very slowly pulled myself to a seated position, keeping my hands hidden. In the dim firelight, I could see that the ropes holding Tenika were tight but wouldn't be impossible to untie. One of my knives would have made shorter work of the rope, if they hadn't taken them from me.

I took inventory, patting down the special pockets of my camouflage. Everything was gone, except my bullet-proof vest and the magazine from Marisa's gun that was in the inner pocket of my pants next to the one that had been holding a grenade. I didn't know if they'd over-looked it because it was so small or because a magazine alone held no danger to them. I wasn't even carrying a gun that size. A small pile of weapons near the bandit leader's feet told me where my stuff had gone. My pack wasn't there, though, so my phone and extra weapons were somewhere else. Maybe outside near the back of the tent where I'd been looking through the gaps. Safe for the time being, but no use to me now.

What I needed was a distraction.

At that moment, the flood of Spanish ended and the bandit lookout headed for the tent opening. I wasn't sure where he was going, but Tenika's fingers spelled out reinforcements, so apparently she'd understood their conversation and knew the man was going for the other two bandits who were still outside somewhere.

I eased up on my knees and the bandit leader shifted his gun in my direction. He barked something more at the lookout, who paused and stared at me, an evil glint in his eyes.

Great. I had the feeling my life was about to get a whole lot worse.

A woman's scream sliced through my thoughts, freezing everyone into place. The lookout turned again toward the tent opening as Marisa burst through, followed by one of the remaining bandits. His gun jabbed into her back, his other hand gripping her arm. With her slender figure, she resembled a small child in Ritter's extra large shirt—a furious child, whose dark eyes sent a thousand needles in every direction.

"Javier!" she began, addressing the bandit leader. More words followed.

The bandit behind her snorted and pulled a second gun from his pocket, which I recognized as belonging to her. Javier took the weapon, checked the chamber, and began laughing. He asked Marisa a question and she pointed at me before responding. Javier laughed again.

I wished I knew what was going on, but I had more important things to worry about. Namely whether I should free Tenika's mouth so she could use her ability, or one of her hands with the hope that she could free her other hand and help me fight. *Hand,* I decided. If her hands weren't too ruined from fighting earlier, she'd be able to free her own mouth.

And where was the other bandit? Why hadn't he come inside to check out the commotion?

Still on my knees, I pushed closer to Tenika, letting my body partially shield my hand that was inching toward hers. Everyone still stared at Marisa.

Whatever Marisa had said made Javier order his subordinate to let her go, and he even tossed the empty pistol back to her. Then Javier motioned to Marisa, and she threw herself into his embrace. Her arms went around his neck as they began kissing. Not just kissing, but *kissing.* She practically sank into him, let him devour her.

My stomach dropped. Not at all what I had expected. No wonder she'd been so intent on getting to the bandit camp. I'd been a fool to believe her story.

Tenika's first hand was free, and I moved forward and over a bit to hide the fact that she was already working on her other one. But I wasn't the only person who had noticed. "The woman, she's—" the Emporium captive began, but before he could utter another word, Marisa turned from Javier's grasp and cracked her pistol into his jaw.

"Pig!" she shouted. "Your friends attacked the airport. They killed Javier's men! They almost killed my father and brother!" She turned and spoke to Javier in Spanish. I recognized only the word airplane and father.

"Ees thees true?" Javier barked at the Emporium agent. "Deed you do thees?"

As the Unbounded calculated the best response, Marisa's face turned to me, her dark eyes catching mine. Something shifted inside me. We both knew she'd lied, but what I didn't know was why. It wouldn't be long before Javier tracked down César and Diego to find out what had really happened. What would he do if he learned she'd lied? Maybe she was hoping he'd believe her and that César and Diego would back up the story. Whatever game she was playing at, she obviously had a history with Javier, one that involved ample lip-locking and a whole lot more.

From the corner of my eye, I saw Tenika shift, a signal that she was free, though the gag was still in place. Behind my back, I moved my hands in my own signal to her. I'd grab the lookout and finish the job I should have done right the first time. She'd be able to take out one of the others, but the fact that they had guns might mean the third would get us both before we finished. Worse, the man she'd knocked unconscious earlier was sitting up, still dazed, but awake enough to go for his gun when the fight erupted.

We had no choice.

I thought fleetingly of my children. I knew they'd be taken care of if I didn't return, but I was going to do everything I could to be the one to tuck them in at night and read them bedtime stories. I had to survive this.

Somehow.

Marisa was staring at me, and I jerked my head toward the tent opening. With Javier distracted, she could probably make it. She shook her head.

So she wasn't going to leave, but she hadn't alerted Javier to me either.

Then what the hell were those kisses for?

No time to consider. I gave a last signal to Tenika: *on the count of three. Two. One.*

I twisted as I jumped to my feet, jabbing my fist up under the ribs of the lookout bandit. His eyes widened, and his gun came around, but I twisted it out of his hand and punched it at his face. The blow landed with a solid clunk and he was down.

I turned to see that Tenika had made short work of the dazed bandit and was grappling now with the one who'd brought in Marisa. Even as I watched, she pulled his arm up so high behind his back that something snapped.

But it was Javier who caught my attention. He fired at Tenika. The first shot slammed into his own man, who dropped to the floor. The next shot hit Tenika in the stomach.

I fired at Javier, but as I did, a body rammed into me,

causing the shot to miss. Obviously, the Emporium agent had decided that Javier was preferable to me.

Even as I hit the still-tied man, Javier fired again, the bullet entering the captive's back. He crumpled and the gun swung around in my direction. "Don't move!" Javier screamed.

I had no choice unless I wanted to die. Tenika lay unmoving, out of the picture for now. Once the Emporium captives awoke, she'd be facing dismemberment or life imprisonment by the Emporium. I had to do anything I could to stay alive and get us out of this.

"Okay," I said, raising my hands. "Look, I'll pay you anything you ask."

"Too much trouble," Javier said. I was close enough to see the muscles in his arm move as he tightened his finger on the trigger.

"No!" Marisa shouted. She jumped toward him.

Without even looking at her, Javier's arm flung out and knocked her to the ground. She lay there in frozen terror, her eyes wide, her mouth open in a silent scream. "You like heem? No?" Javier waved the gun at me. He was staring at her, but I had no doubt the English was for my benefit. "I weel keel heem. You—" He said something in Spanish that was probably the same derogatory words that abusers around the world used to keep those they dominate in line. I wanted to kill the idiot in a slow manner that would give him time to relive every single thing he'd put Marisa through. That terror on her face wasn't just for me.

Slowly, I lowered a hand, feeling in my inner pocket for her magazine. My fingers closed around it.

Javier pulled a knife from his belt, saying something else to Marisa. A whimper escaped her throat. Darting a glance at me to make sure I hadn't moved, he brought the knife to her cheek.

"No!" I shouted.

His attention shifted to me. Crap. Real smart.

I bolted. A bullet whizzed past my ear. I reached the cots along the edge of the tent, dropping and rolling under one of them. Javier thundered after me. In seconds I would be a gonner. I bounced to my feet, picking up the cot and throwing it at him. As a second bullet ricocheted off the metal leg, I turned to Marisa, tossing her the magazine. "Run!" Whatever she felt for Javier, it was my fault she was here. My fault if she got hurt.

She caught the magazine, as if my act had finally freed her from her icy terror.

I hoped the bullets would give her a way to get past that last bandit, if he was still out there, so she could escape into the jungle.

I didn't have time to see if she'd obey. I dove behind the next cot, this time feeling fire explode in my stomach with Javier's next shot. *The vest,* I thought. The thing had been horribly uncomfortable during the hike, and it had better damn well done its job. I couldn't tell past the pain, but if it hadn't, there was nothing left.

At least I was still moving. With all my strength, I pushed against the black eating at the edges of my consciousness and shoved another cot at the crazy man who now stalked me. Then a third and a fourth. But suddenly there were no more cots. Just me and the man with the gun.

He grinned and bent over and put the gun in my face. "Now you die."

CHAPTER 9

THREE RAPID SHOTS CAME FROM BEHIND JAVIER. BOOM, BOOM, *boom!* He toppled on me, his eyes staring in horror. I pushed him off to see Marisa standing over us, her gun in her hand.

"Marisa," Javier said, disbelief in his tone. "Marisa, mi amor."

"That is for three years of hell," she spat. "And this"— she emptied three more rounds into his chest—"is for my husband." Javier was long past hearing by the time a dry click signaled no more bullets, and I knew her words were for me. There was apparently a lot more to her story—and to those kisses.

I breathed a sigh of relief and came painfully to my feet. "Thank you."

"You are wounded." She hurried forward and took my arm. The sleeve was bloody, but the arm only grazed. My stomach and ribs hurt a thousand times more, but that vest had been worth every bit of discomfort it had caused me in the jungle.

"I'm okay. Let's see to my friend."

I hurried to Tenika, who was still conscious despite the steady flow of blood coming through her clothes. I removed my own shirt and bundled it against the stomach wound. She pushed her gagged mouth in my direction, saying something I couldn't understand, but the knot on the gag was impossible to remove, so I retrieved Javier's knife and cut through the cloth.

"Thank you," she said, the barest hint of her native Portuguese coloring the words.

"You okay?"

"I will be."

"I'll get you some curequick. Just let me check all these guys first before anyone else decides to use you for target practice." Or me.

"Good idea."

I covered her with a blanket before going around the tent to examine each bandit. Marisa began cutting one of the blankets with a knife so I could tie them all up. No way was I leaving any free. Except Javier, who wasn't going anywhere ever again. Occasionally, I caught Marisa's gaze drifting in his direction. Every time, her relief was clear, and I wondered again what had been between them.

"I took care of the man who relieved the first lookout," I said, "but don't forget we still have one more out there.

Did you see him when they captured you?" It bothered me that he hadn't yet appeared. If he was hidden in the trees with a rifle, getting out of here alive would be difficult.

"I saw him. He won't be a problem." Marisa's face held no expression as she spoke, but her eyes seemed haunted. I didn't ask her what happened. I hadn't heard any shots, but she likely had a few more tricks in her bag. I know I did. Renegades valued diversity.

I found my weapons and put my nine mil, the backup pistol, the grenade, and two knives back in their places, along with the extra tranque darts. "I'll be back in just a few minutes with your meds," I said to Tenika. With the last bandit out of the picture, I'd take the long way around the tent instead of wasting time cutting through.

"Uh, Chris," Marisa said.

I looked over to see that the other bandit woman, the younger one, had appeared in the tent doorway. She held a gun pointed in my direction.

My stomach tensed. I'd made another grave mistake in forgetting her, in discounting her because of her youth and pregnancy. She spoke now, her eyes wild. Her Spanish was slower than everyone else's, but I still didn't understand it.

"She says to drop your gun," Marisa told me.

The woman looked frightened but determined. The bulge of her child stood out sharply against the thin-ness of her small frame. I remembered Lorrie like that, a mixture of softness and angles, and so vulnerable. I didn't want to hurt this woman, but as long as she held that gun, we were all in danger. I wondered if Marisa could explain to her that we just wanted to leave and take the Emporium captives with us. But that wasn't really true. I wanted to be sure the bandits wouldn't bother anyone again. Short of killing them, my only choice was to turn them over to authorities.

The woman waved the gun, her volume growing now. I stepped closer, and her gun hand shook.

I was contemplating more diving and rolling, and somehow sweeping her feet out from under her—all without damaging her baby—when Tenika, still lying on the floor under her blankets, spoke in Spanish. Her voice held command, and almost instantly, the woman's expression relaxed. She lowered her gun and offered it to me. Closing the space between us, I snatched the weapon. Her face showed confusion now, as though she didn't understand how I'd gotten the gun.

Tenika kept talking. The woman's confusion vanished, tears filling her eyes as she nodded vigorously. A sob erupted. She curled in on herself, shaking, and I sprang forward to support her, afraid she would collapse. She sobbed as she clung to me, smelling of smoke, jungle, and roasted meat.

"Uh, what's going on here?" I asked. I hardly knew where to put my hands; I wasn't accustomed to holding women who weren't Lorrie, pregnant or not.

"I told her we'd take her someplace safe," Tenika

answered. "I just reminded her that she hated living here and that they'd kidnapped her in the first place. She wants to see her family."

I'd heard about Tenika's hypnosuggestion, but I had never seen it in play. She was impressive. I wondered how many bandits she'd won over earlier before someone got smart and gagged her. "Great. Now what?"

A smiled played on Tenika's ruined face. "Help her sit down on one of the cots. Then go get the curequick."

"Right." I didn't sense any compelling in her words, and I could say no if I wanted to—which I didn't—so I guessed she wasn't using her gift with me. I led the pregnant woman to one of the overturned cots. I made sure she was steady on her feet before turning it over, freeing it with a knife when it got stuck in the mosquito netting hanging overhead. I helped her sit, and then, with great relief, headed outside.

Marisa snorted her amusement as she followed me into the darkness. "Good thing no one will need that netting again."

"What, you planning on starting your own bandit club?" I asked.

"No, I . . ." the words trailed away. "Look, about Javier."

"You don't owe me anything." But a part of me felt she did.

"My husband had a farm on the edge of the jungle," she said, her voice losing emotion once again. "It was a beautiful place. Javier came to our farm when I was married only six months. He burned it all because my husband wouldn't pay his peace tax. Javier took me, though, because he knew my father and brother. He used me to get them to do things for him. And also because he wanted a woman. For the first year he kept me here in this camp like a prisoner. I hoped my husband would find me, but then I heard them talking one night." She stopped and the relative quiet in the jungle emphasized the stark pain in her voice.

"You learned he was dead."

"Yes. He'd tracked me here and Javier killed him—after making sure my husband knew I was now his woman. Javier kept me here for two years. Then I arranged a few incidents with his men—he's very jealous—and that convinced him I'd be better kept with my father and young brother. He'd come to visit." The revulsion in her face told me what she thought of those visits. "I had planned to steal their car and some extra gas to get me to my uncle's ranch. He has men and guns, but I was worried Javier would come for me there and cause him trouble."

"And then I came along."

"Then you came along," she agreed. "I should have told you."

Ya think? I wanted to say, but really, why should she have trusted me? Her father and brother had let her down, her husband hadn't been able to save her, and she'd been used for years by Javier. "You saved my life," I said instead.

"You saved mine. He would have killed me. If not today then another day."

On that we could agree.

We'd come around to the back of the tent, where the older woman still sprawled in the foliage. She had a heartbeat, but it was faint. "She's going to need a doctor." Still, I tied her wrists with a length of rope from my pack. I'd learned something with both Marisa and the pregnant woman: never assume anything. This woman had already held a gun to my head once. Between her, Javier, and the pregnant woman, I had almost grown accustomed to it. I definitely understood the adrenaline rush, which was maybe why my Unbounded siblings sometimes seemed to enjoy their battles with the Emporium far more than they should.

While Marisa hefted my pack, I carried the woman into the tent. After setting her on another righted cot, I gave Tenika tiny injections of curequick all along the cut on her arm, followed by two bigger injections in her stomach and shoulder.

"What about your face?" I asked.

"That bad, huh?"

Tenika was ordinarily a striking Angolan woman, but I couldn't see much of her African features behind the mass of bleeding flesh. Only her eyes and the tiny braids of her hair were halfway normal. "Kind of."

Her battered lips stretched in a smile that looked painful. "Better wait an hour. I'll be on a high in a minute as it is with this stuff." Tenika was speaking low, so that

Marisa couldn't hear, but Marisa was watching us curiously from across the room. "She doesn't know about Unbounded, does she?"

"She has to suspect. She saw Irwin come back."

"Ah. Well, you can start putting our Emporium friends in the van." The way she drawled *friends* almost made me laugh. "By the time you're finished, the bleeding in my stomach should have stopped enough for you to help me to the van as well. But make sure you get our weapons back. They took them into the cabin."

I went to work dragging our captives back to the van but left behind all the bandits. I'd stop at the first clearing we found and connect with a satellite to request that Ava send whatever passed for the local sheriff to pick up the bandits. Or I'd leave them for Irwin's guys. I'd accomplished what I'd set out to do.

Marisa shook her head in disgust at the apparently dead Unbounded captives, refusing to touch them, but she helped me with the weapons in the cabin, which were far more numerous than just those they'd taken from us. There was an actual bed in the cabin and a desk, and it didn't take much thinking to know this was where Javier had kept Marisa. I didn't object when she pulled a rifle over her shoulder and pushed a large box of bullets into a shoulder sack she carried. I also didn't say anything when she went to a loose brick in the cabin's fireplace and pulled out a metal box filled with cash. She deserved it, and it wasn't as if Javier could object.

Tenika was looking a lot better when we returned to

the tent to check on her. Even her face had knitted some, though the bruising was considerably darker. I injected a bit of curequick in several spots, and to her credit, Tenika didn't even flinch. I wondered how many times she'd been almost killed, or killed and come back to life. I didn't think it was something I'd ever get used to seeing.

I left Marisa talking to the pregnant woman as I helped Tenika to the van. Like most Unbounded, she didn't carry any extra pounds, but she wasn't a small woman by any means. It said a lot about her condition that she leaned on me at all. Despite the agony I glimpsed on her face, she didn't let out so much as a single groan.

When I'd shut the van door, Marisa and the woman were leaving the tent. "She's going with me," Marisa announced.

I blinked. "You're not coming back with us?"

"To the airport? Or to wherever you are taking those *things?*" She crinkled her nose. "I don't think so. They have a double gas tank in that sedan, and there's a gas can in the trunk. It's enough to get me to my uncle's ranch." The pregnant woman was already checking the gas can in the back of the car.

"Right," I said. "You sure it's safe?"

"The road should be safe enough with this." Marisa patted the rifle. "And now that Javier is gone, my uncle will welcome me on his ranch. It's a good place."

"Okay then." I wouldn't stop her from doing what she felt was best for her life.

She stepped closer until her hip brushed my thigh.

"Chris, I want . . ." Slowly, her face moved toward me, her lips seeking mine.

My heartbeat pounded loudly in my ears, and other parts of my body reacted without my giving them permission. I kissed her back, my arms closing around her slim frame. She was warm and soft and generous. I let it go on far too long before I finally reminded myself that I still had a job to do.

She smiled as I pulled away, her fingers brushing my lips. "You could come with me. You are a good man—I know that. I promise to make you happy, and I will love your children. They will be safe. I bet my uncle has use for a pilot."

For a moment I was tempted. Tempted to run away from the fight with the Emporium and the painful memories of Lorrie. Tempted to lose myself in Marisa's arms and in her world. Her recent life hadn't been pretty, but compared to what the Renegades faced on a daily basis, these bandits barely registered on their danger scale. I longed to raise my children in a place where they weren't at risk of losing someone they loved in a brutal manner that evoked nightmares even for adults. Where there was no chance of them being used in genetic experiments or exploited as pawns in a war that had already spanned centuries. I loved the idea of keeping this simple and generous woman by my side, of falling in love with her. The attraction was there—I'd felt it from the moment she'd appeared on the motorcycle. Maybe before that.

We could be happy. I could finish my duty, take the

cure back to Oregon, and return with my children to see where this relationship might take us. Marisa would never be Lorrie, but I didn't want to replace my wife. I wanted the pain to go away. I wanted safety.

Except there were also my feelings about Stella, however hopeless, and none of that was fair to Marisa. She deserved better. She deserved a man who couldn't sleep for thinking about her, a man whose heart was hers alone. She most definitely didn't deserve someone who was with her because he wanted to hide.

I kissed her again deeply, enjoying a last taste of her sweetness. "In another life, I would."

She gave me a wistful smile. "I know. I hope you will be happy."

I watched her drive away, wishing I had said yes.

CHAPTER 10

I DIDN'T HAVE TO ACCOMPANY IRWIN AND TENIKA TO THE prison compound. By the time we'd retrieved the other unconscious Unbounded captives near the small road, Irwin was up and hobbling around the clearing where I'd left him. Tenika still looked a shadow of her normal self, but her face was already less hamburger and more bruise—a significant improvement from hours before back at the cabin. Irwin and I secured the prisoners, and by then several of his buddies from the prison had appeared, heavily armed.

"You're going to see to the bandits, right?" I asked.

"Sure thing," Irwin said. "We've already called in a few favors." He leaned closer and spoke so no one else could hear. "I'm glad my four-footed friend didn't attack you. I haven't had much experience with jaguars. It's crocs I know best."

"I'm really glad I didn't know that before I went after him."

"I thought you might say that." He chuckled and slapped me hard on the back, making me flinch. "Hey," Irwin said, "Drew over there is a healer. You want him to take a look at you?"

"Naw, I'll be okay. Nothing a few weeks won't heal. Excuse me, I'm going to say goodbye to Tenika."

I went to the van, which was missing a window after the shootout. I leaned through the opening and offered her my hand. "Looks like this is goodbye."

Tenika bumped her fist against mine, a gesture that served for both Renegade greetings and farewells. "Thanks for coming. I owe you one, mortal."

There was teasing in her voice, so I knew the "mortal" wasn't meant to offend, but for a stark moment, I wished my mortality could be otherwise. "Only one?"

"Or two. Just let me know." She gave me a number scrawled on a piece of map she'd torn from someplace. "My direct line. Come see us sometime in New York."

"It might be a while. We have some rebuilding to do after the last attack."

Her face sobered. "We all do."

"I know." She and her group were still recovering from the betrayal of one of our own that had caused Lorrie's death and led to the murder and capture of many Renegades. The same man had been responsible for my captivity. But Renegades didn't leave people behind, and we would find them as they had found me.

"We'll bring them home," I said.

She nodded. "I'll be heading back tomorrow. Maybe when these guys"—she jerked her head to the rear of the van where the unconscious Emporium agents were stacked like so much firewood—"wake up, they'll give us some new leads." Her dark eyes held mine for another long second, and I knew she felt a deep responsibility for the people she'd lost. She wasn't the only one. Maybe all survivors felt that way.

I didn't have the keys to Marisa's motorbike, so I enjoyed a long, humid walk back to the plane, using the time to report in to Ava. I arrived at the makeshift airport as the sun finally broke through the trees of the jungle. There were no signs of vehicles or lights in the small building across the expanse of dirt, which told me César and Diego Molina hadn't returned. It was just as well. I wasn't too happy with either of them after what they'd allowed Marisa to suffer while in their household. As the men in her life, they should have protected her. I would have died before I'd let my sister Erin endure what she had. They would return eventually, I had no doubt, as soon as they heard that these particular bandits were no longer a problem.

Maybe Marisa would even let them visit her eventually. I couldn't help smiling as I thought about her. I didn't doubt that she'd find someone else to love. She was that kind of woman. I envied the guy, whoever he was.

After double-checking the lock on the plane's door, I downed some rations, gulped water and a few pain killers, then fell across three seats and let myself drop into oblivion.

The next thing I knew, my phone was ringing. I groped for it and pressed it to my ear. "Hello?"

"On our way back," Erin said. "Emporium's probably not too far behind. Get the plane ready."

My watch said it was already seven that evening, so outside the plane it'd be dark. "What's your ETA?"

"Twenty minutes tops."

"I'll be ready. But we'll have to touch down for fuel in Mexico again. We're running low, and the fuel here didn't come through as planned."

"Guess we'll make do. Thanks." My sister sounded exhausted. Whatever they'd gone through apparently hadn't been easy.

After a quick preflight check, I had time to swallow more pain killers, rub some of the dry blood from my head, change into a fresh shirt, and pull on a baseball cap. The mirror showed a split lip and a nasty bruise on my cheek, but they couldn't see the bandage on my arm or the huge bruises forming on my chest and stomach. In all I didn't look too bad. No use in causing my siblings alarm. If I kept a low enough profile and didn't move too stiffly, they wouldn't guess how terribly my body ached.

Of course, with Erin, I'd also have to watch my thoughts. She wouldn't delve into my private ones without permission, but if my thoughts shouted pain, she'd easily pick up on it. With a little luck and repeated dosages of pain killer, she might never learn how close it had been.

My hopes of sliding completely under the radar were upset the moment my sister arrived. Erin's face was dirty and cut, her blond hair matted, and her gray eyes exhausted, but her concern for me was immediate. "What happened to you?" she asked as she practically fell from the Pinz—which was short for Pinzgauer, an old European army vehicle that roughly resembled a Humvee.

I walked slowly toward her, purposely clamping down on any thoughts. "Had a little run-in with some local bandits. Tried to steal our plane. Apparently, they were upset about some bad deal they made with the owners here and wanted retribution. But we held them off." I cracked a grin. "I did have to take the guy's sister hostage to make them fight with me, but it worked out."

"You'll have to tell us all about it." She linked her arm around my neck so I could help her up the steps and into the plane. I tried not to wince, failing miserably, and the fact that she didn't notice told me how taxing the day had been for her.

Erin wasn't the only one worse for wear. Our newest employee, Benito Hernández—a mortal like me—was seriously wounded, and Ritter, who was covered in blood, was carrying him. Our healer, Dimitri Sidorov, who claimed over a thousand years of life, hovered next to him with a worried expression.

Looks like we all had stories to tell, but for now I needed to get us into the air. Home to Stella.

The plane had been in flight thirty minutes when broad-shouldered Dimitri came into the cockpit where my little brother, Jace, was asking me questions about flying. Now that Jace knew he had two thousand years to live, he planned to take time to learn a little about everything. Normally, I didn't mind, but today his exuberance was exhausting.

"May I have a moment with Chris?" Dimitri asked.

"Sure." Jace exited the cockpit, curiosity showing on his face.

"What's up?" I asked Dimitri. "Is Benito okay?"

"He's tough. He's going to make it."

I sighed with relief. Jace had told me that Dimitri and the others hadn't been able to save the scientists, but Benito had been instrumental in securing a thumb drive, which we believed held the cure for Bronson, and losing him would have made everything much worse.

Dimitri drew up behind me and placed his hands on my shoulders. "Lean forward."

I grunted with the effort. "How did you know?"

"I mostly guessed after talking to Ava about your report. But I can see you're in pain."

"Don't tell Erin."

He laughed. "Yeah. Not going to do that. She'd want you tied up in bubble wrap until, well, forever. Good thing she's too exhausted to be more suspicious." He closed his eyes as his hand roamed over my chest and stomach. It could have felt weird having another man touch me that way when I was definitely heterosexual, but I knew he healed best by touch, and I was in too much pain to object. Besides, he was Erin's biological father, so he was family in more ways than our Renegade connection.

"Your ribs aren't broken," Dimitri said. "However, they are very bruised. I've done what I can to ease the pain and hurry the healing, but they'll still be sore for a few days."

"Thanks." I was already feeling better.

Finally, he pulled off my cap and began checking my head. "Do you have this thing on autopilot? Because you need stitches. It's going to hurt a bit."

"Guess I'll have to get used to pain."

"Guess so." Did he sound proud? I wasn't sure. But with my own parents out of the daily picture because of the danger the Emporium posed, I did look to him for guidance. If Ava was the leader and mother of our Renegade cell, Dimitri was the father.

I'd had stitches before and Dimitri had been underestimating his gentleness, or maybe his ability as a healer dampened the pain. I managed to endure his ministrations without making a fool of myself or causing the plane to drop from the sky. In fact, by the time he left the cockpit, my overall pain had dipped to a level that the pain killer could handle. I didn't even mind when Jace returned with his incessant, eager questions. He was alive and that was enough.

We had barely entered US airspace some hours later when Ava contacted us with the news: Bronson was dead.

Her words slammed into me, and for a long moment I struggled for breath. All the work, the hurry, the sacrifice. The deaths of the scientists. It had all been for nothing.

We were too late.

WE ARRIVED IN PORTLAND WITH THE MORNING SUN, WHOSE light did nothing to remove the heaviness from my chest. While I dealt with arrangements for the plane after landing, the others went to Stella's apartment, which we were using as a temporary safe house until we moved to the new place in San Diego. I also had to meet the ambulance that came for Benito, and by the time I arrived at Stella's, the place was a hive of activity.

"This location has been compromised," Erin told me, appearing from the back of the moving truck outside the apartment. "But guess what? There was information on that thumb drive we brought back about Tenika's missing people. We know where they're being held!"

A weight lifted from my shoulders. Maybe Mexico hadn't been a total bust after all.

"We're leaving as soon as possible," Ritter added. He jumped down from the truck and turned to offer Erin a hand. At over two hundred and seventy years old, he sometimes had the distinct manners of an old-world gentleman, though I usually didn't see even a glimpse of that because he was otherwise so deadly—a killing machine, really. But I'd noticed that Erin brought out this other side of him, the gallantry from a time long forgotten by most of us.

Erin ignored his hand and came down the ramp, but the look she tossed him at the bottom told me she had been aware of him and wasn't ready to accept him completely. Something had happened between them in Mexico. I hoped it was good.

Ava came from Stella's third-floor apartment, her feet making noise on the outside metal staircase as she descended. I turned to her. "I just need to see my kids, then I'll go back to the airport to get the plane ready for the flight."

Ava shook her head. "No. Cort will take us in the smaller plane. He's skilled enough for that. I want you to load the essentials and take them to the house in San Diego. George and Charles will go with you. I'll arrange for Benito to join you once he's out of the hospital. You might want to send the kids to your parents for a while until you're sure the new place is secure." Her lips tightened. "I want it to be a veritable fortress when you're finished."

Fortress. It reminded me of two days earlier when Erin had begged me to take the kids and leave the Renegades. I'd told her that separating them from those they loved wasn't the answer, but rather making sure it never happened again. I was just the man for creating the fortress. My children could be killed, so I had the most to lose.

However, it didn't escape me that Ava was sending

the mortals with me, while the Unbounded would be going to what would likely be another bloodbath with the Emporium.

"Please, Chris," Ava said, her hand going out to mine. "We must free our people, but after losing Stella's baby and Gaven like that and"—she swallowed hard—"almost losing the kids, and now Bronson, we need a refuge to come home to. Right now we really need everyone to be safe."

The mortals to be safe, she meant.

I looked into her face, with her steel gray eyes so like my own and Erin's. This fourth great-grandmother, who was basically my physical age, had lost so much over the years, and the mortals in our cell were particularly vulnerable, regardless of any black ops experience. I understood Ava wanting to limit further loss. Losing Lorrie had made me seek revenge, but if I lost one of my children now, there wouldn't be anything of me left, and losing more Renegades in the near future might be the beginning of the end in our struggle against the Emporium.

"Okay," I said. "I'll make that house a fortress. You watch over Erin and Jace."

She nodded. "With my life."

I knew she meant it. And not only her, but Ritter, Stella, and the others. "What about Marco?" I asked. Marco Collins was the one mortal employee she hadn't mentioned, one who'd served with Gaven in black ops and who would mourn him the most.

"I'll take him with us. He needs the distraction, and we'll need someone for legwork."

I knew that meant she would keep an eye on him and make sure he was far from any real action. Marco would hate that if he knew, but being left behind would annoy him more. I nodded and started up the stairs.

"We're putting most of the essentials in the vehicles for you to take to the plane," Ava called after me. "We've also hired a driver for the moving truck. We need to be out of here in the next thirty minutes."

I nodded. "I'm ready." We'd lost most of our belongings when we'd torched the old safe house after the Emporium raid, so I didn't have anything to pack that wasn't already in my Jeep. The kids didn't have much left either, except what Ava and the others had pulled from their rooms before starting the fire to cover all the damage. Our concern had focused on electronics, not on stuff we could easily replace.

I went into the apartment, through the front room, and down the hallway to the closet. Inside the closet was a hidden door leading to a room where my children had been when I'd said goodbye before going to Mexico. I wanted to hold them and see for myself that they were all right. But I'd gone only halfway down the hall when they emerged from what had been Bronson's bedroom.

"Dad, you're back!" Kathy exclaimed, throwing herself at me, her blond hair swinging around her face. For an instant, pain shot through me at her resemblance to her mother, but the emotion passed as her arms wrapped around my neck. She was only twelve, but it felt like she'd grown an inch in just the two days I'd been away.

"Bronson's dead!" Spencer hugged my waist, and I dropped to take them both in my arms, nodding a greeting at Charles, the husky man who was watching over them.

"I know, son. But it's going to be okay." My arms tightened as gratitude choked me. I was so grateful to be holding them again.

"We're leaving soon," Charles said, his wide chin set. Sadness radiated from his brown eyes—eyes that looked dark against the paleness of his face. I knew he missed Gaven almost as much as Marco did.

"Look, you two need to get ready," I told the kids. "Charles and I are taking you to Grandma and Grandpa's for a few weeks until we get the security system installed in our new place."

"Ava showed us a picture," Kathy said. "It's huge. A mansion!"

"She says we can have a playroom with a climbing wall," Spencer added. "Can we, Dad?"

"Sure."

"Anyway, we're already packed," Kathy said. "We didn't have much from the old house."

Spencer pulled back, his freckled nose wrinkling and reminding me faintly of Marisa. "Are we going to get new clothes again?"

"Yeah, bud, we are." Reluctantly, I released them and

stood. "If you'll stay with them a bit longer," I said to Charles, "I'll meet you guys in the Jeep. We can drive them to my parents and then meet George at the plane." Though my parents lived in Portland, it'd take a couple hours to follow the precautions necessary for turning over the children. The Emporium had eyes everywhere these days. We'd need Charles for backup.

Charles shook his head. "We're having a brief service for Bronson and Gaven at the mortuary in about an hour, before the others leave for New York. Gaven's family will hold their own service in Alabama, so he'll be sent there afterward."

"Yeah, we need to be there," Kathy said, blinking back tears.

Mentally I began adjusting my plan. The service was a good idea, and I was glad someone had thought of it. I needed closure as much as anyone. "Okay, then. After the service."

"We'll meet you outside," Charles said.

I nodded. "Be sure to take Max," I told the kids. We couldn't forget the dog. He'd love to visit my parents, who were his original owners.

I watched them go before stepping into Bronson's room where his body lay, still and gray-looking. Stella sat in the chair by the bed, appearing almost completely well instead of half dead the way I'd had to leave her. I clamped down to stop the relief; after all, she was Unbounded and healing was expected. But I knew some wounds couldn't be seen.

She was even more beautiful than I remembered. Her shoulder-length black hair was smooth and glossy, her heart-shaped face, sculptured eyebrows, and flawless olive skin perfect. Her Asian heritage lent a kind of mystery to her features that begged me to learn more. I wanted to take her in my arms and protect her.

She looked up and saw me, her mouth curving in a sad smile that I was ashamed to admit did more for me than Marisa's passionate kiss. "They say it helps to say goodbye. I hope it's okay that I let the children see him this way."

"Of course." I trusted her. She'd saved their lives, and in a way that meant they were hers now. If I'd known Bronson's body was still in here, I probably would have talked to them about it, but I suspected Stella and Ava already had—and better than I could have. They both knew more about death than I did, despite my recent loss.

She stood, leaning over to stroke Bronson's pale cheek before straightening and facing me again. "You've probably heard about the service, but I need to stay until Bronson's properly buried. In a few days, I'll join the others in New York."

"You can't stay here. It's too dangerous."

"I know. I'll find a hotel. I'm not sure where I want to bury him. Maybe you can fly him somewhere for me? Maybe to San Diego?"

I would deny her nothing. "If that's what you want."

She nodded.

I stepped closer, then took her into my arms the way I'd wanted to since walking into that room. Well, not exactly the way that I wanted, but it was all I'd ever have. "Stella, I wanted to tell you before we left, but you were still . . ." *Unconscious.* "Asleep. I—you . . . you saved my children. You could have made so many other choices, but you didn't, and I can never, ever repay you for that. Thank you." I didn't mention her lost baby because I could feel it there between us, heavy and aching. I wasn't sure what I would do if she started crying. I wanted smooth her hair, to caress her face, to take away her pain. Love it away. As if that could do it. I knew it wouldn't begin to come close.

She pulled back. "Oh, Chris, I am so glad I was there for them. Whatever happened, I don't regret that. I love those kids, and I know how you feel about them. They are the reason for this fight. I would never let anything happen to them, if I could help it. I don't regret what I did."

"I know." But the cost had been higher than any of us would have wanted her to pay.

"Come with me," I said gently. "Ava will take care of Bronson until the service. We'll go for a drive with the kids before we head over." With the apartment location compromised, I wanted to be sure Stella was out of here long before the Emporium agents arrived. And they would come. It was only a matter of time.

Mutely, she nodded and let me turn her toward the door.

I took one last look over my shoulder at Bronson. I'd liked him, the retired electronics engineer with a steady hand, who'd removed more bullets from Stella and her friends than most mortal doctors. At seventy he looked more like Stella's father or even grandfather than her husband. I knew he'd been married once before meeting her and had two grown children. He'd lived a good life, if short by Unbounded standards. But he looked at peace. Maybe he hadn't been all that unhappy to leave before age separated him even more from the woman he loved.

Goodbye, old man, I thought. *We'll take care of her.*

Ava met us in the hallway with Ritter and Dimitri, who hurried into the room and picked up Bronson. "We have to leave right now. Make sure you're armed."

CHAPTER 11

THREE DAYS LATER I WAS STILL IN PORTLAND—AND STILL ON edge, wondering where the Emporium would strike next. Stella had changed her mind about transporting Bronson to San Diego, mostly because his adult children lived in Washington and driving to Portland for a proper funeral and subsequent visits to his grave would be easier for their families than traveling clear to Southern California. I was glad because I thought having Bronson buried in San Diego, so near our new safe house, might cause Stella more pain.

I stayed with her at first because there was no one else. Then Ava called to let me know the New York Renegade cell had intercepted an encrypted message from the Emporium that mentioned pending activity in our area, and there was no way I was leaving her alone after that. I didn't tell Stella, but I became even more vigilant. I kept

Charles with us and sent George ahead to San Diego to meet with the contractor who was doing the house renovations.

We'd spent the first day making funeral preparations for Bronson. Or rather, Stella made the preparations. Charles and I shared her hotel suite, but we'd consumed most of the time pouring over security options for the house while she'd been making phone calls, hotel arrangements for Bronson's family, and talking to the mortuary. Charles also watched old *Star Trek* reruns, which soon began to make me wish I could beam him out of there. But he was a good pizza buddy, and we consumed far more than our share. He preferred the more exotic kind, like those with kelp and shrimp and white sauce, while I loved pepperoni and sausage.

Even preoccupied as she was with Bronson, Stella did more research than we did into our future security arrangements, vetting companies we might employ to help us create our fortress. I knew she would also ensure that whatever company we chose didn't retain enough information about us in their files to ever betray us to the Emporium.

Dealing with our immediate security problems kept Stella's brain occupied at a time when she desperately needed it. She'd be talking funeral arrangements with the mortuary, and at the same time sending me background checks on all the employees at a security company, complete with lists of their loved ones and associates and charity donations. At the same time, I'd receive a dozen new articles from her on the latest in security options. Having a technopath around had its advantages, but deep down I admitted that her capabilities served mostly to emphasize the gap between us. That was when I wished I could beam myself elsewhere.

Except for when Stella would melt into tears in my arms. Then I was glad that I was with her—whatever it might cost me.

On the third morning, we held the small funeral, consisting only of Bronson's children and grandchildren, four golf buddies, a dozen people from the church he'd attended, and two men he'd served with in the Navy as a teen. Stella dressed the part of the grieving widow in a trim black suit and hat. It reminded me of something worn at funerals fifty years ago minus the veil across the eyes.

She'd Changed early, at twenty-eight, almost two centuries ago, which put her physically at thirty-two, but today she'd directed her nanites to change her appearance, faintly aging her skin so Bronson's children wouldn't wonder at her youth. "Black gloves and my half-Japanese heritage should take care of the rest," she said.

I knew some technopaths could use nanites to slightly alter their faces, and that Stella had enhanced her appearance for years. She claimed that if Cort created faster, more intricate nanites, she might be able to age far more convincingly, but as it was, the nanites had severe limitations, made more difficult by the Unbounded metabolism that worked hard to put everything back the way it was

supposed to be. Even with the aging, she was still beautiful. Seeing her as she might look in a thousand years
brought a lump to my throat that didn't leave for the
whole service.

I told myself I was only worried about the Emporium
crashing our party.

We both wore bulletproof vests under our clothes,
which wasn't nearly the problem it was in the jungle
because Oregon was cold and the added heat welcome.
Our coats hid any unseemly bulk. But there were no
problems at the funeral and no interruptions at the
cemetery.

Finally it was over, and we headed for the airport,
checking for a possible tail as we always did. Charles
was meeting me at our plane with a few more supplies,
and Stella was taking a commercial flight to New York.
I was tempted to go with her, but I had my orders from
Ava, and I was anxious to get to work so that I could
be reunited with my children. Our Renegades were
depending on me to create a safe haven, a fortress, and
that's what I'd do. I'd already directed the contractor to
fill the walls with more cables than my security plans
would ever need, but I was feeling pressure to get there
and make sure it was done right.

There was a little time before her flight, so Stella
dropped me off at the sprawling corrugated metal hangar
that we rented and shared with a half dozen other companies. I still had preflight checks and clearances to undergo
before I followed through on my filed flight plan, and

she'd most likely be in the air on her flight to New York before I took off.

I pushed open the car door, planning to wave a casual goodbye, but Stella killed the engine. I raised my eyebrows. "I'll come in to say goodbye to Charles," she explained. Already her face had returned to normal.

"He should be here," I said, looking around. "But I don't see the rental car. Unless he changed plans, the car company was supposed to pick it up here."

"I can wait."

I didn't remind her that she'd said goodbye to Charles before the funeral, which he'd attended, though he hadn't gone to the gravesite itself with us afterward. I had the feeling her coming into the hangar wasn't about Charles at all, but I couldn't exactly call her on it. Maybe she just liked planes. That I could understand.

I unlocked the hangar and deactivated the alarm. Stella followed me inside a lobby that was really more of a shared hangout where pilots and businessmen would rest between flights when there wasn't time to go home. We had vending machines, a television, couches, and restrooms. It was better than a lot of hangars I'd worked out of. I could tell no one was here at the moment because the heat was off. I reset the alarm.

Opening the door to the main part of the hangar, I turned on some lights that were still far too dim in the vast space. We had more light coming from the windows in the hangar doors themselves than from the artificial lights, even on this cloudy, winter day.

The door closed behind us as we started down the lines of planes, each one backed in like a car in a garage. The hangar didn't have many frills, but we each had a small office and a large wheeled cart to store tools. We also shared a maintenance guy who worked on the planes and went up in the overhead rafters to change the lights. The smell of engines and planes reminded me of my first job in a garage when I was in high school. It was the year the flying bug had bitten deeply after I'd gone up in a small two-seater with one of the clients.

A couple of the newer planes were state-of-the-art corporate jets, and I'd salivated over them more than once or twice. I'd even flown a few on occasions in the two months we'd been here, pinch-hitting for their pilots or riding copilot.

"Doesn't look like Charles is here yet," I said as we reached our plane. Door was shut, no lights inside. "I'd better open the hangar door. Got a lot to do before takeoff."

"Chris, wait." Stella's hand fell on my arm. "Look, thank you for staying here so long to help me with everything. You really didn't have to."

"I needed to research security systems anyway. And, let's face it, you helped me more than I did you."

Her hand didn't leave my arm, and I became acutely aware of how isolated we were alone inside this remote hangar, separated by only the sleeve of my jacket.

"It was the least I could do," she said. "The house in

San Diego is beautiful, but it's going to need heavy reno-vations to become what we need."

"My plan is to have it done in four weeks. Or most of it," I said. "Thanks to Ava pulling strings with that big contractor. I'm meeting the security company there tonight."

"No more running." Stella was keeping up the conver-sation, but her eyes were far away. "It'll be good to have a permanent place."

There was also danger in staying put, but she was right that it felt good. "I'll make it safe."

I'd made a similar promise, though not in so many words, to Lorrie all those years ago when we married. No way could I guess that fourteen years and two children later we would be facing an Emporium hit team, or that Lorrie would step in the way of a bullet meant for me. None of that had been in my plans. Neither could I have dreamed of what Stella would sacrifice for my children. This time I was going to make sure no one got to my family or any of the Renegades.

Something of my thoughts must have shown in my face because Stella said quietly, "It's not your fault."

Her touch still burned through my sleeve. "I know."

Her mouth parted, her tongue wetting her lips. She seemed about to say more but suddenly leaned over to hug me, burying her face in my chest and making it difficult for me to think about anything except how wonderful her hair smelled and how right she felt in my arms. I'd held her quite a few times this way in the past few days, and if I was honest with myself, I didn't know how much more I could take without doing something to scare her away. She was so alive and yet so vulnerable. I didn't trust myself as much as she seemed to.

However, I did understand her—the yearning for children, the cold, gaping emptiness that had once been filled with warmth and love, and most of all the guilt for being the one left alive. Her nearness made me forget all of that, made me forget everything but the furious pounding of my heart. She had to notice its throbbing with her cheek pressed tightly against my chest. I let my hand creep up to touch her silky hair.

"Look, Chris," she said softly without meeting my gaze, "I want a baby. I've already lived more than three lifetimes, and I don't want to wait any longer." A small hiccup marred the last words. She drew back and looked up into my eyes. "I delayed too long with Bronson. I have to live with that, and with him being gone forever, but I can still have a baby, if you'll help me."

Emotions tumbled through me. My body felt alive with them, but my brain warned caution. "What are you saying?"

"This." She put her arms around my neck, stretching up to meet me. I felt helpless as her lips touched mine. Then I was kissing her, pulling her closer, ignoring the twinge in my split lip that wasn't quite healed. If it had been any other woman, wanting her in this way would have made me feel disloyal to Lorrie, but it was Stella, who'd saved our babies' lives, who'd lost so much with Bronson's death. I wanted her. I'd be crazy not to.

Except somewhere in the part of me that was still sane, I knew this wasn't Stella talking. Maybe it would be some day, but not now. Not with Bronson so newly gone and her baby so recently lost. Unbounded or not, she needed more time. Maybe I did too.

I pulled backward until I hit the door to our office, but she followed me, not letting me go. She was soft, so full of life! I wanted her more than I'd probably wanted anything in a long time. My body screamed in protest at my inaction.

It's too soon.

Her beautiful eyes held mine, begging for my agreement. I had to at least try to prevent us from making this mistake. For her sake.

I put my hands on her shoulders, holding her away from me. "Stella," I said with a strained voice I barely recognized as my own. "I know you're missing Bronson, but you're not thinking straight right now. I know because I went through the same thing when I lost Lorrie, and I—"

She chopped at my arms, forcing them from her shoulders. "You don't *know* anything!" Tears started down her face. "I watched Bronson grow old. I watched him change from the vital man I married to an old, sick stranger, who had no interest in going on trips or going hiking or even leaving the house. No interest in sex. I loved him so much, but the Bronson who died wasn't the man I fell in love with—and I couldn't grow old with him or change with him."

She was crying full force now and tearing my heart in two with her anguish. Her pain was deep and raw. "It wasn't fair. It's just not fair!" Again her face buried in my chest, and I held on to her, tears pricking my own eyes. There was nothing I could do but hold her.

After a long time the storm abated. "Yes," she said with another little hiccup, pulling away once more to look into my face. "I miss Bronson, but I miss the man I fell in love with, not the old man who went on without me. I miss feeling his body against mine. I miss being wanted more than food or work or the newest television show. I miss the nights we didn't sleep because we couldn't get enough of each other. I miss camping under the stars, traveling all over the world. I miss it all!" She paused and took a deep breath. "But none of that's new. I've missed him for years. All I could do was to cling to what we had left."

She slumped dejectedly. Wanting to comfort her, I pulled her tightly against me. Her face lifted to mine, her lips beckoning to be kissed, and I wanted more than anything to do that. My thin control vanished, and my lips met hers. This was where I wanted to be, and though I knew I shouldn't be doing this, I didn't know how to stop myself. Her lips parted and I tasted her passion. It took me three tries before I could pull away enough to clear my throat and speak.

"Oh, Stella," I whispered, "you have no idea how much I want you right now. But I won't take advantage of your grief." There, the words were out. I knew I might regret them for the rest of my life. I also knew that if she kissed me again, all my brave words would mean absolutely nothing.

Silence fell for a long moment as she searched my face. When she spoke, her words were calmer. "Then just give me a baby." She didn't add that I owed her, but we both knew I did. She'd saved my children, and if I gave her a hundred babies, it would never be enough to make up for the one she'd lost.

I opened my mouth to speak, though I didn't know what would come out. Whatever the words, they were lost as the sound of gunfire broke through the air, shattering my indecision.

I grabbed Stella and dived with her behind the metal tool station.

CHAPTER 12

I HADN'T BEEN CAREFUL ABOUT OUR TRAJECTORY, AND I landed on my back, with Stella on top of me. Despite Dimitri's earlier ministrations, pain shot through my ribs. I gritted my teeth and reached for my gun.

Stella already had her pistol out. She eased off me, peering around the tool station. "I don't think they're firing at us," she whispered. "Did that come from the lobby?"

"I think so. They must be firing at Charles. Probably attacked him after he entered but before he reset the alarm because I don't hear it. But they'll know someone else is here because of the lights and the car. Look, I'll be right back. Cover me." I stood and darted to the next tool cart and then to a group of light switches. They had them embedded periodically along the wall so that we wouldn't have to go all the way to the lobby doors to shut them on or off. I turned off all four circuits that lit the vast space and returned to Stella.

"How did they find us?" This close I could see her eyes widen with a possibility. "You don't think it was the funeral, do you? Maybe they suspected that Bronson was linked to the Renegades. I tried to keep him away from that side of my life, but they could have identified him and tracked us from the graveyard." She paused, and when she spoke again, her voice sounded panicked. "You don't think they followed Bronson's kids, do you? I'd never forgive myself if—"

"No," I said more gruffly than I intended. "They would have attacked us at the mortuary or at the cemetery. We were there by ourselves. Would have been easy to pick us off. No, I think they've been watching this hangar. Must have traced the flight from Mexico." That meant César and Diego had returned to their little house by the makeshift runway. I hoped for Marisa's sake that the Emporium had left them alive.

"I should have created new numbers and papers," Stella said. "I always do that when there's any possibility of being traced."

"We didn't know there was a need."

My words didn't fool her. All the excuses in the world wouldn't be enough. "I should have done it."

"Must be Marco they're firing at."

"We have to help him."

"They won't kill him. Not until they get inside the plane or find us."

"I hope you're right."

So did I.

I took the lead. After two centuries of training, Stella was more experienced, and in a fair fight, she'd hand me my head on a platter, but this hangar was my domain. Problem was that we kept a fairly uncluttered place, and besides the wheeled tool stations, and the planes themselves, there wasn't much to hide us. Inside the office, we'd be sitting ducks. I opened the tool cart and took out the largest wire cutters I had. "Take whatever you think you might need. You have enough ammo?"

"Two extra magazines." She was putting on her silencer as she spoke. "Never leave home without them."

"Sounds like Ritter."

"I learned from the best. Wish I had an assault rifle, though."

I was glad to hear the panic was gone from her voice. In fact, she sounded almost excited. Yet I didn't like the idea of her in another confrontation so soon.

I motioned to the ladder next to the office door. "I'm going up and over the catwalks they use to change the lights. I'll see if I can drop down behind them when they come in, or maybe shoot them from above. I might be able to cut the wiring to the lights. Darkness is in our favor, especially if they're used to the light outside."

"I'll cover you."

She meant in case they came in while I was on my way up, but I didn't intend to let that happen. I hurried up the ladder, skipping two rungs with every step. It was a long, long way up, but the catwalks came quicker than expected. As I reached the top, I spied the first of the electrical circuits and snipped the wires, then hurried along the catwalk to the next. A thin but sturdy piece of metal formed a halfway decent handrail on one side of the catwalk, but it was a good thing I didn't share my sister's acrophobia—something her Change hadn't fixed.

I'd only snipped two circuits when the door from the lobby slammed opened. "Where are the damn lights?" someone growled.

I sprinted to the wiring of the third circuit and cut it a half second before the lights came on in the farthermost section. Well, I obviously wouldn't make it to that circuit in time, but at least I'd taken out three of the four.

I lay flat on the catwalk, knowing they would soon be looking instinctively upward as they continued to flip the switches, trying to get the other circuits on.

"That's it?" one of the men below growled. "No more lights?"

"It's a hangar," Charles said, "not a hotel."

"Shut up."

The failing lights should let Charles know I was here, but I hoped that knowledge wouldn't make him over-confident. It was still us versus six Emporium agents, all dressed in black, carrying pistols and wearing sword sheaths. Two of them held assault rifles. Definitely an Emporium hit team. I tried to match their faces with the files we had on known Emporium agents, but nothing was coming to me. I didn't know how many were

Unbounded and how many might be mortal soldiers, but I had to assume the worst. That meant six combatants who wouldn't really die unless I dismembered them.

Of course to get that far, I first had to immobilize them. Or temporarily kill them.

Maybe it was better that I didn't know which might be Unbounded and which were mortal. Knowing might make me hesitate.

"You two find the lights," said a big Latino, who seemed to be in charge. "Meet us at the plane."

I stayed motionless as they left the entrance and started down the line of planes. I couldn't risk them seeing me in the dim light. But two staying behind was good because my plane was parked on the very end of the row, and the others would soon be far enough away for me to act safely.

Three men and one woman took off down the line of planes with Charles, while the man and woman who stayed behind continued flipping light switches and staring above them. Nothing to do but wait until they grew bored and tried something else.

"I'll go see if there's a circuit breaker out there," the man finally said, opening the door to the lobby.

"Okay, but keep your eyes open. More Renegade scum could be arriving."

"Got babe here to protect us." He patted his assault rifle and disappeared through the door. The woman took a tool from her belt and began to unscrew the metal plate behind the light switches.

The others were out of my sight, though I could hear their footsteps echoing in the hangar. I eased to my feet and tried to move soundlessly along the catwalk until I was positioned above the woman.

Wait, I told myself as I knelt and took careful aim. I had to make sure her companions were far enough away that they wouldn't hear the soft whoosh of my silenced bullet or notice her go down. I hoped with the positioning of the tool carts near each plane, they might not see her body even if they looked this way. My rifle and a scope would be better for this job, but the nine mil would have to do. The hit team were most likely wearing some kind of body armor, so I had to try for a headshot.

Now. I pulled the trigger. *Whoosh!* She slumped almost immediately, her head making a cracking sound on the cement when she fell. Blood and brains spread over the ground around her head, leaking from her skull, though I couldn't see exactly where I'd hit her.

I stood and moved as fast as I could to the space above the entry. I was in the light now, if anyone had been there to look up, but the Emporium agent was beyond seeing anything. Positioning myself directly above the lobby door, I waited. How long would it take the male agent to discover the breaker wasn't in there? Not long, I hoped. There were no gunshots coming from the other side of the hangar, but I itched to get back there. My own success had proven that the sound of silenced shots didn't carry that far.

The door opened almost before I was ready. My hands

waved into position as the man came through. "I can't find—Sasha!"

He'd taken only two steps toward his fallen companion when I fired. This time two shots, because I wasn't sure of my aim and he was moving. The first hit him near the top of his head and the second embedded in the base of his skull. I felt a momentary triumph, until the urge to vomit nearly made me fall from the catwalk.

Don't think about it. Not yet.

Ritter had been right about all those target practices paying off, but he hadn't told me about this revulsion. Maybe because he'd lost that in the years he'd sought revenge for his own family's deaths.

Stella. Charles. I had to think of them now.

I debated briefly over whether or not I should climb down the ladder and hide the bodies, but there was no way to clean the blood from the cement, so that was rather pointless. Better that I go help the others. Pulling myself together, I started again along the catwalk.

Two down, four to go. The odds had just gotten slightly better.

I had the hangar divided mentally into four parts, corresponding with the electric circuits. I passed gratefully from the first and into the second, going slower now, treading with caution. I'd almost reached the third section when light footsteps below alerted me to someone coming back this way. I paused and waited. An Emporium agent came into view below, walking with exaggerated steps, his hands holding an assault rifle.

He was white and young, probably young enough that he didn't know if he'd Change and become Unbounded or if he'd serve the Emporium as a second class citizen for the rest of his mortal life.

I thought of my brother Jace, newly Changed and, like Stella, younger than most Unbounded. Maybe this man had Changed early too. It didn't matter, though. The hit man below supported the Emporium and there was simply no excuse for coming here with that assault rifle.

Heart banging inside my chest, I waited to fire until he stepped over to the wall and the light switches. My bullet hit him in the head, and he fell against the wall and slid down slowly without a sound. I waited only to be sure he wasn't moving.

Three against three now.

I began moving faster, experiencing a strange urgency. It was a miracle I didn't fall as I tore through the third section. *Slow down,* I told myself. Ritter had emphasized repeatedly the importance of waiting every bit as much as the will to attack, and I had come too far to give up the advantage I held up here in the dark. So far, Ritter's training had not failed me. I popped out my old magazine, still more than half full, and slid in a new one. Twelve rounds in all.

A loud shout farther ahead and to my right urged me on. The sound came from below somewhere near where my plane or the one next to it was parked. I hurried forward as quickly as I could, reaching one of the intersections of the catwalk where it shot out over each parking space.

Below, I heard a flurry of whooshing sounds I'd been dreading. Silenced bullets.

I reached the halfway point on the catwalk where it again intersected another line that paralleled the first. Nothing was under me except a plane, and I couldn't yet see beyond it to my own. I pushed forward along the catwalk. Finally, I caught sight of an Emporium agent standing near my plane, her gun pressed into Charles's back.

"Who's shooting at us!" she demanded, shielding her body between Charles and the stairs to my plane.

"Maybe the IRS? Did you pay your taxes?"

I never knew Charles to be such a wise guy. Maybe all that kelp on his pizza was having a strange side effect.

"I'm going to enjoy killing you," the Unbounded said. "Now get up these stairs and open the door, or I'm going to start shooting off your fingers one by one." The way she said it was more of a promise than anything else, and I suspected that without intervention, Charles would lose all his fingers even if he did open the door. I contemplated shooting the woman as I had the others, but she was too close to my plane. Almost under it now. The angle was poor enough that to hit her, the bullet might first have to go through Charles.

I had only seconds to decide. In the dark, I spied two shadows taking cover behind the next plane's tool station. A flash of a gun going off showed me Stella was firing from behind our own station, the one we'd hidden behind earlier. I wanted to backtrack across the catwalk and drop in behind the other Emporium agents to help Stella, and I knew Charles would insist on it if he had a choice, but my doing so would leave him vulnerable. She was Unbounded; he was not. I knew where my duty lay. I couldn't let my feelings for Stella fool me into thinking she'd thank me for sacrificing Charles. She could hold her own.

"What's the code?" screamed the Emporium woman. "You know what? If you aren't going to help, I'll just kill you right here!" She dug her gun into Charles's neck. "Tell me the code and I might let you live."

Charles shook his head. "Go ahead, shoot me. I'm dead if I let you in anyway."

In a quick motion, she put her arm around his neck and pulled back. Charles began to choke.

I knew what I had to do.

CHAPTER 13

HOLSTERING MY GUN, I GRABBED THE CATWALK AND EASED myself down until I was only three feet from the top of my plane. In all our training, we'd never practiced jumping from heights onto a curved surface, but how much more difficult could it be?

I let go, and my feet clunked hard against the plane. I swore silently, struggling to retain my balance. No dice. I slid off the plane, landing feet first on the ground, remembering at the last second not to lock my knees but to bend and roll. I came up ready to shoot, hoping my rolling angle was enough to give me a line to the woman agent without Charles in the way. I fired.

They both fell, but not before the woman let off a shot that dug into the cement inches away from my head. Only the fact that I was still in motion saved my life. I fired again at the woman's slumped figure and hurried to

Charles, keeping my gun on her. Charles was out cold, but he was breathing and his windpipe seemed intact. I could see no other wounds besides a few punch marks on his face that were going to be nasty bruises in a few hours. The woman stirred and I pulled the trigger again, this time hitting her between the eyes. I stopped only to make sure she wasn't breathing.

I hurried to the end of the plane, where even in the dull light I couldn't miss the drama playing out with Stella and the remaining two Unbounded. She was swinging a large wrench at a man who blocked with a sword. Another agent lay on the ground behind the first, stunned but still moving. They'd evidently used all their extra ammo, or Stella had shot their guns from their hands.

Or not.

Even as I watched, the fallen man lifted a gun. I fired first, missing his head, but hitting him in the shoulder and causing his bullet to go wide. His second shot was better.

But so was mine, and he finally lay still.

The remaining Emporium agent had Stella by the hair, the point of his sword digging into her neck. "Shoot him!" Stella said. "Now!" Blood oozed from the front of her black skirt, a last parting gift from the man I'd just shot. I hoped he hadn't hit an artery.

"Okay," I started to take aim, my movements exaggerated.

"I'll cut off her pretty face," the agent growled.

"Hmm," I said. "Do you think you can cut her into

three before I stop you? It might be an interesting test. If you're a combat Unbounded, you might actually make it before I manage to hit you, but I don't think you can kill her and get to me, no matter how fast you are." I hoped I was right. "Next thing you know, I'll be the one using your pretty sword."

The Unbounded thought about it and then nodded. "Let me go, and I'll free her."

I met Stella's eyes, not his. "I don't think so. Say goodbye."

Stella twisted as I fired. Thankfully, she'd understood my signal. Thankfully, it was enough. The shot hit him in the throat, though I'd been aiming for his eye. Good thing Stella had moved. The last thing I wanted to explain to Ava was that I'd shot Stella and she'd be out recovering instead of flying to New York.

I rushed to Stella, grimaced at the blood seeping from her neck. "It's okay," she muttered. "It's not deep. My leg's worse."

"Lie down. I'll bandage it. Then we'll tie up these guys."

"Not here." She gritted her teeth against the pain. "They called for reinforcements when I started firing. They could be here any minute."

"Okay, but you're coming with me." She didn't argue and I knew that meant she was feeling worse than she let on. "Did you leave anything important in the car?"

"No. I only need what's in my shoulder bag over there."

I scooped up both her and the bag and ran for the plane. It took only moments to punch in the code, while Stella placed her hand on the reader. The door slid open. Ducking inside, I set her on the first row of seats, tossed her a first aid kit, and hurried back down the stairs for Charles.

"Come on, wake up," I said, gently slapping his face. That didn't work. Charles was a rather large man, so I ended up having to mostly drag him up the stairs. My ribs ached horribly by the time I finally laid him on the row of seats that faced those where I'd placed Stella. I set my backup pistol on the table between the two rows, just in case those reinforcements showed up before we were out of here.

Stella had tied a bandage around her upper leg to stem the blood flow, and now had her phone out. She'd also hung a small neural transmitter over her left ear, its metal prongs digging into her scalp. It was a smaller version of her regular headset, which was packed away and sent ahead with the others to New York. Two blinking lights on the transmitter showed it was working.

"Hacking into the airport systems now," she said. "I'll have your flight information and registration numbers changed five times and then some before we're anywhere near landing. You'll look like you came from Arkansas or somewhere in Virginia. In another two minutes, this plane will have never been anywhere near Mexico."

That was good. No way did I want more Emporium agents waiting for us in San Diego. We had measures in place to stay under the radar, from a way to change the actual physical numbers on our plane to getting through security checks with our weapons intact. Part of it involved bribes and connections with people who knew about Unbounded and the secret war being waged, but more was because of Stella's intricately designed back door into their network and her ability to manipulate and process data. She had previously created hundreds of backgrounds for this plane. It was just a matter of choosing one. Or as many as it took.

Of course the Emporium had a similar setup, which was why they had been able to find us and get this close to our hangar with weapons, but they wouldn't be able to trace us or our interference once we erased the connection to Mexico.

"Thanks," I told Stella. "While you're at it maybe you can clear us for flight a little sooner."

I hesitated at the plane door, wondering if I should go back for at least a couple of the Emporium agents, but the worry I'd heard in Stella's voice made me nix the idea. I needed to get her to safety, and that meant out of the hangar and into the sky. I hit the switch to pull the retractable stairs into place in the underbelly of the plane and sealed the door.

"I also need you to go over all the security footage for the hangar," I told Stella. "The alarm wasn't triggered, but it's possible they were here earlier and sabotaged the plane."

"I've already downloaded the footage. It'll take fifty

seconds to skim through the time since you last landed. The data connection here isn't as fast as it should be."

I grinned. "I think I can wait fifty seconds."

I headed for the cockpit, ticking off in my mind all the minimum checks I had to do before we took off. It was standard protocol to keep the plane full of fuel to speed up takeoff in an emergency, and I'd filled it after Mexico, but there were certain things I had to do before every flight. There would also be more security checks before takeoff, including making sure our weapons were secured in the specially lined compartments in the floor. I wouldn't store them until I was sure we weren't going to run into any more Emporium soldiers.

Inside the cockpit, I had an opener for one of the three hangar doors spanning the length of the hangar, but belatedly I wondered if the door was on the same circuit as the lights. I was betting not.

"Go ahead," Stella called through the open cockpit door. "We're clear on the security footage."

I began flipping levers and pushing buttons, and when the time came, the hangar door slid open, verifying my guess, though I'd already planned what it would take to splice back the electric wires and defend the hangar just in case. Finally, something had gone our way.

Twenty minutes later, we were on a runway awaiting final clearance. That we'd only had to undergo one brief physical inspection was a tribute to Stella's ability and genius. Plus, she'd already scheduled herself on another commercial flight out from San Diego. We kept emergency clothes on the plane, so she wouldn't even leave the airport.

I looked up from my readouts as a hand fell on my shoulder. Removing my headphones, I stared into Stella's face, glad she appeared less pinched after a couple of shots of curequick. "You should rest," I said, swiveling toward her.

She was still wearing the neural transmitter, but it emitted a series of flashes and then went black. "About the baby," she began.

So we were back to that. I would be lying if I said I hadn't been expecting it.

"You just saved my life," she continued. "The way I see it, you don't owe me anything. I mean that. But I'm still asking."

"Why me?" I didn't remind her that I was mortal—just like Bronson—or that she could have any number of Unbounded sperm donors who would be more likely to create a child who would grow up to have the active Unbounded gene. She knew all that far better than I did.

Her smile filled me with warmth. "Because you're a good father, and I want that for my baby, whether he's mortal or Unbounded. I want a man who will be there while he's growing up."

She paused for several heartbeats and then rushed on. "For the record, this has nothing to do with Bronson. I wanted his child because I loved him, but he already had children and knew he wouldn't be around for our baby. It never meant the same thing to him. He'd had a vasectomy before we married. He only agreed to let Dimitri heal him for my sake."

I stared into her eyes. I couldn't say no. If she wanted me to father her child, to raise and love him, I would do that gladly. I loved his mother; why wouldn't I love him? Maybe Bronson and I were both fools. Still, I liked the idea of Stella's genes and mine going on forever inside our posterity.

"Okay," I said.

Her lips parted in disbelief, filling me with desire. I struggled with myself not to stand up and start kissing her again, to lose myself in her touch.

Give her more time.

She started to speak, but I reached up and placed a finger on her lips. "First you're going to New York with the others to help free our people, and I'm going to get the house in San Diego ready to protect all of us, especially my children. When you get back, if you still want to, we'll start this baby."

The happiness in her eyes made me catch my breath, but I forced myself to continue because I'd regained enough control to remember that she needed more than just a baby. "We'll create him or her with all the genetic options we have available. And, yes, that means in the lab. We both want this child to have the greatest chance of becoming Unbounded."

An Unbounded female's eggs couldn't be tampered with, but the Renegades had created several processes to alter a man's sperm, raising the likelihood of having an Unbounded offspring by twenty percent. Since I was descended from Ava, our chances of having an Unbounded child would be forty percent after genetic alteration, which was a lot better gamble than she'd had with Bronson, who had no Unbounded ancestry. Stella might not have to watch her child age and die while she remained young.

A smile curved her lips, though her eyes shone with tears. "No relationship?"

"What do you call this?" I moved a hand back and forth between us.

"You know what I mean."

She meant a physical relationship. Sex. I also knew that casual relationships weren't her standard, or something Renegade Unbounded condoned. Family to them was everything, and since all their physical relationships resulted in offspring, they were careful with their intimacy.

I wanted to tell Stella that I was hers. That I loved her like I never thought I could love anyone after Lorrie. That I would wait for as long as she needed. But I'd learned a thing or two in the past months about my Stella, my star. I had to make us something she would fight for, not something connected to a baby, not something she'd feel guilty about later. Besides, a declaration in this moment would forever link us to Bronson and his death, and I didn't want her to see me that way. Mortal. Even if I was.

I blew out a decidedly frustrated breath. "Let's give it a little time."

She nodded, her eyes holding mine. Something passed between us, unidentifiable yet powerful. As if she saw me—the real me—for the first time. I wasn't sure if that was good or bad.

"Okay," she said. "You've got yourself a deal."

Maybe she'd change her mind about both the baby and me once there was a little space between her and what had happened this week. That was okay because at least I'd know I hadn't taken advantage of the woman I loved. It was also possible that after time we could both move forward without the baggage of the past, baby or no.

Whatever happened, I didn't fool myself that it was going to be an easy road for either of us, but I didn't give up easily.

I might be the mortal brother in my family, but I was also a Renegade.

SET
ABLAZE

AN UNBOUNDED NOVELLA

To all those who struggle with addiction of one kind or another, and whose hearts yearn for freedom and release.

CHAPTER 1

THE LITTLE PORTUGUESE TOWN OF MONTE VINHA WAS strange. I couldn't put my finger on what bothered me about it, but the feeling was in every smile directed our way, the stares that followed us down the nearly deserted streets, and even the air we breathed. Yet the quaint buildings, the rich food, the friendly people—everything appeared normal, similar to the other small towns we'd passed.

But I knew something in Monte Vinha wasn't right.

A hundred and eighty years ago, I'd been born in this country, and though I'd returned only a handful of times since after my parents' deaths, it was still my homeland. Even before London, where I'd lived most of the past century, or America, where I had spent the rest of my boyhood and early adult years with my foster father, Ritter Langton.

"It's like we've stepped into some kind of comic horror movie," my partner Kenna Murray said, the lilt in her Northern Irish accent making it sound like a question. "And they're all waiting for night to turn into psychopathic killers and chop us up into wee pieces."

"Exactly," I agreed. "And where are all the tourists? There should be more walking around. They do have a castle here."

Even though I was driving, I didn't miss the roll of Kenna's eyes. "Practically every little town here has a castle," she said. "We've passed a dozen at least." A gross exaggeration since we'd only seen four or five on our drive from the airport. "Seriously, though, it's getting late in the season for tourists."

"Not here, it isn't." Mid-September was still prime tourist season. "The sudden decline in population could be keeping them away. Rumors do travel." I glanced over my shoulder as I turned off the main street, following the directions given us at the café where we'd eaten lunch.

Monte Vinha had plunged from five thousand residents to nearly four thousand in the past five years alone. That abrupt change and the chatter our Renegade technopath had intercepted about Emporium land purchases in the area was the reason we were here. Portugal had a history of remaining untouched in our battles with the Emporium, but after a thorough reconnaissance of the town, I guessed that was about to change.

"Could just be the younger generation moving away

for better jobs in the city," Kenna suggested. "And at the same time the aging population slowly dying off."

The youth in these small cities had historically left for better opportunities, but many returned later in life to take over small businesses from their parents and grandparents as the older generations retired and passed on. "If that were the case, wouldn't there be more older people here? I don't believe I've seen anyone over sixty, have you?" I'd have to check the data we'd been given to see if the population ages matched up with similar cities.

Kenna thought for a moment before shaking her head. "No, I can't recall seeing any really old people. Maybe they had a mini flu epidemic, or some kind of disease the elderly weren't inoculated for. A few hundred dying over several years might not have set off alarms until now. Either that or the Emporium has discovered the fountain of youth and is passing it along to the town, so the old people are leaving in droves for new careers too." We shared a laugh at the implausibility of the Emporium doing anything to help mortals.

Whatever was going on here, I planned to find out exactly what the Emporium was up to—and put a stop to it. That is, unless our initial report made Greggor recall me to London. I didn't fool myself into thinking that I'd been our leader's first choice for the assignment.

Only two days ago, the Emporium had slaughtered twenty of our people during a Renegade meeting in New York City, and our London cell was down five of our strongest Unbounded, four permanently dead and one missing. No, I was by far not the first choice, at least not without more backup. My abilities were extremely useful, but things tended to explode when I was around—literally. Our leader was making the best call he could with the personnel he had left. I just happened to speak the language, and as half-Portuguese, I blended in.

Kenna, by contrast, was a brilliant operative, always near the top of Greggor's list. After two hundred years of life, her fighting skills were impressive even among Unbounded with the combat ability. She spoke as many languages as I did and could lose most of her Irish brogue when she concentrated, though her red hair and all those freckles would be a drawback here without her disguise.

"Oh, wait, remember that old guy we passed in the park?" Kenna said. "He had to be a least seventy." She gave me a grin that twisted something in my gut. "Guess that takes the fountain of youth idea off the table."

I turned our rental car down a short dirt road, which should lead to our vacation rental. I'd have preferred a bed and breakfast, but a villa meant no prying eyes as we came and went, and no neighbors to run into at mealtimes. We couldn't risk Emporium agents hearing through casual conversation that we were here.

Dust billowed up the sides of the car, mostly kept out by the closed windows. A little whitewashed villa with a tiny patch of grass in the front yard appeared in the distance.

Kenna squinted through the dust. "Look, someone's waiting for us."

She checked the mirror and adjusted her long, dark wig. I could still see her myriad freckles under her thick makeup, and every one of them fascinated me.

I pulled my mind away from those thoughts. I was so far out of her league that even thinking about her that way was a waste of time. As a combat Unbounded, she was disciplined, unforgiving of weaknesses like the one that was already making my hands start to shake. I'd have to do something about the unsteadiness sooner rather than later, but I would put it off as long as possible.

I wasn't wearing a wig, but I'd grown my hair several inches longer, and let three days of beard cover my normally clean-shaven face. For an Unbounded, that meant I looked like I hadn't shaved in three or four weeks. I could pass for a thousand different Portuguese men.

Bringing the car to a stop in front of the villa, I jumped out and made my way to the narrow cobblestone pathway leading to the porch. The stocky woman sitting on a chair came awkwardly to her feet, smoothing her dress and the apron she wore over it. Her hair was still mostly dark, but her face was wrinkled by long exposure to the sun. I guessed her age to be mid-fifties.

"*Boa tarde*," she said with a smile, ducking her head slightly.

"Good afternoon," I repeated, slipping easily into the language of my youth. "I guess we're your tenants for the week."

"Ah, I can tell by your speech that you are Portuguese," the woman's smile grew wider, her Portuguese flavored with the accent of the Alentejo. "Welcome. I am Dona Mafalda." *Dona* meant missus, but as was often common, she'd used it with her first name and not her last. Hearing it reminded me of long sunny days and simpler times.

"My husband and I take care of this house for the owner," she continued. "There are clean linens on the beds and more in the cupboards if you need them. I brought bread, cheese, ham, and the other things you requested and put them in the refrigerator. Keys are on the table. If you need anything, please call the number by the phone."

She glanced at Kenna and added, "If your wife doesn't speak Portuguese, my daughter knows English, and she can call to tell me what you need. Her number is also by the phone."

"I speak Portuguese," Kenna said, her accent passable, but with a hint of her Irish brogue. "But thank you for your kindness."

"Good, good." Dona Mafalda said. "You live in Portugal then?"

"In Leria." I chose a significantly larger city farther north, one definitely not close to where I'd been born in nearby Évora.

"Ah, that's good. It's so nice to have young people here. Monte Vinha is so beautiful, but our youth don't see that. They always want to leave."

At first, I suspected Dona Mafalda's remark was a subtle

jab at our youthfulness—an illusion since Unbounded age only two years for every hundred we live—but there was really nothing in her tone to indicate this, and her semi-vacant smile never faltered.

The woman leaned over to scoop up a very large cloth shopping bag. "I hope you will enjoy your stay. There are two bicycles on the back deck, a soccer ball, and inflatables for the pool. Let me know if you need anything." Tipping her body forward in a partial curtsey, she stepped past us and hurried down the cobblestone path to the dirt road.

When her figure disappeared, Kenna drew one of the guns we'd picked up at the safe house in Lisbon this morning. I did the same. Opening the door to the villa, we stepped carefully inside. The entryway opened into a large sitting room, featuring an aged floral couch, two matching chairs, a long black coffee table with a stack of magazines, and an oversized TV. Kenna motioned that she'd check out the two bedrooms, so I ducked into the kitchen. The room took quaintness to a new level, every gleaming surface decorated with hand-crocheted doilies like my grandmother had once made. No sign of danger.

Kenna met me back in the sitting room and together we headed for the large cobblestone deck off the back of the villa. She checked the perimeter, while I gazed at the glittering water in the pool. The water beckoned, promising to soothe the growing ache inside me, but I knew it couldn't. There was only one thing that could stop the ache.

"Let's bring in the equipment." Kenna returned to my side, holstering her gun.

"Yeah, right." But I didn't move to join her as she started to leave. The cobblestones, the whitewash of the house, the red tiles of the roof, and even the interior setup was very like the house my parents had owned in Portugal—the house I still owned—passed down first to my parents and then to me by a great-grandfather I'd never met.

The water in the pool undulated with a light breeze. I'd been swimming in the river with my friends the day the gardener had brought the awful news that my Portuguese mother and English father were gone. Killed in a fire on their trip to Lisbon, he'd said. That was long before I'd heard of Unbounded, or learned my parents' deaths weren't accidental.

"Blaze, is everything all right?" Kenna asked.

I turned to look at her, aware that the minor shaking in my hands had now become flashes of heat. Moisture washed over my entire body. "Of course."

But everything wasn't all right. These memories made me feel more out of control. Hopefully, nothing a swig of curequick couldn't dispel, but I wasn't going to drink it now. *I can wait just a little longer.* I would end up taking it because I'd never jeopardize the mission, even if drinking the curequick meant hurting myself. It was almost like a game I played at times, a deadly serious game. One I always lost.

I strode past Kenna and added, "I'll grab the computer while you sweep for bugs."

Setting up the laptop and the projector didn't take long. Soon I was staring at a large satellite image on the white wall of the sitting room, where I had removed a painting to give us more space.

Kenna came into the room with a teapot full of water. "Is there some special place that Portuguese customarily keep the matches? I was going to make some tea, but I can't light the gas burner until I find the matches. Would you like a cuppa?"

"Sounds good."

Like all Unbounded, we didn't need to eat to survive. Our bodies were continuously absorbing bits and pieces of the world around us, but we still derived comfort from food and especially the familiar. Sometimes a juicy cheeseburger helped push back my demons.

"Here." I approached her, reaching for the pot. I could see lemon rinds already floating in the water.

"Wh—" She broke off, a smile playing on her mouth. "Oh, this I have to see."

I gave a little effort, and the pot in my hand instantly heated, the water beginning to boil violently. Oops, too much.

As a *roaster,* my Unbounded ability was to manipulate matter in one specific way—heating. The ability was remotely similar to the talent of pyros, who could set fire to anything flammable, but my manipulation extended to any matter. I could increase the temperature of an object by touch, either scorching, boiling, or melting it. Bursting objects into flame was the most obvious part of the ability, though not the most effective, thus my nickname Blaze.

A side effect was that my skin could withstand incredible heat before it began to burn. Not that I was impervious to high temperature, but I could normally work through the discomfort and pain. The ability made me valuable to the Renegade cause, but using it excessively as I'd done meant I often ended up incapacitated and in dire need of curequick, which in turn had allowed the "medicine" a chokehold grip on my life.

Still smiling, Kenna went to retrieve the teacups and a plate of ham and cheese sandwiches made from the welcome package left by the landlady.

I set the still-boiling teapot on a hot pad and returned my attention to the map on the wall. Splashes of yellow marked the areas our intel had pinpointed as possibly being connected to the Emporium. Some of the purchases dated back over ten years, but it was the recent large purchases marked in red that had flagged our attention.

"With both the red and yellow, it means they own most of the land surrounding the city," I said.

"If the yellow really belongs to the Emporium."

Sometimes I wondered if Kenna disagreed with me just for the sake of argument.

"I'm betting it does, and whatever they've been doing

here, it's been successful enough that they've decided to expand." I reached to touch the teapot again, giving it a final shot of heat because it hadn't boiled quite long enough yet.

"That's farmland, isn't it?" Kenna pointed to the red areas on the satellite image.

"According to the data, it was all vineyards and cork trees at one time. And one olive grove. But you're right. The satellite images Greggor gave us don't show trees on the new land they purchased, though there are some on the yellow areas." I paused before adding, "Cutting down cork trees? That's almost a crime. It takes three harvestings of nine years apart before the very best cork is grown. That's twenty-seven years of work and patience thrown away."

"Vineyards take time too." Kenna sat on the floral sofa, crossing her knees, her eyes still fixed on the map. "And it's difficult to cut down trees at all. So what are they growing instead that is so important? Maybe some kind of GMO?"

"Genetically modified organisms? Could be. The background I was reading on the plane says Portugal has increased their use of GM crops every year."

"I thought Europe banned the use of GMOs."

"Publicly, maybe. But most countries have them in some form or another."

Kenna gingerly tested the handle of the teapot before pouring a cup for each of us. She'd found a sack of sugar—most likely left by past vacationers—and put one spoonful in mine and two in hers. I wondered how she knew my preference, but before I could ask, she was talking again.

"Still, cutting down trees hardly seems something the Emporium would waste time on. Why not just go somewhere else? With American companies pushing for GMOs, it isn't really an agenda the Emporium needs to help along. Something else is going on. Something bad."

"Well, that's what we're here to find out." Like most Unbounded gifted in combat, she had great instincts. I would trust her even if my gut wasn't giving me the same feeling. "I already emailed Greggor a request for a population comparison with other towns to see if that brings up anything." Our technopath in London could come up with the information we needed in a fraction of the time it would take us to research it.

I gulped the hot tea and eyed the sandwiches, but my desire to eat had deserted me. I couldn't push back the need for curequick any longer without endangering my ability to function. Besides, in a minute, Kenna would see that I was suffering.

"You up for a bike ride?" I asked her. "Let's see what they have growing in their fields now."

Kenna's laugh was genuine. "Actually, I haven't ridden a bicycle in fifty years."

"Don't worry. It's like . . . like . . ."

"Riding a bike?"

I laughed. I'd spent most of the last decade largely avoiding working with a single partner. Mostly, I was sent in alone, while a team worked the same op from another angle. My goal was to complete whatever missions I was assigned until I was too damaged or too exhausted to continue, and then I'd spend weeks in my flat recovering. That meant a lot of solitary moments. It felt good to be working with a partner again.

"I'll just change into some shorts," I said. "Trifle hotter here than in London."

Grabbing my duffel, I headed to the smaller of the two bedrooms. I forced myself to wait until after I changed, my body flushed and sweating, my stomach cramping, to get the curequick from my pack. Curequick was a staple for all Unbounded regeneration, despite its addictive properties, and we usually carried it in both drinkable and injectable versions. Made primarily of sugars and proteins reduced to their most usable forms, it allowed us to regenerate at five times the rate of our already increased regeneration level. It also gave the user a pleasant buzz. The mixture had been designed by a scientist in one of our American Renegade cells, strictly formulated for use after taking wounds in combat. Unfortunately, Unbounded who used it too often found themselves victim to the severe withdrawal symptoms.

Unbounded like me.

For years, I'd told myself I was different from the new generation of Unbounded, who used curequick as a recreational drug, not as a way to heal after battle, but in the end it all boiled down to the same thing. Too many missions, too much curequick, and I was no longer reliable. The only thing left was to check myself into a certain hospital in London for treatment, and I'd be damned if I was going in that direction. No, I'd fix myself.

After this op.

It was always after the next op.

I downed the contents of a pouch, and the warmth spread through me, at first a trickle and then a rush.

I loved it—and I hated myself for needing it.

Of course, if I had been reliable and not in the habit of avoiding extended meetings because of my dependence, I would have been in New York with the others when we were betrayed to the Emporium. I might have been one of those slaughtered. Instead, I'd have to live the rest of my two thousand years—twenty-five lifetimes of guilt— knowing I hadn't been there to protect our people.

A noise at my door had me reaching for my gun, but it was only Kenna, her eyes narrowing as she spotted the pouch in my hands. "Look, if you can't do this . . . I heard about your . . . trouble."

"My addiction, you mean. It's not a problem. I'm dealing with it, okay?"

"Sure." The firm line of her jaw told me if there came a time when I wasn't handling it, she'd make sure I didn't endanger the mission.

"Anyway, right now we have a bigger problem," she continued. "I was moving the bikes out to the path behind the house, and I found something. Remember those old people we were looking for? I found another one, but he's dead."

CHAPTER 2

THE MAN'S LEATHERED FACE POINTED UPWARD, HIS EYES open and unseeing.

"You sure he's not just smashed?" I asked, kneeling to check his pulse.

"Of course I'm sure. And for the record, he doesn't even smell like alcohol."

"He can't be older than sixty." I rummaged through his pockets. "Wallet's here . . . with money."

"No obvious signs of trauma, either. Looks too young to have died of old age." Kenna glanced around. "We have to move him. Can't let the authorities come to the house or think we're connected."

"We're not connected."

"No, but if the Emporium owns all the land around the city, I bet they own the authorities. This will call attention to us."

"I'll get the gloves in my pack."

Gloves and a white bedsheet were all we needed to carry the man through the deserted grove of thin-leafed olive trees bordering the property. Tall bushes that were almost trees themselves often barred our way, telling me this particular grove wasn't cultivated. We deposited the body far enough away from the villa that we wouldn't be suspected, but close enough to a small grouping of houses that someone was bound to find him soon.

"Careful where you step," Kenna said as she folded up the sheet we'd used. We'd have to dispose of it later, not that I was expecting much from local law enforcement.

"Poor guy," Kenna added, staring down at him. "Hey, what are you doing?"

"Taking a blood sample." I inserted the needle into his calf, where the hair should go a long way toward hiding the mark. "How many other dead mortals have you discovered lying around on other missions? We both know something is going on in this town. It might be—"

"Connected," she finished. "I know—it's just that I already took a sample before we moved him." She shook her head and sighed. "It's so peaceful out here. Hard to believe the Emporium chose this place."

"They're everywhere." I purposely made my voice hard. "Let's go."

Back at the villa, Kenna tossed the sheet in the bathtub and filled it with water and bleach. Then she changed her clothes. She always did that after any kind of fight or op, as if changing wiped away the memories.

Whatever she needed to do.

"What are you staring at?" she asked, as she climbed on one of the bicycles.

I dragged my eyes from the legs that emerged quite compellingly beneath the patterned shorts with the oversized pockets. I'd been attracted to Kenna for most of the past five years, but even if I didn't have a problem with curequick, Renegade Unbounded were careful about their relationships—and for good reason. Our genes ensured that children would invariably result from almost any union, and there was no guarantee the offspring would be Unbounded. We'd all learned too well that having a family meant watching most of them grow old and die before we'd aged two years. It meant stress-filled years of actively protecting loved-ones from Emporium slaughter. I'd seen many of our people watching over their posterity for six generations with the hope that someone in their line carried the active Unbounded gene.

No, even if Kenna was interested, a relationship wasn't something I could risk until I got myself under control. I wasn't reliable.

I flashed her a grin. "I'm not staring. I'm just hoping we aren't going to be climbing in the bushes, or we'll both be uncomfortable."

"The satellite images show paths all around this area and most of the fields. We only have to get close enough to see what's going on, and take a few samples."

Hopefully, not more blood samples.

"Let's check out the buildings last," I suggested.

There was only one set of buildings large enough to be of interest. "I bet we won't be able to get too close."

"Probably not."

The first field was only ten minutes away, but the crop had already been cut down. "Corn," I said, squatting down to examine the remaining stalks.

In the next field, cabbages were being harvested by a dozen Portuguese who loaded them into a long, wagon-like trailer pulled by a truck that showed more rust than green paint. Only one woman glanced our way as we pedaled by. We waited until they were out of sight to gather a sample and put it in my pack.

We passed fields of potatoes, carrots, and tomatoes before coming to wheat fields that went on as far as we could see. I took a sample as I had with the other fields and said, "I think we've seen enough here. Fresh daily bread is a staple in Portugal, so these probably go on for a while. I'd like to look at those vineyards and the olive grove we saw on the map. If the Emporium is behind those, they've been here for at least ten years."

"The buildings are near the vineyards too. We need to see those."

We reached the olive grove first, and the beautifully tended trees brought a lump of nostalgia to my throat. Olive oil was as common as water here, and I still used it whenever I had time to cook.

Next came the vineyards, the sweet grapes beckoning to us on the vines. I was already experiencing the faint taste of grapes through absorption, as my body sucked in nutrients from the world around us, but I couldn't resist stopping. Picking and eating grapes from the fields on the way to our swimming hole was straight out of my childhood. Hopping off the bike, I grabbed several bunches of the bulging fruit.

Kenna settled next to me on the remains of a crumbling stone wall that had once encircled the field. "Don't you think it's stupid eating these without knowing what the Emporium is doing here?" she asked as I held out a cluster to her.

I laughed. "I guess I'm too accustomed to being immune to everything. Besides, it's not Unbounded who are dying here."

"Just because severing our focus points is the only proven method for killing Unbounded doesn't mean another way isn't possible. I'm fairly certain Emporium experimentation is how we learned about the whole lock them in a sealed room for decades until the body falls apart approach." Taking a tube from a back pocket, she dropped in one of the grapes before adding a squirt of liquid from a vial stored in yet another pocket. Even Kenna's casual clothes were especially designed for combat, and I was betting she had at least ten other pockets holding different weapons and tools. I used to order similar clothing, but more often than not, they ended up burned and unusable after an op, so I'd given up on them.

Shaking the tube, she smiled. "No toxins at levels that should hurt us."

"Course not." I threw a grape at her, intending to catch her off guard.

Her hand, barely a blur, shot up to catch the fruit. "I didn't say there aren't *any* toxins. This test isn't that sensitive." She popped the grape into her mouth. "Mmm," she said with an exaggerated sigh. "Whatever they're doing here, they haven't compromised on taste like most of the genetically modified foods in the world today." She shook her head. "I don't even bother with strawberries anymore unless they're straight from my own garden."

"You have a garden?"

She shrugged. "I dabble. Just a few years now."

Right. And I'd been trying to stay away from her for at least that long. "It doesn't make sense, all these different foods. I mean, there is no sign they're exporting or even selling outside the region. They might own the land around the town, but in the scheme of things, it's only a tiny bit of land. Really not more than enough food to feed this town and maybe a few more. They can't be making money."

"We need Drew." Kenna's voice caught on the words, but her expression was even.

Drew Gunnel was one of those we'd lost in the New York raid. I knew he and Kenna had been close, but I didn't know how close. He'd also been a scientist who could do wonders in the lab. Normally, he would have come along on this op; now we'd have to send our samples to his mortal assistant in London.

"We'll figure it out," I said. "But I think our answer is over there." I jerked my head in the direction where my GPS had pinpointed the buildings.

Kenna nodded and brought up on her phone the notes we'd made earlier. "According to the records Greggor pulled, the original main building was built at the same time this vineyard was purchased ten years ago. But in the past two years, they've doubled its size and added a bunch of what might be large storage barns."

I swallowed the rest of my grapes. "Let's go see." The sun was low in the sky, but there were still several hours left of daylight.

"Be careful. They'll have cameras."

When I didn't respond, she added, "Sorry, force of habit."

Combat Unbounded liked running the show, which was often annoying for the rest of us who trained just as hard and knew the rules. "I don't mind. I'll be careful."

Her smile sent heat curling through my belly, a burning sensation that had nothing to do with my ability and everything to do with how much I liked being with her. I hadn't been in a relationship to speak of in fifty years, and I would be blind not to be attracted to Kenna.

Leaving the bicycles, we wound our way through the vineyard, careful to keep the vines between us and the buildings that rose in the distance. Finally, there was only one row of grapevines left to shield us, and we squatted down to peer around them with our binoculars. The place was surrounded by a chain-link fence topped by razor wire. If that wasn't a big enough clue, the uniformed guards standing at the gate and intermittently around the fence were a clear indication that this wasn't your average agricultural company.

I counted at least eight newer buildings, made from corrugated metal or wood instead of the brick and cement typical to the region—probably hastily constructed. There were also two crumbling brick buildings, and nearest the main gate, an older, squat edifice with fresh mustard stucco. Guards came and went from the yellow building, some strutting with an overt confidence that hinted at an Unbounded nature.

"Well, look at that," I said as the workers we'd seen earlier picking cabbages drove up with their wooden wagon full of produce. The guards let them through the gate, and I followed the wagon with the binoculars until it reached a wooden barn-like structure behind the main yellow building. The double doors opened wide to reveal stacks of crates.

Before the workers finished sorting their cabbages into the crates, four other groups arrived with what had to be more produce. The workers looked happy and smiled as they waved to the guards. One of the female employees jumped down from a truck and ran toward a guard, who swept her up in his arms and kissed her, his hands eagerly groping her body. The other guards poked each other playfully and pointed at their comrade, goading him on.

I wasn't surprised. The Emporium always left a slew of abandoned women and illegitimate babies in their wake. Babies they'd only send someone to check on after thirty years, in case they carried the active Unbounded gene and Changed.

"The workers don't seem afraid." Kenna put down her binoculars, fitting them into a zippered side pocket in her shorts.

"The Portuguese are hard workers, and the economy here isn't great. I bet they're glad to have jobs." I hadn't seen any old people in the mix of workers, though I didn't point it out. The Emporium would naturally employ people they thought could endure hard work.

"Obviously, they're not planning on making this a real business," I said, returning to our earlier conversation. "Or they would have brought in more machines and purchased even more land. There's not even enough wheat to supply more than the city with flour. Whatever they're doing is localized."

"Testing, then."

"That's my bet." I suddenly became aware of how close we were sitting. My mouth felt dry as my gaze locked onto her face. Much of the makeup she'd worn was gone, and a trickle of sweat sliding from under her wig hinted at the reason. Usually we dyed our hair every other day during ops, to account for rapid hair growth, but we'd expected this to be more of a reconnaissance than a combat operation.

With the dead man outside the villa, all that had changed. Meaning the op was working up to be pretty average fare for Renegades. Most of our ops had casualties, though we tried to make them happen on the side of the Emporium and not the innocent mortals we protected.

"I'll text the courier to meet us at the villa," Kenna said, drawing out her phone. The courier service we'd contacted this morning in Lisbon employed a driver in a nearby town who would come for the samples and fly them back to London. The exorbitant price tag on the remote pickup was more than worth getting the samples there before noon tomorrow, and they had promised to send the courier in civilian clothing so as to not attract attention.

We zigzagged across the field, keeping low until the buildings dropped out of site on the horizon. At the bikes, I dug into my pack and took out the samples I'd gathered from the other fields. "Why don't you take these and meet the courier at the villa? No sense in both of us waiting around. I'll go into town and see what I can learn about the man we found."

She opened her mouth to protest, and I wondered if Greggor had warned her to keep me in sight.

"I'll be fine," I said before she could speak. I had plenty of curequick in my pack, if I needed it. Being a native, I was the obvious person to snoop around, and getting the samples to the courier was vital, which meant it was Kenna's responsibility.

"I was just going to say we have company." She looked past me as she spoke, shifting her body into a defensive stance.

I adjusted my position casually, catching sight of two men coming toward us. The heat built inside me as I prepared for a fight.

CHAPTER 3

THEY WEREN'T DRESSED LIKE EMPORIUM AGENTS, AND THEY looked Portuguese, though that didn't say much. The Emporium had many mortal employees. These men didn't look any different from the field hands we'd seen earlier.

Workers, I guessed, *going home for the day.* I didn't relax my readiness, though. The Emporium could be using them.

"*Boa tarde,*" they murmured, nodding.

"Good afternoon," I echoed in Portuguese.

One of the men hesitated, but when his companion didn't pause, he hurried on without stopping. We watched them disappear down the narrow dirt road.

"That's weird," I said. "Portuguese in the country *always* stop to chat. They want to know everything about you."

Kenna laughed. "Ah, give 'em a break. They look knackered. Probably worked all day."

"That's just it, they should be excited about going to a pub or something, but they're heading away from town."

"Maybe they need to go home and shower."

"I guess." The path leading back to the villa was in the same direction the men had taken, and now it was me who was reluctant to let Kenna go, though she could best me in a fair fight. Those two didn't look like Emporium agents, and twenty just like them wouldn't be a match for her.

"I'll see you later then. Stay out of trouble." Climbing onto her bicycle, she rode off without waiting for a response.

I headed in the other direction. It was only ten more minutes before I reached the edge of town. The few people out and about stared at me as I passed, smiling and nodding. The stares weren't unusual. In the larger cities, you almost never saw a Portuguese riding a bicycle—the traffic on the roads and the crush of humanity on the sidewalks made it too difficult. While bike riding was more common in smaller towns, walking was still the preferred mode of transportation for all but the very young. Clearly, I'd been pegged for a tourist. Not exactly the best way to blend in, but there was no changing that now.

I'd ridden up and down almost every street in the town, finding nothing unusual besides the stares, before I steered toward the hospital. An ambulance was pulled up there, and I recognized Dona Mafalda standing near it with a vacant smile on her face.

Leaving the bike, I went to her side. "Hello again."

She turned toward me as if trying to remember who I was.

"I'm staying at the villa? Just came in a few hours ago."

"Oh, yes. Are you enjoying your stay? Do you need something?" Her gaze pulled toward the hospital door, and then back to me.

"No, we're getting along fine. Is everything okay?"

"Yes. It's a beautiful day, isn't it?"

"Someone's not sick I hope," I said.

A fleeting frown and another glance toward the hospital. "No, not sick."

I was about to press further, when a little, bubble-shaped orange car screeched up to the curb and a woman in her mid-thirties jumped out. She was thin, though tall for a Portuguese woman, and mad as hell.

My hand moved toward the gun tucked in a holster at my back, the bulge hidden beneath my T-shirt, but the woman didn't glance at me as she rushed to Dona Mafalda.

She threw her arms around the older woman. "He's dead? Really dead? I told you something would happen, that you needed to leave this town. It's a death trap. Why didn't you listen?"

Dona Mafalda enfolded the newcomer in her embrace. "Everything is fine, daughter," she said, using the term daughter like an endearment. "Everything is fine."

The younger woman pushed away. "It's *not* fine. Papa's dead. DEAD! And you call me like he just has a cold."

"Bridida, calm yourself. It was his time, that's all, my love."

"No it wasn't! Mother, can't you see? Something's wrong here. I'm worried about you."

"Me? But I'm perfectly fine." Dona Mafalda's brow wrinkled with confusion.

"You're not fine. And you're coming home with me. I'm getting you out of here. Something's in the water or the air. Papa's gone, and I'm not losing you too."

"But my café, and the villa . . . new guests arrived today." Dona Mafalda's gaze moved in my direction, as if asking for help.

Her daughter whirled around to glare at me. "Who are you?"

I made my voice as mild as possible. "Paulo. I'm staying at the villa. Your mother takes care of the place."

"Not anymore. I'm sorry. Just leave the key under the mat when you leave. I'll tell the owner." The anger in Brigida's eyes pierced me. "But I wouldn't stay here if I were you."

This brought Dona Mafalda out of her daze. "Oh, dear, don't say that. Monte Vinha is a beautiful town. You always said so. I thought someday you and the kids were going to come back and run the café."

"Not anymore, we're not. Let's go. You're coming with me." Brigida put her arm around her mother, urging her toward the funny orange vehicle. "Wait in the car with Rute and Zezinho while I go inside and take care of things."

"I guess I can come for a visit," Dona Mafalda murmured, smiling as they passed me on the way to the curb.

Two young children were now peering at us from the car, their noses pressed against the window. A boy and a girl, maybe a year or two apart, both preschoolers.

"Don't let them out of the car," warned Brigida with the voice of someone who expected to be obeyed. "And don't tell them about Papa . . . I'll talk to them later."

Once Dona Mafalda was inside the car, her daughter strode purposefully toward the hospital, her fists clenched at her side. I stepped in her way.

"Oh!" she said, apparently having already forgotten I existed.

"Please. What's going on?"

Her jaw clenched and her nostrils flared. "What happened is that my father died today."

"He was sick?" Her father had to be the man we'd found outside the villa, which explained why he'd been there in the first place.

My comment enraged her. "No, he wasn't sick! At least not with anything the doctors could find. I talked to one of them on the phone, and he said my father was simply old, but both his parents and grandparents lived passed their nineties, and he has four older brothers, all still in great health. He was only sixty! But this town is cursed—hardly anyone makes it to seventy."

She had to be wrong, of course. Living in another town meant she wouldn't have kept up with all the residents. "Has anyone else you know here died?"

"Of course—that's the problem."

"How many?" Maybe she was talking one or two more.

"Let me see. There was Dona Ana, Senhor Gato, the eye doctor, the guy who ran the bakery by our house . . ." Her fists unclenched and her fingers popped out as she spoke each name. "Then my friend Monica's parents and Fatima's father and what's-his-name's uncle—I can't remember his name, but we're all friends on Facebook—"

By the time she ran down the list, she had used the fingers of both hands—twice.

"Are these older people? In their sixties? Fifties?"

"Sixties, like my father. They have children and grandchildren. It seems every day there's a new death. My friends and I talk about it all the time."

"Do they get sick first? Go to the hospital?"

"Sometimes. But mostly they just . . . slow down and don't wake up one morning."

She could be describing old age. "So no one else is getting sick? No children?"

"Not that I've heard about." Her eyes widened. "Are you saying the old people are dying? Is it some kind of virus?"

I wasn't suggesting that, but from what she was describing, a virus was a possibility. Except viruses that affected the old often affected children too. Then again, whatever experiments the Emporium was conducting in their fields might eventually kill everyone. Maybe older residents were only the beginning.

"Do-do-do you think it's going to spread? Oh, dear Lord." She looked heavenward and crossed herself. "My mother might already be sick. Maybe that's why she never gets upset when her friends die. She doesn't seem to really understand that her own husband is gone."

The woman looked ready to faint, and I put a steadying hand on her arm. "I saw an old man in the park today. He was fine. Just take your mother home with you and take care of her."

"Right, right." Her head bobbed up and down quickly, as if clamping onto my words. "I have to go inside and make arrangements for my father, but I'll take her back to Évora with me. I can't lose her. My children would be devastated. They're already going to miss their grandfather. He was their favorite." The tears I'd been expecting from her all along began to fall as her anger faded.

"I'm sorry for your loss." I hated seeing women cry. It made me want to melt metal or burst something into flames. Heat built inside my body, and I took my hand away before she felt it.

There was nothing I could do for her or her mother that she wasn't already doing, but I wished I could tell her I would fix the town. Problem was, where the Emporium was concerned, repairing what was wrong might not be possible because they didn't care about mortal casualties like we did. Still, even if it meant killing every last Emporium agent with my bare hands, I would try to make things right here.

"Thank you." She stepped around me and continued her journey into the hospital, wiping furiously at her wet face.

I glanced at Dona Mafalda to see how she was taking her daughter's orders to remain in the car. She sat there smiling, staring through the window with a blank expression and looking for all the world like a sweet grandmother. Apparently, whatever was insulating her from the death of her husband also made her accepting of Brigida's stronger will.

It was downright creepy.

The little boy had climbed into the front seat of the car and was playing with the steering wheel. His older sister still pressed her face against the window, her forehead wrinkled with concern. I hoped they told her sooner rather than later about her grandfather. A hundred and eighty years had taught me that the truth, however devastating, was better than wondering why the adults were suddenly acting crazy.

As I started to turn away, the girl's small hand came up to wave at me. I nodded and waved back, feeling a little silly but glad I did it when a smile replaced the worry on her face.

Back on my bicycle, I headed out of town, realizing that the plastic on the bike handles was melting away. I was also beginning to feel jumpy inside.

I needed to calm down—and I needed more curequick

from my pack. The cravings came faster each day, no matter how I tried putting them off.

That was when I noticed a guy on a moped following me. Not glancing again in his direction, I made a few turns just to make sure.

Yep.

And he didn't look Portuguese.

Losing a single tail might not be a problem, especially now that night was setting in. If there were others set up around the town, I might be in trouble.

It bothered me was that I had no idea how long the man had been following me. Since the hospital? Or maybe the two Portuguese Kenna and I had seen by the vineyard had reported us. Someone could have even spotted us dumping the old man's body, though they'd have to be better at tracking than Kenna to have tailed us that long.

But that really didn't matter. What did matter was if they had tracked me, Kenna might have been followed too.

CHAPTER 4

THE FIRST COURSE OF ACTION WAS TO LOSE THE TAIL. I stopped at a random pub to consider my options and called Kenna while I ordered a beer for cover.

No answer from Kenna. I sent her a text: *Tail.* That would say it all.

Why didn't she answer?

Casually, I scanned the café. The men and women looked like natives, most of their faces bronzed dark by the sun, and their vague smiles reminded me of Dona Mafalda. There was no loud laughter or drunken behavior that typically punctuated these places in the evening, though the night was still young. Not one person appeared over fifty.

A trip to the pub in Portugal was sometimes a family endeavor, but this town seemed to take that to extremes. Children were at almost every table, sitting as docilely as their parents.

Exactly what we'd seen during our first walk through the town, only more accentuated in this environment. I cranked my neck to see if my tail was still out there. He was, and he was chatting on a cell phone.

Great. I wasn't sticking around for his backup to arrive.

I downed the rest of my curequick-laced beer. Already I felt the buzz, soothing my jitters and enhancing my metabolism as it purged the alcohol from my system. Even without curequick, it was impossible for Unbounded to get inebriated with regular-strength alcohol, so at least I had clear senses going for me.

Outside, I jumped on my bike and started pedaling, wishing I'd taken the rental car. That reminded me of Kenna, who still hadn't answered.

I steered down a road, through a narrow alley, and into a park at the center of town. The problem with the moped was that he could go anywhere I could. My only advantage was that I could choose where to stop running. I slowed and let him catch up to me in the park. Night had fallen in earnest now, and given the inevitable confrontation, I was glad for the cover of darkness.

I slipped off my bike, but I didn't step away from it. The metal beneath my hands slowly heated. It wouldn't be long before the tires and seat melted. Would he even notice?

I waited until the man approached. He was grinning, but the expression was nothing like the vacant smiles in the pub. It was knowing and cruel, taunting. He was taller than me by a foot, and his hair was light brown, his eyes blue. With those pale features, he was definitely not native.

"Can I help you?" I said in Portuguese.

He paused, obviously not expecting me to sound like I belonged.

"What were you doing snooping around my fields today?" His Portuguese was fast, but heavily accented. He was English by the sound.

"I'm here on vacation. It's a lovely town."

"We don't get many tourists."

No, because the whole town is nuts, I thought. "That's too bad. It deserves more." I meant that literally. Everyone here deserved more than what the Emporium conglomerate had in store for them.

He stepped off his moped, still not going for a weapon, but the gleam in his eyes told me I'd been made. Maybe he detected the scorn in my voice instead of the fear he was accustomed to hearing. I doubted it. He didn't look that smart. More likely, his ability was combat and his instincts told him I was a serious threat.

I'd have to gamble on having the advantage of surprise. Otherwise, I might be the one roasted.

"So, what brings you to our town?" He jiggled the key to his moped in his left hand like a nervous tic.

"Your town?" It came out a half snort. "Oh, that's right—you said the fields were yours. But you don't sound native. How long have you lived here? A few months?"

His lips came together in a grimace that told me the

poor baby imagined he had a decent command of the language.

Closer, closer, I thought at him.

He obliged, his right hand moving toward the gun he'd have hidden at his back. I couldn't let him get too far.

Now. I released my grip on the bicycle.

The man instinctively put out his left hand to catch the handle where the rubber guard had long dripped to the ground.

His scream was instantaneous, as was the smell of searing flesh. Part of the handle bar came away, fusing with his hand. That he still managed to draw his gun said a lot about his skill and confirmed my suspicions about him being Unbounded. But the pain was too much even for him, and almost immediately, he curled over his wounded hand. The seat of the bike scraped his leg on the way down, smearing the hot remains of the padding and metal underneath.

His screams somehow grew louder. Definitely going to draw a crowd. My gun was already in hand, so I fired two shots into his torso. The screaming stopped.

Really, I'd done him a favor. If he was lucky, most of the damage caused by the molten metal would be healed before his heart started beating again. Depending on how much curequick he might already have in his body.

Furtively, I scanned the park for movement, but no one was running in my direction or shouting. I heaved a sigh of relief. Except I couldn't just leave him here. Even if no one stumbled on him tonight, he'd be found by morning when the women cut through the park on the way to Saturday market. The townspeople might be complacent, but they couldn't ignore an apparently life-less body in the middle of the walkway. But if I somehow managed to take him back to the villa, there was no guar-antee I could find and destroy his tracking chip before his comrades found him.

A greater concern was Kenna.

The thought of her decided me. For now, this guy could wait in the bushes. They were a little too sparse to hide much during the day but were adequate by night. It took only fifteen seconds to drag him to the densest area.

The bicycle was useless, but the moped was a better choice anyway. I ran to it, nearly colliding with a dark figure. At once my hands burned with readiness, my gift eager to be used. I reached out.

And stopped.

It was the old guy Kenna and I had seen earlier in the park. He stood in front of me dressed in a dark coat that draped on his thin frame. His gray hair was slightly askew, his face brushed with a day or two's growth of stubble.

How much had he seen?

Protocol indicated that I incapacitate him so he wouldn't jeopardize the op, but he looked just like my short, wizened grandpa, and there was no way I was going to punch him, or even drug him. For all I knew, I would accidentally kill the only aged person in the entire town.

"Keep quiet," I told him. "The whole town is at risk. I'm trying to fix it."

His dark eyes glittered in the moonlight, his face expressionless. He didn't reply but looked past me right at the bushes.

I was screwed.

Nothing I could do about it. Jumping onto the moped, I prepared to flee. Where was the stupid key? Belatedly I remembered it in the Emporium agent's left hand. No doubt it was part of the fused mess of my bicycle now.

The old guy was still watching me.

"Do you have a car?" I demanded.

His eyes went to my gun. I wasn't pointing it at him, but I would if I had to.

"Come with me," he said, his words garbled by either age or fear.

I followed him from the park and down a side street until we came to a squat motorcycle with a ridiculously huge, tightly-woven wicker basket bolted to a homemade frame on the back. Similar setups had once been more familiar in Portugal, their owners often stacking an entire pickup load of wares into these homemade baskets. If the situation had been different, I would have been amused at the quaintness.

Five large cardboard boxes half full of vegetables crammed into this particular basket. Interesting. Did the old man grow them himself or did he work for the Emporium?

He took a key from a ring and handed it to me. "I would like it back," he said, "when you are finished. Please."

I nodded. I was trying to protect humanity, but I was taking what was probably his entire livelihood. "I'll leave it here with the key in the basket."

He reached in and heaved out one of the boxes. "Room for the body," he muttered.

I wanted to tell him to stop, that I wasn't going back for the agent, but I had a few questions. Grabbing a box, I asked, "You're a farmer? You grow these?"

"All my life." He set down another box. "Used to do good business before that man and the others came." He jerked his head toward the park.

"They sell vegetables in town?"

A brisk nod. "If you can call it selling. They practically give food away. People won't buy my veggies anymore. I mostly take 'em to friends."

"You eat your own?"

He chuckled. "Of course. They taste better."

I doubted that—I'd eaten the grapes in the vineyard— but he was still alive. That was more than I could say for Dona Mafalda's husband and the others her daughter had listed.

"You never eat any of their food?"

He spat out his disgust. "I make it a point not to."

Which was good for me, since he didn't seem too concerned about reporting my assault.

"What about bread?" Surely the old man bought bread

here, and with all those wheat fields, the Emporium had to be selling flour locally as well.

"One of my cousin's sons owns a bakery, next town over. I go there twice a week."

We'd finished unloading the boxes, and I threw my leg over the motorcycle. "I would keep eating your vegetables," I said. "And that guy in the park? I don't have time to deal with him now, but if things work out, I'll be back for him."

"I hope before he wakes up."

I stared, forgetting whatever I'd been going to say next. Apparently the old guy was sharper than I'd given him credit. Sometime during the past years, he'd witnessed something he shouldn't have, and the Emporium's carelessness about keeping our existence a secret said volumes about the fate they planned for the town. I was betting no one was meant to survive.

Yes, they will.

I dipped my head to the old man, and kicked the engine to life. *I'm coming, Kenna,* I thought. Finally.

She'd better be okay, or I *would* be coming back for the Emporium agent, and he'd regret the day he'd Changed.

CHAPTER 5

I LEFT THE MOTORCYCLE A HALF MILE FROM THE VILLA AND ran the rest of the way. When I reached it, the place was utterly dark. A sedan that didn't belong sat outside the house next to our rented one with no sign of an occupant. Dread crawled across my shoulders.

Drawing my gun, I headed around the back. Kenna's bike was neatly stored on the cobbled deck where we'd found it—and in a lot better shape than mine. Everything looked peaceful, from the moon reflected in the rippling water of the swimming pool, to the whispers of the wind through the leaves of the trees lining the patio.

I didn't fool myself that Kenna was resting. If she'd finished here, she would have joined me in town. Besides, there was that little matter of the extra car sitting out front. I stepped to the back door. Sure enough, it was slightly ajar.

Dropping my pack to the ground by the door, I eased into the house, pausing just inside the door to allow my eyes to adjust to the dark. Already I could see evidence of a struggle. Two figures sprawled on the floor, the sofa was overturned and a swath of ripped fabric hung from its side. Everything else was too dark to see. I inched forward.

A dark figure hurtled at me from behind the couch. The next instant, a blow threw my gun across the room. My first punch was blocked, but I landed the second. So did my opponent. Breath rushed from me as pain spread across my chest. I kicked out, but nothing was there. A fist landed on my jaw from the other direction. I feigned right and punched left, but the blow only grazed my opponent, who'd dodged out of the way.

Combat Unbounded, I thought. No way for me to beat him without using my own ability.

Heat gathered in my hands. All I needed was to touch the Emporium agent for more than a few seconds and this would be over. Finding those few seconds, however, might be fatal.

I took two pounding blows, trying to find an opening. A third blow met my ribs with an agonizing *crack!* But exposing myself afforded the opportunity to latch onto an arm. My opponent struggled to pull away, gasping with pain. I held on. My whole body burned with heat.

"Blaze," the figure screamed. "Stop!"

Kenna.

Damn.

The next moment, we were falling, and I was sucking back the heat. It was easier to turn it off than to begin, but her grunts of pain as we fell told me I wasn't fast enough.

At last, she lay pinned under me, soft in all the right places.

I'd hurt her. "Are you okay?"

"Fine. *Get off!*"

Right. I rolled off her, clenching my jaw against the pain in my ribs. "Is anyone else here?"

"No. I took care of the last one right before you arrived. I thought you were their reinforcements." Her voice was faint, and her rapid breathing told me she was hurt badly.

"Do you think they called backup?"

"I don't know."

I left her side and crawled to the lamp that was on the floor next to the overturned sofa. Every movement sent needles of pain through my ribs and chest. As long as I took shallow breaths, the pain was bearable, but with my luck, I'd get to the stupid lamp and it would be broken.

Too slowly, I passed the two sprawled figures, both men, dressed in black from head to toe. They were definitely dead, at least for now. I'd need to secure them before they awoke. I reached the lamp, flipping the switch, and to my surprise, light flared into the room. I crawled back to Kenna, trying not to breathe too deeply.

Kenna still lay where I'd left her. Her wig was gone, revealing red hair pinned tightly to her head. A large section of her bare left arm was blackened, and I guessed the damage was deep enough to kill the nerves because she was moving the arm without sobbing. She'd need time to regenerate. The rest of her skin was only little reddened, so I hadn't damaged her anywhere else, but sometime during the evening, she'd taken a bullet in her thigh. How she'd managed to fight me at all was a testament to her ability.

Searching the room, I found a nine mil on the carpet—not mine or hers. I checked the magazine; six out of ten bullets left. "Here," I said, giving it to her before climbing painfully to my feet. "I'll get the kit." I was back in a minute, locking the doors and closing the shutters and curtains on the way. I wanted a warning if we had any more visitors.

From our medical kit, I took out several syringes of curequick mixed with pain killer. Deep wounds always benefitted from curequick injections, and she'd need them to get walking again. My hands shook as I fitted a needle.

I glanced to see Kenna watching me. "You'd better take some first."

Grimacing, I looked away, unable to meet her gaze as I tried to remember where I'd left the pack with my curequick. An injection into my bloodstream would be better for the pain, but in a way, it was nice to feel something besides the buzz from the curequick or the horrible aching need addiction left in my gut.

Kenna fished something from a pocket near her waistband. "Here," she said, tossing it.

I barely caught the tiny pouch of curequick, flattened and still warm from her body. Nodding my thanks, I ripped the top open with my teeth and sucked it in.

My shaking easing, I injected her leg first, checking to see how bad it was. The bullet had gone in, but there was no exit wound. "I'm going to have to remove the bullet." Removing it would aid in healing, which we needed her to do fast.

"Give me two minutes. I won't feel anything by then."

She was right. Our pain killers had to be strong or they wouldn't stick around in our bodies long enough for surgery.

"I should have known it was you," she said as I made tiny injections around and in the blackened skin on her arm. She didn't flinch.

"Why's that?"

"You make a lot of noise."

I glanced toward the fallen men. "They didn't?" Why was she still alive then?

"No noise, but I stopped to look at the watering system on one of the other fields and caught a glimpse of them. No mistaking an Emporium hit team. So I came in the front and snuck around the back and waited for the one who tried to enter there. I would have had them both but . . . but . . ." Sudden moisture filled her eyes. She closed them, her expression becoming rigid, impassive.

"Did I hurt you?" I pulled out the empty needle.

She shook her head. "It's not that. The courier service sent a woman, but the other Emporium agent picked the front lock, and he was inside when she arrived. He answered the door, let her in, probably thinking it was me. I didn't get to her in time." Her gaze strayed to her leg, and I guessed she had taken the bullet trying to save the woman.

"Where is she? Maybe . . ." Standing, I saw the very young woman dressed in khaki pants and a blue shirt. She was curled up on the other side of the sofa, one of the cushions obscuring half her body. A black bag lay open near her, papers spilled over the floor.

"She's gone," Kenna said before I could move toward the girl. "I was checking when you came." Her voice was devoid of emotion but somehow told me more than if she'd let the tears fall. "We're supposed to help mortals, not send them to their deaths."

I thought of the old man and knew exactly how she felt. I hadn't hurt him, but I would have if it had meant saving all the others in the town.

"I'm sorry," I said.

She nodded. "Me too."

A single silent tear strayed down her face. Swallowing hard, I turned and retrieved the sofa cushion that wasn't covering the courier and worked it under Kenna's head.

"You can only do what you can," I said.

When she didn't respond, I pushed on the edges of her gun wound with my finger. She didn't stiffen but looked away as I took a scalpel from the medical kit and cut into her leg deep enough to remove the bullet. I followed the extraction with a few stitches and a bandage.

She studied me as I scooted next to her on the floor. "It's not your fault, you know," she said.

"What?"

"The addiction."

"Of course it's my fault."

"You forget I've been a part of the ops. I've seen what Greggor and the others did to you, sending you in again and again. And you coming back dead or so damaged they had to submerge your entire body in curequick to get you to regenerate in time for the next op."

I couldn't look away from her mesmerizing eyes and those pale cheeks. "It was my choice. I knew the risk."

"You were in mourning."

I didn't need to tell her what it had done to me to watch my wife age and die. In her lifetime, Kenna had already experienced that same loss. Older Unbounded said it got easier.

"They should have given you more time between ops."

"Maybe."

Grimacing with pain, she moved toward me until our bodies touched along the length of our sides. "Not maybe. Definitely. The fact that they keep sending you proves you're capable, but I think they've pushed you too far. After this, you have to tell them no. You have to take care of yourself first. You need to get free."

She was so beautiful. I wanted to kiss each of those

freckles, taste her lips, explore her body. I wanted to eat grapes off the vine and take her to the second house I owned on the Portuguese coast. It would never happen unless I was free.

"Okay," I said.

She rested her head on my shoulder, and I slipped an arm around her, gently pulling her closer. My chest felt tight. How long had I wanted to hold her this way? Even this afternoon the idea was out of reach, but now staying this way forever seemed like a possibility.

Except it wasn't. Kenna needed a few more minutes to heal and for a little of the numbness to recede before we could move, but in the meantime, we had to come up with a plan.

I dragged my attention back to our situation. "I was followed too." I told her about Dona Mafalda's daughter, the man on the moped, and the old guy in the park. "I think they've genetically modified the food. To kill. I don't know if it's a poison or a virus or something else altogether, and I have no idea why it's killing older people, or if there are other casualties we aren't aware of."

"But the Emporium is going to need mortals in the new world they want to create. A virus might kill too many workers the Emporium would need to provide special services."

"Yes, but they don't need old people—and they won't need mortals forever. Without the war between Renegades and Emporium, we'll multiply, and sooner or later our longer lives mean we'll far outnumber mortals. Then the Emporium won't need any of them."

"But even with genetic manipulation, only half our offspring Change."

"Exactly. More than enough to fill any grunt position. The Emporium has never been above using their own children."

Kenna looked thoughtful. "If you're right, the Emporium plans to have mortals work until whatever is in that food does its job and kills them. The money saved on health care alone would be astronomical."

"And you've seen how weird everyone is here. Docile, absently friendly, smiling at everything."

"No rebelling. No protest."

"Exactly."

"We have to stop it."

"They'll be coming for us," I countered.

"I know. Let's call Greggor for a quick update; he's waiting for our report. I only need a minute or two more. I should be able to move then."

"Even if he can send backup, they won't get here in time."

"I know."

I put in my password and dialed the number. Nothing. "There's no cell service."

"Try the laptop. Maybe you damaged your phone when you melted the bicycle."

I had a feeling it couldn't be that easy. It never was when we went head-to-head with the Emporium.

Leaving Kenna, I went to retrieve my laptop. Already I was breathing a little easier, and by tomorrow, my ribs wouldn't even twinge.

My laptop appeared miraculously undamaged on the floor by the coffee table, and as I reached for it, I couldn't help seeing the face of the courier. She looked so young, so peaceful, despite her violent death. We'd have to make sure her family was taken care of, if she had any.

Seated again next to Kenna, I attempted to link to the Internet over my laptop's internal data connection, while she patted herself down, looking for her phone.

"Nope," I said. "Not working either."

"Then I guess it won't help to find my phone. I was trying to text you when I got busy with those agents. I've no idea where it ended up. We'll try the satellite connection when we get outside, if they haven't blocked that too." She rotated up onto the knee of her good leg. "Let's go."

I wanted to protest that she wasn't ready, but I knew it didn't matter. We'd already stayed too long. When these Emporium agents didn't report in, someone would come looking for them. Besides, combat Unbounded were better than the rest of us at pushing through the pain.

At that moment we heard the chopper.

We were too late.

CHAPTER 6

KENNA WAS UP BEFORE I WAS, REACHING FOR THE GUN I'D given her earlier and dragging her wounded leg behind her. I hit the destruct button on my laptop, snatched up another gun, and barely beat her to the back door. "We have to get into the trees," she said. "Before they trap us."

I yanked open the sliding glass door and put one arm around her waist, the other arm scooping her legs out from under her before she could protest. Without checking the sky, I ran from the house, carrying her. Bullets sprayed us from the approaching chopper, but they were still too far away to be accurate. My ribs screamed, and every bruise Kenna had given me in our fight burned with renewed pain. I pushed myself harder.

With relief, I watched the trees rise up before me. Kenna struggled in my arms, and I let her down before she broke any more of my bones, keeping my arm around her waist for support. The trees were planted too far apart to be decent cover, but at least they gave us something to dart in and out of as we headed for the denser patch of wild olive trees farther in.

I glanced back once and saw men perched on the edge of the chopper, rifles in hand.

Something sliced into the fleshy part of my upper right arm, and agony rippled through my body. From long habit, I bit down hard on a scream.

We made it to the thicker grove, where the heavy brush between the trees afforded better cover but made our flight more difficult. I half carried Kenna as we fought our way through, and it became clear that I wasn't the only one hit. Kenna's arm was also bleeding where she'd been grazed. No time to take care of either of us.

"Wait," she said after a moment. "They'll be dropping men to come after us. We need transportation they won't expect. Otherwise, we won't be fast enough to escape."

The old man's motorbike came to mind. It wouldn't go fast, and with the basket it was an awkward ride—not to mention a substantial target, but it would be better using it on the open road than traversing the countryside on foot.

"I left a motorcycle half a mile from the house, but in the other direction, on the way to town." Even as I spoke, I didn't know if she could make it that far fast enough to stay ahead of them.

"Let's backtrack and then circle around for it. We might be able to temporarily throw them off our trail."

"I've got a better idea." I held up my hands. "Let's make a distraction."

She nodded. "Okay, wait until I tell you."

"Yes, boss," I mocked, but without any bite in the words. Her guess would be more accurate than anything I could come up with.

We retraced our steps until we could hear the men moving through the brush, then we angled off to the left. We'd stumbled along exactly two minutes in the new direction when she stopped us. "Here. Do it here."

Releasing her, I squatted and rubbed my hand over some brush, dry from a long hot summer. In seconds, the heat transferred and the vegetation burst into flames. A bit of fire raced up my arm, singeing the hair, but I rubbed it out and repeated the process on the next clump of bushes, working in a line. Flames crackled, gobbling up the dry patches first before spreading to the greener bushes and trees.

Kenna touched my shoulder. "Enough."

Right. The flames were moving in all directions, coming dangerously closer. I put an arm around her and we ran.

Her leg seemed less numb now as the drugs worked through her body, but that meant more pain, and all this running was only making her wounds worse. My own arm and shoulder throbbed and there was enough blood that I'd need to tie it up soon. My shirt would do the trick for both of us once we got a chance to stop.

The end of the trees came sooner than expected.

Smoke filled our lungs, making it difficult to breathe, but my anxiety lessened when I spied the old man's motorcycle behind the tree where I'd abandoned it. Ripping off my shirt, now damp with sweat, I handed it to Kenna and dug for the keys in my pocket. Blood dripped down my arm to the ground, and shaking was already setting in. For the first time in a very long time I didn't have my pack or any curequick with me. My mouth went dry at the thought.

Wordlessly, Kenna ripped my shirt, tying a folded strip around my upper arm. I tore off another strip and fastened it around the blood seeping from her arm. Already I could see pink skin eating away at the edges of her burn on the same limb, but the healing wasn't coming fast enough for either of us.

She mounted the bike, taking control, and I climbed on behind her. Kenna's faster reflexes made her the best choice for driving, while I could cover us with the gun I'd taken from the villa.

On the dirt road, out of the trees, we were a clear target, but we reached the end of the road without incident and turned onto the paved one, heading out of town. Part of me regretted the choice to run from the Emporium agents, even while I knew it was the only responsible option. We had to regroup and decide what to do. Since we'd been compromised, I suspected Kenna would make the call to retreat and wait for backup, no matter how she felt about it personally.

It wasn't a terrible decision. While our mission hadn't

exactly been a success, we had an idea of what we were up against, and our Renegade cell could make an intelligent decision about how to proceed. Even if the Emporium took all their research and began again elsewhere, they no longer had the element of secrecy.

The downside was that we still didn't have a clear idea of what the Emporium was doing here or why this area was so important to them. Without knowing more about their experiments, we might not be able to help the townspeople who were already damaged. Understanding what was in the food and how long the townspeople had consumed it would make it easier to stop the progression and possibly reverse the damage. It would also help us know what to look for the next time the Emporium set up shop to experiment on mortals.

Thoughts banged around inside my brain, pushing to be heard, but that contrasted with the surprisingly pleasant fragrance of Kenna's pinned hair and the feel of her body in front of me. Between her closeness and the pain, I could barely think.

As if on some sort of signal, Kenna eased off the gas. I scanned both sides of the road in search of what she must have spotted, but we were alone. She shifted into neutral with her bad leg and cut the engine altogether, her body tensing in reaction from the movement. We hurtled forward for another half minute before coming to a stop at the side of the road.

"What is it?" I asked, putting my feet down on either side of the bike to balance it, not trusting her leg.

"I think I see something up ahead." She reached into the pocket of her shorts for the small set of binoculars she'd used earlier. The idea of her hidden pockets brought me a sliver of hope. Maybe she had more curequick.

"Yeah," she said, peering through them. "Two trucks parked across the road. A car too. Can't see how many men, but I'm betting they're Emporium." She smacked the gasoline tank. "I bet they have all the roads covered. And any other likely exit points. No easy way for us to get out of town. Looks like we've made right bags of this op."

Meaning we'd messed up. She was right about that, but testing the populace and the produce in the fields would reveal a lot, so maybe we'd done enough.

Or maybe that was my need for curequick talking.

"We just need to stay clear until Greggor realizes we've missed our report and sends backup," I told Kenna. I wasn't sure who he could send, but we had enough Renegade allies in Europe that he would manage to round up an able crew.

Scowling, she offered me the binoculars, then swung her good leg over the motorbike and stood a bit awkwardly, still holding onto one handlebar. "They're looking this way, but I don't think they've identified us yet. Must have heard the motorbike. We can hide in the trees until we decide what to do."

I knew she was waiting for me to move the bike, but I was staring at the familiar orange car in front of the trucks. The bubble-fronted vehicle was parked askew in the middle of the right lane, as if halted abruptly. It didn't look like anyone was inside.

One of the men broke away from the others and started toward us. Time to go.

I returned Kenna's binoculars and began pushing the motorbike into the trees. They'd be able to track us if they looked hard enough, but given the distance, they might assume we'd driven back the way we'd come. If it came to it, I could always start another fire to mask our trail.

"We might not be the only ones they're preventing from leaving," I said to Kenna. "Remember Dona Mafalda's daughter? That little orange car looks exactly like hers. You think they stopped her because the guy following me saw us talking?"

"Maybe, but if it's only about keeping everyone here, why not just make her turn around? Why is the car still there?"

I had no answer except that Brigida had probably put up some kind of fuss about not being allowed to leave, and the Emporium hadn't reacted well.

My fault. I should have soothed Brigida's worries, not asked questions that emphasized them. For all I knew, she and her family were lying dead on the floor of that car. Except there was no obvious damage to the vehicle—and the Emporium had never been known for "neat" kills.

Kenna let out a sigh. "The way they've come at us, I don't think the Emporium is going to back down. Even if they catch us, they know it won't be long until our people come to find out what happened."

A thought stopped the reply on my lips. "That old guy in the park? He knew the agent I killed would regenerate."

"So the Emporium hasn't been careful about hiding their abilities." Kenna's voice betrayed her anger. "That means they don't intend to leave. No wonder they've locked down the city. My guess is they'll either fortify the town with more agents so we can't get close, or they'll destroy the entire town."

Leaving no witnesses, and no people or crops to test.

I'd fought against the Emporium long enough to know their methods, but shock struck me anyway at her words. The people in this town were my kinsfolk. *Mine.* And this was my fight.

I took a steadying breath before saying, "The daughter knows something's going on here, and she was vocal about it. She had two kids with her." In my mind, I could still see the girl, her hand lifted in a trusting wave. The thought that she might never go home to her father, that she'd likely not survive the coming battle, made me ill.

Kenna gave me a sympathetic glance. "I was hoping the agents would be slow to realize the threat, but it seems I underestimated them."

"We can't let this happen," I said. "Those townspeople are like children themselves."

"You know the protocol. We don't have a choice. I'm sorry."

I knew she was.

We stumbled through the increasingly dense foliage, mostly bushes and an occasional olive or oak tree. We couldn't see the road now, so this was as good a place as any to stop and talk.

The faint sound of a siren reached our ears. "Looks like they're responding to the fire at least," Kenna said. "That's a sign they'll be fighting for control of the town, not running."

"In the end, it'll all be the same to the people."

"I know."

I came to a stop and faced her. "I have to go back."

"No you don't."

"I can't let them hurt those kids. Or the town."

She stared at me for a long moment as the darkness pressed in around us, her face only half lit by the overhead moon. Being a combat Unbounded, she had final say in our tactics, but I was going whether she agreed or not. Finally, she said, "You're a good man, Blaze Vincent."

I wasn't so sure of that, but I'd be damned if I'd stand by in relative safety while Dona Mafalda's family was being held somewhere by the Emporium because of their connection to me. These people were simple country folk, and the Emporium had no business messing in their lives.

"I'll cause more distractions," I told Kenna. "That'll keep them busy until you can contact Greggor and arrange backup. That way the Emporium won't have time to plan a resistance." I extracted my phone from my pocket, showing her the passcode that would open it without triggering the self-destruct. "Even if you can't make it to a place where you have service, Greggor should still be able to track your chip once they get close enough. Then you can all come for me. I'll meet you here, if I can."

Kenna pocketed my phone with barely a glance. "I'm going with you."

If the situation were reversed, I'd never let her go alone either, but this was my element. I'd successfully completed many similar ops. Going in as a distraction while the rest of the group carried out the real mission. Blocking the fear with swigs of curequick, not really caring what happened to me. Maybe even hoping, just a little, that the end would come swiftly.

I forced a smile. "We could both get caught."

She swallowed hard, and for a moment I was distracted by the motion of her throat and by the expression in her eyes. I wanted to kiss her, to trace her throat with my mouth, to taste her lips. Maybe she'd even let me.

No. I wouldn't try. The bullet wound and my body's struggle to repair the damage had increased my ever-present desire for curequick, and the yearning made me unsteady. The fear the curequick buzz normally kept in check careened rampant through my brain like some kind of crazy game of table tennis. She'd feel that I wasn't okay if I got close. She'd remember what kind of man I really was.

Kenna's face was unyielding. "We're partners. Together we have a better chance of finding what we came for—and more chance of getting away if we get caught."

Partners. We were that. I felt it as I hadn't with anyone else for years. "Okay."

We trudged back through the trees with the motorcycle, angling farther down the road in the direction of the villa. Kenna seemed to be walking with more ease now, which boded well for our new focus.

A cloud drifted over the moon, plunging us into darkness. Still, I saw her in my mind, the length of her throat, her eyes delving into mine. Tomorrow, maybe I'd kiss her.

If either of us were still alive.

CHAPTER 7

ALREADY I WAS PUSHING BACK THE JITTERS THAT TEMPTED me to curl up on the ground and howl like some rabid dog. So far, we hadn't run into any sign that we'd been pursued, but I was beginning to worry about how we'd get to Dona Mafalda and her family.

"The Emporium could be keeping them anywhere," I said. "*If* they've taken them." There was a chance they hadn't, but only a very slim one because of the abandoned car.

Kenna's head shifted in my direction, though I couldn't make out her features. "The only area we've seen them guarding is the compound near the vineyard. I'd say that's the best place to start. It's probably also where they're keeping their records." Kenna might care about helping me find Dona Mafalda's family, but her mention of the records told me she also hoped to complete our original mission.

Getting to the Emporium's compound meant at least a mile to town and another few miles beyond. With my wounds, walking was torture, and I suspected Kenna was experiencing a similar pain. Using the motorcycle might be worth the risk of the Emporium hearing us, but the basket made it impossible to drive through the trees, unless we traveled close to the road where the vegetation was sparse. Closer to the road was infinitely more dangerous.

I could remove the basket, but there was only one way to do that without tools, and that included the possibility of exploding the gas tank and ruining our only means of transportation. If only I weren't shaking so badly.

"We're wasting time," Kenna said, apparently coming to the same decision. She stopped walking and went down on her good knee. "You can melt the bolts holding this basket, right? Without blowing it up?" Trust her to get right to the point.

"Maybe. You have any curequick?" I hated to ask.

A quick shake of her head. "All back at the villa. I gave you the only pouch I had on me."

"Right." Forcing a smile, I squatted and peered under the motorcycle. *Steady,* I thought, reaching out a finger to the first of the four huge nuts. It melted without incident, followed by the second.

I was reaching for the third when a sudden crack of a branch made me careless, and the nut melted in a rush, liquefying also the bolt and the metal plates protecting the wicker, and leaving a fist-size hole in the basket itself. So much for my promise to the old man.

"This way! I hear something!" a voice called. Maybe in English or German—I was in too much of a hurry to do anything more than understand the meaning. Definitely not Portuguese.

Kenna drew her gun, placing her body between me and the voices. Leaving the last nut intact, I jumped on the motorcycle and started the engine. Kenna hopped on behind me, one hand wrapping around my bare chest as I popped the clutch, almost throwing us off the seat with the abruptness. The basket bounced, sending the three loose bolts flying.

I caught a glimpse of two men and assault rifles in my peripheral vision. I pushed harder on the gas, hurtling us forward through the trees. The basket twisted to the side, slamming into a tree and then back again.

Shots rang out after us, and Kenna fired back, emptying her entire magazine before turning to reload. The gun was one an Emporium agent had dropped at the villa and the magazine was different from her own, so she couldn't just slam in a new one from her endless pockets. By the time she'd reloaded the magazine, the men were long behind us.

I headed for the open road, urging the old bike to its limit, the engine screaming under the strain. The horizon in the direction of the villa was aglow, but not raging, so they must have the blaze under control. I was glad for that; I didn't want to hurt any of the Portuguese residents.

The expectation of seeing headlights from an

Emporium truck behind us was so great it was almost a relief when they finally appeared. I was nearly at the town, which was strangely deserted, though everyone must have heard the fire engines. I drove into an alley and out the other side, losing the black truck but running into another one two streets later.

I screeched to a sliding stop, turning as we skidded toward the truck. Shots fired from the windows, one ricocheting off the gas tank. The basket, still attached by that one bolt, jerked to one side and back again. Kenna let off only one return shot this time, apparently preserving ammunition.

Tearing down another alley, we came out just in front of a third truck. They were closing in on us now. More shots had me ducking and tensing for a possible impact.

If they caught us, they would kill us—but not permanently. Not yet. I would only wish they had. No, they'd torture us for information and breed us for our talents. Keep us in a locked cell for decades or centuries until they had no use for us. Then they would chop us up, severing the three focus parts of our bodies. A final death.

Neither of us would go easily. Kenna let off another shot, blowing a tire on the truck behind us.

Only two more streets. There. I could see the end of the town. If I could make it to the countryside, the trucks wouldn't be able to follow so fast through the trees, and we might stand a chance of reaching our target. One truck was still hot on our tail, and I glimpsed another on a parallel road through the side streets. To my left, the swift river and the three-foot wall bordering it cornered me every bit as much as the trucks.

But the way in front was still clear.

Then it wasn't. A dark truck squealed to block the end of the street, men with rifles piling from the back. No way could we run that gauntlet. I had my gun, and Kenna had whatever bullets were left in hers, but they would be useless against so many.

That left only one option.

I swerved sharply to the right and then to the left, gunning the engine. Kenna's hands dug into my sides. Seconds seemed to turn into minutes as we careened toward the short wall that bordered the river. With a sickening screech, metal ground into concrete. The impact sent us flying up, up, and over—into the rushing water. The bike stayed behind on the road, but the wicker basket, finally shaken loose, came splashing into the water after us.

More shots peppered the river. Kenna dived, and I followed, letting the water bury me and carry me away. Unbounded could absorb oxygen from the water, so we could stay under longer than the average mortal, but after twenty or thirty minutes, we'd eventually lose consciousness and surrender to the water.

The river was swifter and colder than I'd expected, and scattered rocks along the bottom battered at me as I passed. When I finally came up, trucks, town, and bullets had been left behind. The *whomp-whomp* of a chopper reached my ears, but it was still some distance away by the sound.

"Grab on," Kenna called.

She clung to the damaged remains of the wicker basket, and I reached for it myself, floating with the current for a few blissful minutes. The basket was definitely the best option to keep afloat and preserve energy for now. I might even be growing fond of the stupid thing.

The adrenaline blasting through my body had temporarily masked my need for curequick, but the craving would return soon, and I needed to remain strong. And warm. My ability couldn't heat the entire river, but I could heat the water around me, even turn some of it into steam, if needed. Letting off only a bit of energy, I heated the water immediately around us so our muscles wouldn't lock up with the cold.

Kenna threw me an amused glance, telling me she'd noticed, but she didn't comment.

The sounds of the chopper faded—a good sign, I hoped. The river would take us closer to the vineyard, but I knew from studying the layout earlier that it veered off before reaching the buildings. We needed to get out before then—and on the left side.

As the adrenaline rush eased, my shaking increased. The bend in the river approached, and Kenna took off swimming in an angle toward the bank, but I waited a second too late. I struggled, the rush of water pulling me past the bend. Maybe I'd drown after all, and the Emporium would be waiting with an interrogator when I revived.

No.

I took a deep breath and plunged into the water, pushing outward with my hands until the water around me boiled, steaming away like water in a pan on the stove. In that instant, I pushed against the river bottom and drove myself upward, popping out of the water and catching onto the branch of a scraggly tree growing halfway down the bank.

Crawling onto solid ground, I collapsed, sucking in air and pulling back my gift before I melted the earth and rocks and set fire to the forest. The shaking in my body grew worse, and so did my pain. All I wanted was another swig of curequick so I could do my job.

Only the image of the little girl waving at me from the car urged me to my feet, to join Kenna at the top of the bank. "Ready to do this?" she asked, seeming remarkably chipper in the face of our dire circumstances.

This. It was what we were born to do—fight, protect, serve.

"Yeah." I unholstered the gun I'd taken from the villa, hoping it still worked after my dip in the river, and started forward. My stumbling pace eventually worked into an awkward jog. Kenna was no longer even limping.

Reaching the vineyard, we bent over and crept to the last row of vines. My gut twisted in protest and my internal voice told me to wait until backup arrived. But I had a vested interest in these people, and Dona Mafalda's little family in particular.

Kenna had lost the binoculars in the river, but we couldn't see anyone patrolling this section of the fence.

Maybe all their guards were out searching for us. These buildings were probably the last place they expected us to go. Crawling on my belly, I made it to the fence, reaching out to melt enough of it to open a good-sized hole.

So far, so good.

"Which building?" Kenna asked.

"I doubt they have a place to keep prisoners in the storage barns or processing facilities. So I'm guessing there." I pointed to the squat building we'd seen guards going in and out of earlier. The yellow paint on the building's stucco looked a dull gray in the darkness.

"As good a place as any to start." Kenna lead the way, sprinting across the open space to the yellow building. I followed with a lot less grace.

We found a darkened window toward the back. Kenna stood watch as I heated the glass, feeling it start to buckle under my touch.

With a warning hiss, Kenna tugged me back from the window. She jerked her head in the direction of two guards swaggering toward the building next door where the cabbage workers had unloaded their harvest.

Pressing myself to the ground close to the building, I gripped my gun and waited until they disappeared inside. My head buzzed with a need that was growing harder to ignore. I had to hurry and finish this.

Kenna gave the all clear, and I climbed to my feet. Reaching out to the window, I finished heating the glass, sending a molten mass dripping down both sides of the sill, glowing with the intensity of my ability.

As we waited for it to cool, another guard rounded the building, giving a surprised shout as Kenna launched herself toward him. Her movements were liquid and sure, but the Emporium agent met her stroke for stroke.

Combat Unbounded, I thought, watching this strange and deadly dance.

Kenna spun and offered a final kick in the stomach that sent him careening backwards into the building. His head slammed into the stucco with an echoing *crack!* As he slid down the side into a messy heap, Kenna bent over him, her hands coming up with a gun and more ammo.

Climbing through the window, we found ourselves in a small, deserted kitchen. Kenna raced across the room toward the door, opening it to reveal a narrow dimly-lit hallway. No one in sight. Kenna took two steps, but jumped back before I could follow. Her hand signaled for silence.

Clop, clop, clop. Measured footsteps came down the hall. A man spoke, his voice soon joined by two others, the tones urgent. More footsteps. We waited, my heartbeat sounding like a drum in my ears. This time the adrenaline didn't seem to take even the edge off my craving.

Far too soon, Kenna moved forward in a blur, shooting a woman and sending a man to the ground with a few choice kicks. I pushed the remaining man against the wall, my gun pointed at his pale face.

"Don't move," I ordered in English, almost hoping he'd disobey so I could shoot him.

"Okay! Okay. Don't shoot!" His entire body shook.

"Your people stopped two women with a couple kids trying to leave town," I said. "Where are they?"

"I don't know what you're talking about." His glance strayed to his fallen companions. "Please don't hurt me," he pleaded. "I'm mortal. Not like them. Please, don't kill me."

He was probably telling the truth. The Emporium typically employed more mortals than Unbounded, and though their leaders normally chose Unbounded for the most important ops, they always needed someone to make coffee and clean their toilets.

Kenna put her hand over his throat, bringing her face close to him. "I'm giving you two seconds to tell us where they are, or I *will* shoot you."

"Someone said something about a woman and some kids over the radio an hour or so back. I don't know anything more, I swear! There isn't a woman here. I would know."

Kenna seemed to accept that. "The Emporium is killing people here. How?"

"I-I-I don't know."

"Wrong answer." Kenna pushed harder against his neck, making him gasp for air. "Another wrong answer, and I'm going to put a bullet in your leg—and then in every other part of your body until you tell the truth. What are you doing here? It's in the crops. That much we know. Is it a disease? Some kind of virus?"

The man gagged, his breath coming in huge panicked

gasps. I didn't blame him. Kenna was scary—it was downright awesome.

"Not disease. The crops have been engineered to enhance a few natural toxins. I-I don't know the science. I just manage the harvest workers." He paused, as if waiting to see if that was enough information.

Kenna pointed her gun at his thigh. "And?"

His voice rose to an annoying squeal. "It accumulates in everyone who eats it—mortals, I mean." A slight curl of his lips hinted that he might not be as content with this as he might have led his employers to believe. Of course, that would be a matter of self-preservation. One never left Emporium employ, unless it was in a casket.

"It kills all mortals?" I asked.

He shook his head. "Mostly it depresses the neurotransmitters in the brain. I don't know the science, but it makes people calm. It's only fatal to older people as their organs age. Their systems can't handle the accumulation—but that's a sign they are becoming less effective anyway."

I sneered. "So you murder them."

"It's better than other alternatives," the man said, his eyes haunted. Sweat sheened across his forehead. "Believe me."

"You're sure it doesn't kill anyone else?" Kenna asked the question before I had the chance.

"Well, there is also a fifty percent higher fatality rate in the babies of the women who consume—"

Kenna's grip on his throat must have increased because

he choked off and his face, even in the dim light, was bright red.

"Please!" he gasped.

Kenna eased off and leaned forward to speak in his face. "You're going to help me get the crop information. Now."

His eyes darted wildly. "I don't know the computer password! I don't have access to the print records."

"I'll get access. You show me where."

He flung out his left arm. "Down that way. The office."

Kenna pulled him from the wall, grabbing the back of his shirt. To me, she said. "Look for Dona Mafalda and her family. I'll get the records."

Without seeming to look, she fired down the hall as a figure rounded the bend. "They'll track us here eventually," she added. "We don't have much time. Get out as soon as you find them or determine they aren't here. I'll meet you in the vineyard."

Our captive turned slightly toward us, stiffening as he hit the barrel of her gun. "Try the barns. They sometimes sport with locals there."

"Get going." Kenna pushed at him.

I went back inside the dark kitchen. Kenna would check rooms here as she went, clearing a path to the office, and if she found the family, she'd get them out. My best bet was to do as the mortal agent had said and search the other buildings.

I had almost reached the melted window when a terrified scream shot through the night.

CHAPTER 8

KENNA! WAS MY FIRST THOUGHT. BUT KENNA WOULD DIE before she gave that kind of satisfaction to an Emporium agent. No, the scream was coming from outside, and I was guessing it was Dona Mafalda or Brigida.

I sprinted the remaining steps to the window and peered out into a deceptively quiet night. The faint stench of smoke filled the air, but there were no guards in sight. Another high-pitched scream split through the calm, coming from the cabbage barn the two guards had entered earlier when we'd arrived. I vaulted through the window and darted across the open space, expecting at any minute to feel the hot slice of a bullet piercing my body. But I reached the barn doors in safety—and none too soon. Two of the black trucks were rolling through the main gate, stopping out of my sight behind the stuccoed building. Kenna was about to have more visitors.

Nothing I could do to back her up. Not with the

panicked cries and whimpers now leaking from the barn. I pulled one of the massive doors open a crack and peered in. Not more than a car length away, a guard gripped Brigida's arm, keeping her in place while the other guard held his gun to her little boy's head. The child stood on unsteady feet, crying for his mother, but each time he tried to go to her, the guard pushed him back with the gun. The little girl clung to her mother's leg, whimpering.

"Please," Brigida said in broken English. "I no know this man. I see him today. I no know anything. Please, please, no hurt my baby!"

"If you got nothing to tell us, we don't need any of you." The guard jabbed his gun into the boy's head, sending him sprawling backwards onto the ground. The child's scream was garbled with tears.

"I don't know," the other guard said with a smirk at Brigida, jerking her back as she tried to run to her sobbing child. "She's awfully pretty."

"So are dogs," retorted the other. "But you do whatever you want. I'll get rid of the kids."

"No!" Brigida cried.

I fired, hitting the man with the gun in the forehead. He crumpled at the same time Brigida yanked away from the second guard, rushing to her son and snatching him up in her arms. The second guard pulled out his gun, aiming at me, but I was already firing. One bullet slammed into his left shoulder. The second shot brought only a *click!*

Grinning insanely as if he didn't notice the bullet, the

guard pulled his trigger. I dove to the side, heating and throwing my gun at him. I missed his face, the molten metal hitting his chest instead. He screamed but didn't retreat, his leather jacket apparently protecting too much of his skin. Lunging at him, I punched hard at his face, leaving a deep burn across his cheek.

His returning jab to my ribs felt like being hit with a sledge hammer. Biting down on the pain, I drew closer, slamming him with first one fist and then the other. His clothing and skin blackened wherever I touched. He fought back with viciousness, his hands blurs that barely registered in my vision. He knew the places to hit that would bring the most pain and struck relentlessly. Blackness threatened to plunge me into unconsciousness, but I pushed it back, just like I did with the cravings. If I could hold on for just a few seconds more.

Blood dripped down my face, obscuring my vision. I lashed out, connecting with his jaw. The skin melted in a rush, burning away his entire face. His mouth opened in a scream—one he never uttered as he collapsed to the floor and lay there unmoving.

Brigida stared in horror, both children now in her arms, their faces pressed to her body. "You," she said hoarsely.

The heat seeped from me in a rush. "Where's your mother?" I asked her in Portuguese.

Brigida shook her head, her face crumpling. "She said she didn't know anything. They didn't believe her."

"I'm sorry. But you have to get out of here now."

Shouting outside told me it was already too late.

"Come on!" Jumping to my feet, I grabbed Brigida's shoulder. She resisted at first, but when I pulled her daughter from her arms, she stopped fighting me. We ran behind the large wagon the workers had used to haul the cabbages, coming up far too quickly against the wall. "Look for a door!"

"There's none. I looked earlier when they first left us."

Pushing the little girl at her mother, I strode to the wall, calling on my ability. It answered my demand, eager and willing. Almost immediately as I touched it, the wood burst into flame. Ignoring the renewed sobbing from the children and Brigida, I grabbed a shovel from the wagon and struck the burning wood until I cleared a hole large enough for them to exit. The fire spread faster, greedily consuming the dry wood.

I peeked outside and saw no one. "Get your kids out," I told Brigida. "There's a break in the fence leading into the vineyard. It's by one of the poles opposite the short building." I pointed in the general direction to be sure she understood. "Run to the fence and work your way up until you find it. Go into the vineyard. If you see a woman with red hair, you can trust her. No one else. If you don't see her, run as far away as you can. Hide until it's safe."

Would it ever be safe? Had Kenna even gotten out?

Brigida hesitated, her chest heaving. Behind us, both double doors burst open.

Brigida needed no more convincing. She bounded through the hole in the wall, as if the children in her arms weighed nothing more than a couple of kittens.

I turned back to the wagon, sending my heat into it. Between the blood drenching my face and the effects of my withdrawal, I was having trouble seeing, but my ability was working well. The wood of the wagon burst into flames, the metal parts beginning to melt. I pushed the entire thing in the direction of the oncoming men, hoping the wheels held up long enough to deliver my little surprise. Then I dived through the hole in the wall, summersaulting into a squatted position. Brigida was nowhere to be seen.

More shouting, but still no guards in sight. I headed for the next building, also setting it on fire. Kenna and I would be harder to catch if they were worried about saving their new buildings. They might even think twice about staying in Monte Vinha if they had to start completely over. I ran to the next building, tripping twice on my way and hitting the ground with a painful crunch. I was still having problem seeing. Bile rose in my throat.

The shouting was now accompanied by wailing sirens. Additional people arrived in trucks and began running around purposefully. Two strode in my direction, but I ducked behind the building I'd torched and hurried on. I risked melting two of the metal buildings, touching all the sides to hasten the collapse, and set fire to a third wooden barn. The last building I touched was an older one made of brick, and as heat funneled through it, the entire wall exploded in a rush of falling bricks and flaming debris, nearly trapping me in the process.

Coughing up smoke, I stumbled through the rubble to the fence and melted another hole, falling through it into a field of wheat. I was tempted to set it on fire as well, but I was already worried about Kenna, and about Brigida and her children. And the whole town.

Had my distraction been enough to save them from the Emporium? Or had I just hastened their deaths?

Every part of my body ached with agony. I crawled until I could no longer see the wheat around me.

Finally, I let myself collapse.

CHAPTER 9

ANGUISH PIERCED MY AWARENESS AND FORCED ME TO CRAWL from the blackness. I was on fire, pain filled my entire body, except my hands and feet, which felt blissfully numb.

Oh, God in heaven, please let me die.

"He's coming around," said a female voice. "Now that he's awake, we need to get him into the curequick."

Yes, dump me into an ocean of curequick. My body shook with need.

"No." The single word, spoken by a man, was completely unyielding. Somehow the voice was familiar, or maybe the tone, but I couldn't place it.

"He needs to heal," insisted the woman. "He's burned far too badly to give him much comfort otherwise. After he's better, we can worry about his addiction. It's too much all at once."

The man didn't back down. "Giving him curequick will only prolong his dependence. It's been five days since they found him. With our metabolism, five days is halfway there."

The blackness I'd crawled from invited me to return, but I clung to the familiarity of the man's voice. It was the only thing that seemed to cut through the cravings and the pain of . . . what? I didn't remember doing anything that could bring this agony.

"Not with his level of addiction, it isn't," the woman said. "Our bodies record the need for curequick in a way similar to how they record our memories even if our heads are severed—as long as our other two focus points, the heart and reproductive system, are intact. His recovery will take at least two months and maybe up to six."

"Look, I know your first priority as a doctor is to make your patient comfortable, but do not give him curequick, or you'll answer to me." The man's voice betrayed controlled anger, and I knew he had every intention of fighting for what he believed.

"I'm sorry, but my patient is an adult, and he has the final say." The doctor's voice moved closer. "Blaze, I'm Dr. Strout, I'm here to look after you. I can give you curequick with the sedative. Would you like that?"

I wanted to say yes. In fact, I wanted to beg for the curequick. But all at once I placed the other voice as that of my foster father. "Ritter?" I whispered. The effort sent shards of glass rippling down my throat.

"I'm here, Blaze. Your partner called me when they found you."

I struggled to open my eyes and could almost make out his face through a thick haze. "Where . . .?"

"You're in London. I flew here as soon as I heard."

That wasn't what I meant. "Kenna?"

"She's safe. You want me to get her?"

"No." The last thing I wanted was for her to see me like this.

There was more I wanted to know—about Brigida and her children, and the town. But my ability to even think had fled, and the torture I was experiencing cranked up a notch.

"Would you like the curequick?" The doctor asked again. "I wish I had an alternative to offer, but there isn't one. We can wean you off it later when you recover. It'll be easier then."

"Blaze, don't," came Ritter's voice, both firm and soft, punctuated by a pleading I hadn't heard from him for over a hundred and sixty-seven years.

I remembered the day he'd arrived in Portugal, standing in front of me with an uncertain expression as he explained that he'd been a friend of my grandfather's—great-grandfather's, I would find out later—and was there to take me with him to America. If I agreed.

I had. He had saved me then when I'd trusted him, and maybe he could help me now.

"No curequick," I said, the words barely a whisper from my parched throat. Never again.

As if to taunt me, the agony in my body became all encompassing. *I need it now!* I screamed inside my head.

"Give him a painkiller," Ritter ordered.

"It won't help. Not much. A sedative would be better, though it won't last."

"Give him both."

I didn't feel the prick of a needle, and it wouldn't have made a bit of difference if I had.

"You staying?" I asked Ritter.

"I'll be right here. You can do this, I promise."

From the moment he'd taken me in at thirteen, he'd kept every promise he'd made to me. Maybe I *could* do this.

The darkness threatened to take me, and this time I dived in.

Time passed with the ever-constant, agonizing torture, a need so deep I didn't know how I'd make it through another second. As my body healed from the burns, the demand for curequick increased tenfold. Every hour, I questioned my decision, but each time I thought to give in, Ritter was there, a barrier between me and any chance of curequick.

I lived for the moments of blessed unconsciousness, though these were haunted by images of a crying toddler screaming for his mother, and a little girl with a bullet hole in her chest.

Then after what seemed like an eternity, the haze partially lifted, like the dawn after a storm, and I awoke from a fitful sleep with only the familiar cravings instead of the blinding ones that made me want to curl into a ball and weep. I still wanted curequick—and quite badly—but it was nothing compared to the hell I had endured.

I looked over to see not Ritter but Kenna by my bedside, tucked in a chair, her red hair fanned over her face. Sleeping, she looked vulnerable, nothing like the tough warrior I knew her to be.

I must have made a sound because her eyes popped open, her hand sliding almost imperceptibly to her gun inside its holster. Without shifting position, she scanned the room until her gaze fell on me. Abruptly, she sat up. "Oh, you're awake."

I wanted to tell her to leave almost as much as I wanted to beg her to stay. The need to see her won out. "Was I dreaming, or was my father here?"

"Oh, he's been here nonstop until today. I finally made him leave to take a shower." She made a face. "Believe me, after seven weeks sitting in here, he needed it."

"Seven weeks," I mumbled. *Only seven?*

"I know. A long time."

I wasn't about to admit that it had felt like much longer. A year in purgatory would be a vacation after the past seven weeks.

"Ritter made me swear on my life to protect you from any offers of curequick. Though the doctor is just as happy as we are that you've made it this far."

Even the mention of curequick conjured a desire so strong I wanted to leap up and go find the drug myself. I pushed the need down, and to my surprise, it receded to a manageable level. "So, what happened in Portugal?"

A smile spread across her face. "You saved everyone, is what." She scooted the chair close enough that if I had been able to focus even a little bit better, I could have counted her freckles.

"I wasn't able to break through the codes on the Emporium's computer system with my limited tools," she went on, "but they had plenty in hard copy that I was able to steal, thanks to their preoccupation with your fires. Apparently, you destroyed nearly all the Emporium's buildings, including a brick one they were using as a lab. A good portion of their fields burned as well. Cities all around had to come help put out the fires. By the time Greggor and the reinforcements he called in from Italy arrived the next day, the Emporium was already pulling out. Best we can figure, they decided to cut their losses when they realized how far we—or you, rather—were willing to go to send them packing."

"The town burned?"

"The town lost a few dozen buildings when the fire spread, but the great thing is that almost everything there is made of cement and stucco, so it spread slowly. All the people are okay—well, besides those who died before we arrived. Better yet, they came out of their odd stupor a few weeks after they stopped eating the genetically modified food. Believe it or not, in the past month, the police had to arrest five people for being a public nuisance." She laughed.

I couldn't join her mirth. Not yet. "And Dona Mafalda's daughter?" I held my breath, seeing again the little children who'd stalked my dreams.

"Actually, Brigida's the reason we found you. Your tracking chip was damaged when you were burned, so at first we suspected the Emporium took you with them. But she reported to the police about you disappearing into a wheat field after saving them, and we had ears out waiting for just that kind of intel. We searched the field and found you. Burned to a crisp I might add. You must have been passed out there when the fire jumped to the field."

I might have also accidentally set it ablaze. "Her children?"

"They were a little hungry and a lot scared, but they're fine. Thanks to you. Often it's the wee ones who are the most resilient."

I let out a sigh, releasing the tension that had built inside me since waking. "That's good."

"The town will recover before too long, though the depressant will remain in their organs for years to come. However, only the pregnant women and their children are at immediate risk, and with the formulas I stole, we've managed to come up with some countermeasures to save the babies." A slight frown marred her face. "Some of the older people may still die before their time, but they're lucky we caught it when we did."

"At least it wasn't a virus that could spread like a biological weapon."

Kenna grimaced. "That's probably next on the Emporium's list." Her voice was light but deadly serious. "Regardless, we'll keep a sharp eye out for any more unexplained decreases in population. By the way, you were right. All the documentation points to their intention of eventually getting rid of any sick or aged who might be a drain on society. And they were pleased about the side effect of infant mortality because they felt it would help them control the mortal population."

"That control will never happen. Not while we're still alive."

Her hand slid into mine, sending a different kind of sensation pulsing through my body.

"You might have a fever," she said. "Your hand's burning."

"No, I . . ." How embarrassing to show my reaction to her this way. "Just a few overheated atoms."

"I like the sound of that." She leaned forward and kissed me. My hand went up around her neck pulling her close, enjoying the taste of her lips. She felt so good, and smelled even better. Far better than any drug.

I was about to investigate her mouth further when Ritter reentered the room, his hair still wet from his shower. "Feeling better, I see." His smile mocked, but his dark eyes danced with amusement.

Releasing Kenna reluctantly, I reached out and shook his hand. "Thank you for coming."

"How are you feeling?"

"Not great, but I think I'm going to be just fine."

"I knew you would be once you made the decision. I'm proud of you, son."

Ritter never gave praise unless it was merited, so this, and the way Kenna watched me with her baby blues, her lips moist and reddened with my kiss, finally made it all real. I had fought both the Emporium and my own personal dragon and had come up the victor.

"Is there anything I can do for you?" Ritter asked.

I started to shake my head and then remembered. "Well, there is this old guy I borrowed a motorcycle from. I really need to get him a replacement."

THE END

TEYLA BRANTON GREW UP AVIDLY READING SCIENCE FICTION and fantasy and watching Star Trek reruns with her large family. They lived on a little farm where she loved to visit the solitary cow and collect (and juggle) the eggs, usually making it back to the house with most of them intact. On that same farm she once owned thirty-three gerbils and eighteen cats, not a good mix, as it turns out. Teyla always had her nose in a book and daydreamed about someday creating her own worlds.

Teyla is now married, mostly grown up, and has seven kids, so life at her house can be very interesting (and loud), but writing keeps her sane. She loves writing fiction and traveling, and she hopes to write and travel a lot more. She also loves shooting guns, martial arts, and belly dancing.

She has worked in the publishing business for over twenty years. Teyla also writes romance and suspense under the name Rachel Branton. For more information, please visit http://www.TeylaBranton.com.